MAGIC
—⊙ON THE⊙—
CARDS

THE CARTOMANCER'S GUIDE TO WEREWOLVES: 1

MARINA FINLAYSON

FINESSE SOLUTIONS

Cover design by Book Cover Artistry
Editing by Larks & Katydids

Published by Finesse Solutions Pty Ltd
2023/05
ISBN: 9781925607123

Author's note: This book was written and produced in Australia and uses
British/Australian spelling conventions, such as "colour" instead of "color",
and "-ise" endings instead of "-ize" on words like "realise".

A catalogue record for this book is available from the National Library of
Australia

For Mal, because you always make me laugh.

1

*T*here's a give and take to magic: if you craft a smart spell, the universe is supposed to help you out.

Apparently, magic didn't get the memo.

I glanced up at the two vampires and clenched my hand around the cards. Ethan gave me an encouraging smile, but Raquel was tapping her foot. I really needed this to work. There was a monster out there, preying on the people of Kurranderra, my adopted hometown. If my magic played ball, I could help find the rogue before it killed anyone else.

I laid the Three of Earth next to the Seven of Air in my circle, then added the Ace of Air over the top. Air was my weakest suit, but *this* time, surely? The Three represented Ethan, Raquel, and me working together. I smiled a little wistfully, hearing Mum's voice in my head saying, *Team-work makes the dream work.* The Seven was the secret we wanted to steal, and the Ace would activate the spell.

"Aren't there supposed to be more cards in the deck?" Raquel asked, her red lip curled ever so slightly.

The blond vampire's bare arms were folded across her chest, and she was wearing a sleeveless top and a tight leather miniskirt. In September. In the Blue Mountains. Honestly, just *looking* at her made me break out in goosebumps.

I was rugged up like a bag lady in layers of clothes and I was *still* cold. The chill of the ground seeped through my jeans where I knelt in the grass, and the night air nipped at my face. September in the mountains was technically spring, but during the middle of the night, it was cold enough to freeze the balls off a brass monkey out here.

"Aren't vampires supposed to clean up their own messes?" Ariel sniped. "Shouldn't she at least *pretend* to be grateful that you're helping them find their stupid elder?"

Neither of the vampires reacted, of course. I cast Ariel a sideways glance. She stood beside them, her pale, silvery hair drifting around her head as if she were underwater. She was wearing the same T-shirt I was, neon pink with *Nap Queen* splashed across the front, though mine was covered by a jumper and a heavy jacket.

Ariel's bare arms didn't make me feel colder, though; she wasn't like the rest of us. She'd been my constant companion since I was six years old, but no one else could see or hear her—and I'd given up trying to convince people she existed long ago. Whatever she was made of, it wasn't flesh.

Calm your farm, I told her in my mind. *She'll come in handy when I find something. If I find something.*

2

I shot Raquel my best disdainful look. "You know a lot about cartomancy, do you?" I'd been trying different card arrangements for ten minutes, pulling ever more creative combinations from my slim deck, trying to pinpoint the rogue's location. Some of them were sheer genius, if I did say so myself. In a sudden burst of inspiration, I slid the Four of Air under the Ace. *There. That should winkle out your hiding spot.* "If you've got any better ideas, I'm all ears."

Raquel huffed in annoyance, her breath billowing white in the night air.

"Sunday's very experienced," Ethan said mildly.

"Experienced! She's an infant. How much experience can she have?"

"I'm twenty-three," I said, stung. "Being as old as dirt doesn't make vampires better than humans, you know."

"Sunday's doing the best she can," Ethan added, though he, too, had started shifting impatiently from foot to foot. He didn't feel the cold any more than Raquel did, but he wore a leather jacket with his jeans. Vampires like Raquel liked to flaunt their otherness. The more cautious ones preferred to blend in and appear non-threatening. Ethan was the second kind, so he'd dressed for the weather.

For a vampire, he was a pretty good guy.

"A pretty sucky boyfriend, you mean," Ariel said.

Which is why I broke up with him, I pointed out.

"Ha! 'Sucky boyfriend.' Did you see what I did there?"

I rolled my eyes and turned my attention back to my spell. I'd drawn my circle on the concrete path with chalk —cartomancers always had a bit of chalk in their pocket—

but I was kneeling on the grass, hoping that the connection with Earth would help.

Cartomancy was a finicky kind of magic, and my results were often underwhelming. Raquel was right—not that I'd tell *her* that. My deck was missing a lot of cards. None of the big guns would work for me at all, so I'd given up carrying them. In one of those cosmic jokes the universe liked to play, one of the world's most powerful cartomancers had given birth to ... me. Sunday Armitage, cartomancer very much *un*-extraordinaire.

Raquel sighed as I blew gently on the Ace and tapped it to activate the spell.

"Focusing here," I said tartly. "Why don't you go sigh somewhere else?"

The three of us—well, four if you counted Ariel, but since she was as reliable as a toddler on a sugar high, I usually didn't—were in the deep shadows behind the public toilets at Kurranderra Falls, a popular local picnic spot.

It was a lot less popular since the body of a young guy had been discovered here three nights ago, completely drained of blood. The vampires insisted it wasn't them, of course, and even though vampires had raised lying to an art form, I believed them. It wasn't in their interests to prey so blatantly on humans. Since preternaturals had come out to the world in 2000, vampires had been very carefully rehabilitating their public image. No one wanted a return to the days of pitchforks and angry mobs.

"How long is this going to take?" Raquel asked.

"You know there's thousands of acres out there to

search, right?" Ethan said. He slouched against the wall of the toilet block, hands jammed in his jacket pockets, outside the tiny circle of light from my candles. Long blond hair fell across one eye. "If it saves me having to trek over every one of them, I'll happily stand here all night while Sunday does her thing."

"I can't believe I gave up clubbing for this," Raquel said.

"Maybe if you people didn't lose track of your elders right when they were about to tip over the edge from *nutcase* to *homicidal maniac*, none of us would have to be out here," I said. The cold was making me cranky. I should be curled up on the couch at home, not chasing monsters after midnight.

"We're not sure yet that it *is* an elder," Ethan said.

"Sure you're not." Ever since the body had been discovered, the vampires had been running around like ants whose nest had been kicked. If that wasn't an admission of guilt, I'd be a monkey's uncle. "And Santa might bring me a new pony for Christmas."

Ariel crouched down beside me, watching the cards. A faint white glow was growing around them. Finally! I'd cracked it.

I stood up and brushed off the damp knees of my jeans. They'd probably have grass stains, but who cared? I'd sacrifice every piece of clothing in my wardrobe if it would help find the elder before it killed again. I felt fiercely protective of this little town and its people. I'd travelled all over Australia, never spending more than a few months in one place for as long as I could remember. I'd never had a hometown before. I wasn't letting some senile, blood-crazy vampire lay waste to it.

"Is it working?" Ethan asked. He pushed away from the wall, curiosity lighting his face as the glow spiralled up like smoke from a fire.

He'd never seen me work magic before. No one had, apart from my aunties. The world wasn't a safe place for people like me. Preternaturals came in all flavours, some good, some bad. Most of them had a live-and-let-live attitude toward each other.

Except for the Soldiers of the Light, the so-called guardians, who were the closest thing the preternatural world had to a police force. They were obsessed with cartomancers, and not in a good way. *Witches*, they called us. Those jumped-up werewolves thought they were God's gift to the world, and their divine mission was to get rid of us.

Hence I'd spent most of my life always on the move, keeping my magic hidden. No cartomancer wanted to come to the attention of the Soldiers—that was a one-way ticket to the grave.

I couldn't believe it when Ethan had shown up with Raquel in tow. He *knew* my magic was secret. I'd almost called off the whole thing, but that wouldn't change the fact that he'd already told her. And I wanted this monster found as much as they did.

The faster we got rid of the elder, the less likely that the Soldiers would come sniffing around Kurranderra looking for a monster and find *me* instead.

The pale glowing magic flowed through the air

towards the trees surrounding the picnic grounds, and I felt a tug in my chest, urging me to follow. Ariel came with me, the two vampires close behind.

Under the blackness of the trees, a track led to a viewing point above the falls, and that was the path my magic followed. I'd done this walk a few times; the falls were a good half-hour away. In the daytime, the twists and turns of the track led through some very pretty bushland, sometimes following the river and sometimes veering away from it.

Right now, it felt spooky as heck. The eerie light of my magic didn't illuminate more than the track, and even that was dim. There were noises all around, little rustlings or the occasional shifting of pebbles, the odd call of a night bird. They were only animals, and nothing that I would even have noticed during the day. But now they made me feel like a sitting duck, aware that everything out there had better night vision than I did. Anything could be watching me from the dark, and I wouldn't be able to see it.

So, I was grateful that Ethan stayed pretty close. Raquel soon pushed on ahead, following the magic trail, and disappeared. Not that she was any great loss, but Ariel went with her.

"You okay?" Ethan asked, after the third or fourth time I tripped over something I couldn't see properly in the dark.

"Fine. Just not blessed with magical night vision."

"Could you do a spell for that?"

"Maybe? I mean, someone *else* might be able to. I don't think *I* could." My Air magic was already fading, that tugging sensation disappearing. I walked faster, trying to keep up with it and hoping I wouldn't faceplant and make a complete idiot of myself.

"Then it's handy that our monster seems to have stuck to the track."

"Very thoughtful of him. Or her," I added. I was all for equal opportunity, even in monstering. "You have any idea who we could be tracking?"

He shook his head. "None of the local elders are missing, and I haven't heard any reports from other hives. Doesn't mean much, though. Elders aren't exactly party animals."

I nodded. I knew what he meant. Elder vampires tended to retreat from society, so one might have gone rogue without anyone noticing if their local hive wasn't keeping a close enough eye on them.

"I hope you didn't mind me bringing Raquel," Ethan said after five more minutes of me stumbling over rocks and twigs in the dark.

"It wouldn't matter if I did or not, would it? Since you didn't give me any choice."

"She won't tell anyone about your magic. I told her it was a secret."

I rolled my eyes. "Yeah, it *was* a secret. That means you weren't supposed to tell anyone, Ethan. That's how secrets work."

I hadn't even wanted *him* to know, but that's what happened when a vampire glamoured you. Suddenly you were spilling your guts all over the joint. That's what had ended our brief relationship. I was still mad at him about that, actually, but I'd thought I could at least trust him to keep quiet about my magic.

"I thought you'd realise I'd need backup," he said. "If it's an elder, there's no way I can take it down on my own."

"And Vampirella will be a big help in those heels?"

He snort-laughed then tried to cover it with a cough. "She's actually a great person to have your back in a fight. I'd trust her with my life."

"Well, I guess that's reassuring, since you've trusted her with *mine*."

He winced at my acidic tone and shut up. *Good call, Ethan.* I was Not Happy with him.

Raquel reappeared, so suddenly that my heart thumped uncomfortably.

I put a hand to my chest. "Don't sneak up on people like that! You scared the crap out of me."

"Sorry," she said, but her smile said she wasn't.

"Are you sure you're not cold?" I asked, eyeing her smooth, bare shoulders. My breath was making white clouds in the air as I spoke. Surely even a vampire would feel a little chilly in these conditions? "I could lend you my scarf."

I started to unwind it, and a look of revulsion crossed her face. I stopped, the thick wool clutched in my hands. It was still warm from my body heat. What was her problem? She didn't like scarves? Or just chunky bright pink ones? At least I'd dressed for the outdoors, unlike her.

"Vampires don't feel the cold," she said, tipping her nose up.

I shrugged and looped the scarf around my neck again, snuggling into its softness. "Your loss."

My magic began to pulse like a strobe light.

"Is that supposed to happen?" Raquel asked.

I pushed past her, drawn by a change in the tugging sensation in my chest. It almost felt as though a tug of war were going on inside me, as if someone else were fighting for control of my spell. Strange. I'd never had a finding spell do that. "No idea."

"Maybe we're getting close," Ethan said.

Raquel looked at me the way a headmistress looks at a disappointing student. Trust me, I'd seen that look *plenty* of times. "You're not a very good witch, are you?"

Air was my weakest suit—I was far better with Water. But I wasn't taking any sass from Vampirella.

"We prefer the term *cartomancer*." Only the Soldiers of the Light called us witches. Usually right before they killed us. "And I've never searched for a rogue before. I've never *had* to. And I wouldn't be here now except you vampires can't seem to find your butts with both hands. So maybe save your criticism for someone who cares."

"Ladies, ladies," Ethan said, flashing a bright, fangless smile. Most people caved when he brought out that smile. He'd been a good-looking guy even before he became a vampire, and I was guessing people hadn't often told him no. "Let's not argue. Why don't we spread out from here and see if we can pick up a scent?"

"I'm not a sniffer dog," Raquel said. He just kept smiling until she shrugged. "Whatever."

The two vampires faded into the darkness so suddenly

I didn't know whether to be impressed or scared. I followed the pulsing light, sure that we were close, doing an awkward half-run, half-power-walk thing. Still, I had no chance of keeping up with them.

And then the light started fading. I was stumbling, almost blind, when I came to a little cleared area right on the edge of the river. An old gum tree leaned out over the dark water, its trunk almost horizontal. There was no one there. No sign of either of the vampires, or even Ariel.

The insistent tug in my chest winked out, the tug of war over. Had my magic just run out of juice, or had I found the right place?

Gradually, my eyes adjusted to the darkness. The moon, still a week from full, cast a tiny bit of light, though it made the shadows deeper and twisted trees and branches into alarming shapes. I moved closer to the river, scouring the ground for any hint that an elder had been here.

The cold crept through the soles of my boots and crawled up my ankles. I stamped my feet, trying to warm them. Every time I breathed out, a pale cloud billowed in the air in front of me. Wishing I'd brought gloves, I shoved my hands deep into the pockets of my jacket. If this was the right place, where were Ethan and Raquel?

As the seconds ticked by, I started to feel an uneasy sensation of being watched. I strained to see into the darkness under the trees, my hand clenched around the cards in my pocket. They were just pieces of cardboard covered in pictures, lovingly drawn by yours truly. They couldn't protect me unless I took the time to set a spell and activate the magic, but the familiar feel of them was comforting.

Everything was quiet. I couldn't hear anything moving towards me. In fact, I couldn't hear anything at all. Those little noises that had bothered me so much earlier had all died off, as if the trees were holding their breath.

A tiny crackle, like someone stepping on dry leaves, broke the silence. A shiver ran down my spine as I slowly turned my head. There, on my right—behind that big gum with the ghostly white trunk. What was that?

"Uhh, guys? Where are you?" Too late now to run. I'd never make it back to the car.

I backed up right to the river's bank. Could vampires cross running water or was that inability another one of those myths that people had made up? I'd wade straight in and never mind the cold if it would help.

A twig snapped off to the left somewhere.

Was it circling me? "Ethan? Are you there?"

A bush shook as if something big had just brushed past it. My breath was coming faster now, my heart racing.

And then the something growled—a low, rumbling noise that vibrated through my very bones.

"Ethan!" I yelled. "Raquel! A little help here?"

The big problem with cartomancy—apart from how phenomenally *bad* I was at it—was that it was *slow*. No sudden hurling of fireballs like wizards did in stories. Real magic took time, which was why we always liked to work our magic from a safe space. Preferably with back-up. I'd helped deal with a few monsters in my time, but usually with my aunts at least, if not the full coven.

I crouched down and groped around for a weapon. If magic wasn't coming to my rescue, it was time for a Plan B. My hand closed around a hefty rock, and I stood up.

Man, that river was looking better and better by the moment.

My gaze darted from one side of the clearing to the other, trying to be ready the minute something appeared. The longest moment in the history of time passed. Nothing happened. That was good, right?

There was a sudden flurry of movement in the bushes, and I hurled my rock.

2
_____

I opened the fridge and stared into its disappointing depths for a long moment. Four rashers of bacon. Four eggs. A half-empty bottle of milk, assorted jars, and a head of lettuce that had definitely seen better days. I closed the door with a sigh, then abruptly re-opened it.

"You know that won't make food magically appear," Ariel said.

I glared at her. "Do you have to be so annoyingly chirpy in the mornings? Morning people *suck*."

She was sitting on the countertop behind me, her legs swinging. Her silvery hair floated around her head as if it were stirred by a gale that no one else felt, but I was used to her oddities by now.

My own hair was the deep brown of dark chocolate, but right now I was fairly certain it looked as though I'd been dragged backwards through a hedge. I'd only just gotten out of bed, and that was my standard morning look.

I was doing pretty well to be dressed already, actually, after the late night I'd had.

Ethan had been supremely unimpressed after I'd hit him in the head with the rock, but hey, whose fault was that? If he wanted to sneak up on me when I was armed and dangerous, he deserved everything he got.

Raquel hadn't reappeared for a while after I'd clocked Ethan in the head. He said they'd seen no sign of the elder, so she'd gone off to check another trail, but *something* had growled at me. I insisted on waiting for her back at the cars like a sensible person, instead of hanging out in the bush with a big sign around my neck saying *monsters, plz come eat me.*

Ethan had thought that was a good idea, too, though maybe he'd just been scared I'd rock him again if he disagreed. I hadn't been exactly calm by then. And it was all for nothing—the elder was still out there somewhere, and we were no closer to finding it.

"Maybe I'll have strawberry jam on toast." I'd run out of cereal at the beginning of the week, and I was sick of peanut butter.

"Eat the bacon." Ariel eyed me critically. "You're getting all bony again."

She turned into a skeleton and showed all her teeth in a horrifying smile. I was used to her changing forms on a whim and just rolled my eyes. She laughed and flickered back into her usual waif-like appearance.

"I'm saving it." Weekends were the only time I got to sleep in, and I liked to follow my sleep-ins with a big, cooked breakfast. I wasn't wasting good bacon on a rushed *cram it into your mouth and run out the door to work* kind of a breakfast. The big weekend breakfast was a tradition that had begun when I lived with my aunts Ling and Ivy, or the Dynamic Duo, as I liked to call them.

My mouth watered a little at the thought of one of Ling's breakfasts. Hash browns, grilled tomatoes, and her special pancakes with a little bit of everything thrown in. As much bacon as you could eat—which, in Ivy's case, was quite a lot—plus pickled cabbage and tiny little sausages bursting with flavour.

Sadly, my budget didn't run to those kinds of extravaganzas. My pay cheque from the shop didn't leave a lot for food once I'd covered the rent, so the last few days before pay day were always kind of lean.

I got some bread out of the freezer and put it in the toaster, shoving the electricity bill out of the way. That was another thing that would have to wait until pay day.

Waiting for the toast was a pretty intense activity at my place. You had to be as prepared as a catcher in a game of baseball, because when the toast was done, the toaster launched that mother fluffer as if it were trying to send it into orbit. That's what came from buying your kitchen appliances from Second Chances. What could I say? It had been cheap.

I'd developed a habit of angling the toaster so that my body blocked the toast from falling into the sink or onto the floor if I fumbled the catch. Once, before I'd figured this out, the corner of a piece of toast had smacked me right in the eye, and Ariel had laughed so hard she could barely stand.

Once the toast was safely wrangled, I slathered it with butter.

"What's the plan for today?" Ariel asked, watching me pile strawberry jam on my toast. For someone who never ate, she was surprisingly interested in everything to do with food—buying it, preparing it, eating it. Her idea of heaven was lying on the couch watching cooking shows on TV.

I shrugged and spoke around a mouthful of toast. "The usual. World domination, that kind of thing."

"Really?" Her unearthly blue eyes lit up.

"No. Of course not. I'm going to work. In fact"—I glanced at the clock on the wall and crammed the rest of the toast into my mouth in a sudden panic—"I need to leave in five minutes. Are you coming?"

"Probably. Someone's got to make sure you don't leave the house with strawberry jam smeared all over your face."

I raised my hand to my mouth. "Have I—?"

She grinned. "No."

I ran into the bedroom to grab my shoes. Ariel hadn't understood humour when she'd first turned up in my life, but she was the queen of the comeback these days. I blamed all the sitcoms she'd watched over the years. I quickly brushed my teeth, checking my face in the mirror for jam, just in case. She'd gotten better at lying, too.

Then I snatched up my keys and hurried out. My tiny little one-bedroom apartment was on the ground floor, and I almost bowled over my upstairs neighbour as I raced out the door. He'd just reached the bottom of the stairs and took a hasty step back as I appeared in the foyer like a one-woman whirlwind.

"Sorry, Mr Garcia! I didn't see you there."

"Sunday! You're the best day of the week." He was almost as short as Ling, which was saying something for a man, and could easily have been in his nineties, judging by the shrivelled walnut appearance of his face. A few wispy strands of hair straggled out from under the blue beanie he always wore. They were dyed a dark brown that wasn't fooling anyone, but I guessed even ancient old men had their vanities.

He made the same joke every time he saw me. I wasn't sure if that was because his memory was shot or if, at his age, he just didn't give a crap. At least he was always in a good mood.

I sidled toward the fire door that led down to the basement car park. If he got talking, I could be stuck here for half an hour. "I didn't hurt you, did I?"

He smiled brightly at me. "There are worse things in life than being bumped into by a pretty young woman. Where are you off to in such a hurry?"

"Gotta get to work. I have to unlock the shop, so I can't be late." I jiggled the bunch of keys in my hand for emphasis, then ran down the fire stairs, giving him an apologetic wave before the door clanged shut behind me. My boss Cheryl had only started letting me open and close the shop a couple of months ago, and I wanted to live up to her trust. I never ran late if I could possibly help it.

In the underground car park, I climbed into my little green Corolla and turned the key. *Come on, Bugsy, don't let me down.* After a couple of ominous splutters, the engine caught, and I reversed out of my spot with a sigh of relief.

Bugsy was a temperamental old girl, and her cough had been getting worse the last few months. When she finally carked it, I'd be back to catching the bus, which would be a nuisance. I was only a five-minute drive out of town, but the bus followed such a winding route that it could take half an hour to cover the same distance.

I'd done more than my share of driving in my lifetime. The Dynamic Duo had dragged me all over Australia in their motorhome after Mum died. There was no Dad on the scene—he'd died before I was born. Mum had always refused to talk about him, saying only that he was a deadbeat not worth our time.

For a little girl, my new life had been fun, in some ways —living in a little house on wheels and getting to see so much of the country—but it had also meant that I'd changed schools with depressing regularity. Kurranderra was the first place where I'd stayed longer than a year since I was six years old.

I was cruising down the wide main street of Kurranderra a few minutes later. Cherry trees were planted in a strip all the way down the middle, and they were in full bloom. The soft pink blossoms made me itch to get out my sketch pad. Business would be booming this week with all the tourists up from Sydney to take photos.

I parked Bugsy in the council car park behind the row of shops, then hurried down the alley to the back door of the shop and unlocked it.

Shopping at Second Chances was always a bit of a

lottery. That was the thing about a secondhand shop—you never knew what you were going to find. Sometimes it was trash and sometimes treasure, but the constant flow of new stock arriving kept things interesting. As well as clothes, we sold china, jewellery, and secondhand books, which, in my opinion, was where the real treasure was to be found.

Ten minutes later, I was busy behind the counter when the bell that hung above the front door jangled violently as Bethany burst in. As usual, she was out of breath and full of apologies.

"Oh my gosh, Sunny, I'm so sorry. My first alarm didn't go off, and then the second one didn't either. Thank goodness I always set three alarms, or I'd still be asleep."

Bethany's alarms were like old friends to me—I'd heard about them almost every day that we'd been working together, which was going on eleven months now. I'd realised pretty fast that the problem wasn't Bethany's alarms, but Bethany herself—she just slept through them.

"It's fine," I said, as I did every morning. "The morning rush hasn't started yet."

Kurranderra was a tourist town, and things didn't get busy for us until the tourists had finished their breakfasts in the cafés that dotted the main street.

"What has she done to her *hair*?" Ariel asked, appearing out of nowhere and staring at Bethany's short bob in horror.

I ignored her—and Bethany did too, of course, since she couldn't see her.

"Love your hair," I said to Bethany. "Did you do it yourself?"

Her hand crept up to play with a lock of her hair. Yesterday it had been all black, but this morning the tips were dyed a pink that was even hotter than my T-shirt. "Yeah, I did. Do you like it?"

"It suits you. You look like a manga character."

"Awesome!" The diamond piercing in her nose winked in the light as she smiled with pleasure.

"I thought she was a goth," Ariel said.

She just likes wearing black, I thought fiercely at Ariel. Carrying on silent conversations with Ariel at the same time as out-loud ones with other people had given me a reputation as a scatterbrain who checked out of conversations on the regular.

"And single-handedly keeping the black eyeliner companies in business, too," Ariel said.

Whatever. Why don't you go home and watch one of your cooking shows?

"Because you didn't turn the TV on for me before you left."

That was the problem with Ariel. Well, there were a lot of problems with Ariel, like her disregard for personal space and her habit of always wearing the same thing I did but looking better in it dammit—but that was the one that bothered *her*: no physical body to punch buttons for herself.

Then go play in the traffic or something. I'm busy working here.

Around midday, Bethany brought me a cup of tea from our tiny kitchenette and slumped onto the stool next to me with a dramatic sigh. "Did you hear there was another attack last night? Some poor tourist out on Ridge Road."

"Another one?" My heart sank. Someone had died because we'd been searching in the wrong place.

"Yeah." She nodded vigorously, her pink-tipped locks bobbing up and down. "Crazy, isn't it? So much excitement in little old Kurranderra."

"You sound as though it's a *good* thing that people are being attacked."

"Well, it's not for *them*, obviously, but you've got to admit, it's a *little* bit exciting. Nothing ever happens here."

The fact that nothing ever happened in Kurranderra was one of the things I liked so much about it. It had an olde-worlde charm and a relaxed pace of life that had made me feel at home from the moment I'd arrived with all my worldly belongings in boxes on Bugsy's back seat.

There hadn't been many boxes. For as long as I could remember, I'd been on the move. Every few months, a new town, a new set of people to get to know. After a while, I'd stopped bothering. What was the point of trying to make new friends when we'd only be moving on soon anyway?

"Kurranderra doesn't need that kind of excitement," I said firmly, taking a sip of my tea.

"Do you think it's a vampire?"

I shrugged.

"Sometimes the elders lose their marbles and go on a killing spree," she continued.

"True." Elder vampires were way scarier than your everyday run-of-the-mill daywalker.

"Did you know that almost everything we thought we knew about vampires was wrong?"

I always tried to act as if I didn't know any more than the average person about the preternatural world, so I just said, "Really?"

"Yeah." She tugged absentmindedly on her eyebrow ring. "I wish I'd been around when the preets came out. Would have been crazy, huh? Can you believe everyone was losing their minds about the Y2K computer bug and then, wham! all of a sudden vampires and werewolves and stuff are real? I bet that put things into perspective."

"Yeah, I bet."

"So, you know vampires aren't actually dead, right?"

"Of course."

They weren't dead, or undead, just completely changed. Their hearts still beat, they could still walk in the sun, and nobody slept in coffins. You could be sitting next to one in church and never know, since crosses weren't actually vampire kryptonite. They weren't even allergic to garlic.

They could live for centuries, assuming nobody staked them, but as they grew older, sunlight bothered them more and more. What started as a preference for overcast weather became a full-on aversion to daylight by the time they were about five hundred years old. And after another couple of centuries rolled around, they'd mostly either killed themselves out of boredom or gone completely mad.

The mad ones were the ones who'd given vampires such a bad name and, luckily for the rest of us, they were rare. Vampire queens kept a careful eye on their elders. But occasionally, one would slip through the safety nets, and then we had a killing spree until the local daywalkers managed to off them.

"But I heard the elders start to rot because they've been alive so long, and they need more and more blood to keep going. That's why they go so crazy."

"Pretty sure that's an urban myth," I said, torn between wanting to set her straight and letting on that I knew the truth.

"So were vampires a couple of decades ago," she said triumphantly.

"Well, it might not be an elder anyway," I said. "Could be a banshee, maybe, or a black widow. They had one of those last year in Katoomba." There was a lot of bush around here—like thousands and thousands of hectares of it. We were a tiny town in the middle of a vast national park. "Why does everyone always blame the vampires?"

"Aww, look at you standing up for them. Are you sure you don't still have a thing for Ethan?"

"Are you sure *you* don't?" I'd dated Ethan for a few weeks when I'd first arrived in Kurranderra, but that had been a year ago and Bethany still mentioned him constantly. "Seems to me that someone has a crush. You're the one who can't stop talking about him."

"Well, I mean, have you *seen* that cute little butt?" She slapped her forehead with her palm. "Of course you have —you went out with him."

"Bethany," I said warningly.

She laughed. "Okay, okay, but he is *seriously* gorgeous. I can't believe you turned him down. He could suck my blood any time." She shot me a sly glance. "Or anything else he wanted."

"Bethany! He's twice your age."

"So? That means he's twice your age, too, and it didn't stop *you*."

"Can't argue with that logic," Ariel said, hoisting herself onto the counter between us. She seemed to prefer having her feet off the ground whenever possible.

"Can we please stop talking about him?" I asked. "We have work to do."

"The store is empty. Chillax." A moment of blissful silence followed. I thought she'd dropped the topic, then she added, "You know, I reckon we're meant to be."

I blinked. "Who? Us? Beth, you're a sweetheart, but you're really not my type."

She gave me a scornful look, while Ariel cracked up in silent laughter. "Not *us*. Ethan and me. Like, his name is a part of mine—it says *Ethan* right there in the middle of Bethany. I think it's a sign."

"A sign you've been drinking too much, maybe. What's in that tea?"

"Speak of the devil," Ariel said as the door chimed.

"Hear the rustle of his wings," I murmured as Ethan walked in.

"What?" Bethany asked.

I jerked my head towards the door, and a slow blush crept up her cheeks as she suddenly became super interested in the contents of her cup.

"Tell her mentioning their names summons them," Ariel joked.

You're such a jerk, I told her.

Today Ethan was wearing faded blue jeans and a T-shirt that had seen better days. The shaggy hair that brushed his shoulders was streaked blond by the sun, and his smile was as warm—and un-fangy—as his tanned skin. He looked more like a surfer dude than a vampire.

The only thing that marked him as a vampire was his eyes. Even then, you had to know what you were looking for. They were a soulful brown, but stare into them too long and you'd be caught up in his vampire glamour. I'd had a couple of embarrassing dates with him before I'd realised what was happening. Luckily for me, he was young by vampire standards, and his powers of persuasion were still resistible for the strong-willed.

I'd like to claim that it was the strength of my own will that had come to my rescue, but it had actually been Ariel's. She was occasionally good for something other than snark.

"You're *sure* you don't want to go out with him?" Ariel asked as he strode towards us, looking like something out of a model shoot despite the holey T-shirt. "He's pretty hot stuff for a dead guy."

I only just stopped myself from rolling my eyes. *You know they're not dead. You watch too much trashy TV.*

"Morning, ladies," he said, bathing us in the glow of his smile.

"Morning," Bethany squeaked without looking up, all her teasing and insinuation gone now that the object of her crush had turned up. She had a death grip on her teacup.

"Hi, there," I said, putting on my helpful customer service voice. "What brings you to Second Chances? Can I interest you in a prom gown? How about a nice pants suit? I have several with those eighties shoulder pads that are all the rage at fancy dress parties. You'd be the talk of the hive."

"I'm already the talk of the hive, baby." He gave me a cheesy grin and then I *did* roll my eyes. "They can't resist me over there."

Whatever his other failings, one thing you could say about Ethan was that he didn't hold grudges. He'd tried some moves on me, they'd failed, and he'd simply shrugged and moved on with his life. And we'd stayed friends. Lately, he'd been treating me more like a kid sister than an ex-girlfriend.

That was fine with me. I'd always wondered what it would be like to have siblings.

"Bethany was just talking about you," I said, watching her blush creep higher with satisfaction. Take *that*, Bethany. That would teach her to suggest I still had a *thing* for Ethan.

"Oh, really?" He turned a megawatt smile on her, which was totally wasted since she was focusing on her tea as if her life depended on it.

"Yeah. She was wondering what you thought about the latest attacks," I said, diverting his attention back to me. I wasn't totally heartless—poor Bethany would melt into a puddle of mortification in a minute. "Did you hear about the tourist last night?"

"Ah." His smile faded. "Yes, I did."

"What's the hive doing about it?" The three of us stumbling around in the bush last night hadn't been part of the hive's official response. I just hoped whoever was running the search was having more luck than we had.

He shifted restlessly, clearly uncomfortable with the question. He probably wasn't supposed to talk about hive business—but if the elder had struck again so soon, the vampires needed to throw all their resources at finding and stopping it. People's lives were at stake.

"Good one," Ariel said. I glanced at her in confusion. "Lives *at stake*? You know, like a vampire joke?"

I hated it when she eavesdropped on my thoughts. *It's just an expression. No pun intended. And can you please stay out of my head? It's creepy when you listen in to my private thoughts.*

"Don't think so loud, then."

"The queen has called a meeting for tonight," Ethan said. "Trust me, we're taking this seriously. We need to remove the threat before the crowds with the torches and pitchforks decide that maybe the world would be a better place without any vampires at all. I just dropped in to make sure you'd heard about the latest attack. I know you sometimes leave the store after dark."

"Aww, he still cares about you," Ariel said. "You should totally make a move on him. Look at all that hotness, going to waste." She hopped off the counter and stood next to him, leaning in close to run her tongue slowly up his cheek, then shooting me a sidelong glance. Thank goodness he couldn't feel that.

You're disgusting.

She grinned hugely, mission achieved, and wandered off. Her attention span was mercifully brief.

"Thanks," I said to Ethan. "That was nice of you, but you don't need to worry about me."

"Why? Have you suddenly turned into a sword-wielding ninja who could defend herself from an elder vampire?"

"So it *is* an elder vampire?" Bethany asked, curiosity winning out over her shyness.

Ethan took a step back, hand to his chest, feigning shock. "The baby goth speaks!"

A wave of red flooded her pale face, all the way up to the dark roots of her pink-tipped hair.

"Knock it off," I said. I had no problem with teasing her myself, but I came over all protective when someone else made her blush like that. "I don't need to wield a sword. I just have to not go wandering around on lonely bush roads by myself."

"You sure?" His eyes softened, and I hastily looked away before I changed my mind about dating him again. "I'd be happy to come over at closing time to make sure you got home safely."

"I'll be fine," I said. Making sure I got home safely could all too easily turn into being invited in, and who knew where that would end up? I did *not* like the loss of control that being under a vampire glamour brought with it. It was worse than being drunk, because you could remember every embarrassing thing you'd done the next morning and obsess over each one in excruciating detail for weeks afterwards.

Ask me how I knew.

He shrugged. "Suit yourself. But the offer's always there."

"Thanks."

Bethany went to help a customer, and Ethan studied my face carefully.

"You look tired. Too much excitement for you last night?"

"About that ..." I'd been thinking about it, and it seemed to me that the two vampires had deliberately left me alone in the middle of the bush as bait. "You set me up, like a goat staked out for a T-rex."

"You weren't tied down." He grinned. "Although that's a tantalising thought."

"I should stake *you*," I grumbled. "What if you hadn't come back when you did? I could have been attacked."

He grimaced. "Not by the elder, since it seems it was busy on the other side of town. Are you sure you didn't imagine there was something there? All I heard was you screaming. I didn't sense anything else."

"I wasn't screaming. I was *calling* your *names*, thank you very much. Which I wouldn't have had to do if you hadn't abandoned me, hoping to attract the elder with a nice little snack."

"You were never in any danger."

"Easy for you to say. You're not the one walking around full of juicy, enticing blood."

"Stop it, you'll make me hungry."

He was grinning, but I frowned at him. I wasn't ready yet to forgive him for setting me up, and I knew I wasn't mistaken. There *had* been something in those bushes. I hadn't imagined that growl.

"Johnny's is next door. Go and buy a pizza like a normal person. I'm not on the menu."

"You're no fun today. And pizza doesn't taste like it used to." He checked his watch. "I've got to run. I'll talk to you later."

"Tell me what the hive decides at the meeting," I said.

Maybe talking about food had scared him off. I'd have to remember that. Vampires could eat, but they rarely did, since they didn't need food to sustain themselves and most things tasted like sawdust to them. All they required to survive was blood.

The rest of the day passed in a steady stream of customers. Bethany left, and at 5:45, I tidied away the last things and straightened a few jackets on their hangers. However messy I was at home, I always left the shop looking immaculate. After a last satisfied look around, I switched off the lights and headed out the back door.

It was full dark outside, and the air was crisp and cold. I huddled a little deeper into my puffer jacket, grateful for its warmth. One of the perks of working at a secondhand store was that you got first dibs on anything that came in, and the jacket had been one of my best purchases, even if I'd had to eat noodles for two solid weeks to pay for it.

The back door opened into a narrow alley between the shop and Johnny's Pizzeria next door, which led out to the car park. It was very dark once I'd switched off the shop lights, but I strode towards the beacon of the single lamp post that lit the car park with confident steps. By its yellow light, I could see my breath forming clouds in front of my face. We were in for another cold night.

A shape flitted across the rectangle of light at the end of the alley, momentarily throwing me into darkness. My heart stuttered a little, but I didn't slow. It was probably just Toby, the delivery guy from next door. He often parked his little yellow car with its pizza sign on top next to Bugsy, and we'd wave to each other in passing.

Nevertheless, I dug my car keys out of my bag as I walked, clenching them tight in my hand. All that talk today of elder vampires and dead bodies on the road was playing on my nerves.

Don't be an idiot, I told myself. Whatever was out there preying on people was doing it on the lonely roads, where only the trees saw how you died. There was nothing to be scared of here, in the heart of town, with people all around.

Delicious smells of pizza cooking drifted on the cold air from next door. Further down the street, half a dozen restaurants clustered around the civic centre. There would be people everywhere at this time of night, looking for a meal.

Even the quiet little car park was half full. See? Nothing to be scared of. *Hordes* of people. I picked up the pace, my boots on the concrete loud in the silence. I wasn't scared; I was just in a hurry to get home to my warm apartment.

I emerged from the alley into the open space of the car park. Several large industrial dumpsters hulked in a line along the back of the buildings. A few half-dead weeds clustered around them, poking up out of cracks in the asphalt surface of the car park. I stumbled in the dim light —the ground here was more pothole than asphalt these days. It was about time the council did something about it.

In the blackness between the bins, something moved with a sound like metal scraping on the ground.

Or claws.

I froze, suddenly aware that none of those hordes of people were here in this car park, and peered into the dark, trying to make out what was there. A cat? But cats didn't make noises like that. And whatever that was, it was *much* bigger than a cat.

Two red eyes blinked very slowly, and I froze, unable to look away, the keys clenched so tight in my fist that it hurt. I swallowed hard. Why was Bugsy so far away?

Ariel appeared beside me. "Don't just stand there, you idiot. Run!"

3

"*E*than? Is that you?" I had never wanted to run more, but my feet were glued to the spot.

A low growl was the only response.

Nope. Definitely not Ethan.

"Why would Ethan be hiding behind the dumpsters, you numpty?" Ariel shouted directly into my face, breaking the spell of those blazing red eyes. "Move!"

I sprinted for the car as a massive gale sprang up out of nowhere, whipping leaves and small pebbles into my face as I fled.

The gale roared, rocking the dumpsters. They crashed together, making a sound like the end of the world. A lid opened, slamming against the wall behind it with a metallic clanging as I reached the car and shoved my key into the lock with trembling hands. One day, I'd be able to afford a car that I could unlock without a key, but that magical day was nowhere in sight yet. I wrenched the door open then slammed it shut behind me, locking it with desperate haste.

I sagged against the seat. "Well, that's my exercise for the week."

A small tornado had formed in the parking lot behind the pizza shop, its tail firmly planted in the open dumpster. It had sucked up boxes, bits of old metal, basically everything the dumpster had contained, and was hurling it all at the space between the dumpsters where the eyes had been.

"Thanks, Ariel." My hands were shaking so much I missed the ignition on the first try, but I finally got the car started. Ariel might not be able to turn on TVs, but she could sure raise one heck of a windstorm when it counted. I threw the car into reverse and lit out of there, still shuddering at the memory of that menacing growl.

Bugsy's tyres squealed as I turned onto Main Street. *Okay, Sunday. Calm down before you cause an accident.*

The streetlights and the sheer normalcy of Main Street reassured me. The clock tower on the civic centre glowed softly, and neon signs for the various restaurants flashed in garish colours. A group of young men laughed outside the pub while another man hurried out of the Thai restaurant, swinging a plastic bag full of takeaway. An older couple strolled slowly along the street hand in hand, stopping to check the menus posted in restaurant windows.

I drew in a deep breath, and then another, trying to slow my racing heart. Should I warn them? But what would I say? *I saw some eyes, you'd better beware.* Maybe it had only been a possum. Maybe I was panicking over nothing.

"Yeah, and maybe we'll win the lottery tomorrow," Ariel said.

I jumped as she appeared in the seat beside me without warning. "Don't *do* that. My nerves are already shot to pieces."

"Sorry," she said, clearly not. "I can't believe you! You have the survival instincts of a cardboard box. *Is that you, Ethan?*"

"He said he wanted to make sure I was safe after work! And I did *not* sound that whiny."

"Sure you didn't. Why didn't you introduce yourself and invite that thing to dinner while you were at it?"

"It had some kind of hold on me—I couldn't move! Was it the elder? Did you see?"

"I'm not sure. It didn't look right for an elder, but I didn't get a good look at it before it got into the trees." She gave me a pointed look. "I was kind of busy saving some idiot's life."

"Thanks for that," I said, deciding to ignore the fact that she'd just called me an idiot. I could be grateful. I *was* grateful. I looked at her more carefully. "Are you okay? You look a little ... see-through."

When Ariel had first shown up in my life, she'd looked like a figure etched in glass, almost completely transparent. But in the years since then, she'd fleshed out—if you could call a being without a physical body *fleshed*. Most of the time, she appeared as real as anybody else, but right now I could see the outline of the door handle through her. I looked back at the road, swallowing. I'd forgotten how disconcerting that could be.

"I'm fine," she said. "Might take a bit of a nap. If you're okay, I'll see you at home."

"Sure." But I was talking to empty air. She'd already gone.

I turned out of Main Street and crossed the railway line. The railway and the highway that ran alongside it connected all the towns of the Blue Mountains to Sydney down below on one side, and to the vast farmlands of the Western Plains on the other. The mountain towns were scattered along the railway line like jewels spaced out on a necklace. But it was a very thin necklace.

Each jewel was a little pocket of civilisation along the spine of the mountains. On either side, gorges fell away into impenetrable bushland. There were still vast tracts of land up here where humans had never set foot. It meant we had more preternaturals than in the city, but the beauty of the area was worth a little extra risk. And not all of them were dangerous, for that matter.

But as the houses disappeared and the trees closed in on either side of the road, such reassuring reflections began to fade, and those baleful red eyes dominated my thoughts again. Was it the same thing that had found me last night in the bush? And if it was, did that mean it was stalking me?

Yikes. What a comforting thought. I felt very alone among the towering gum trees, conscious that Bugsy was all that stood between me and the empty night. Her dashboard lights glowed a reassuring green, but outside, the night pressed in. Visibility wasn't great. Mist was creeping out of the trees and spreading pale fingers across the road. Bugsy's headlights only lit it up, making it even harder to see what was actually out there.

My hands had clenched tight around the steering wheel, and I forced myself to loosen my grip and shake them out. *Come on, Sunday. Relax. You're almost home.*

And when I got there, the first thing I'd do would be to ring Ethan to let him know about the monster. If we were lucky and it hadn't gone far, the vampires might be able to find it. If I hadn't been so focused on fleeing, I could have done it before I started driving, but hopefully a few minutes' delay wouldn't matter.

The road swooped down into a gully, then climbed back out, Bugsy's engine labouring as she carved her way through the swirling mist. I hit the bend by the Rogersons' old place a little fast and felt Bugsy's back wheels skid out.

Heart in my mouth, I fought the car back onto the road and braked gently, my whole body trembling. I caught a glimpse of something out of the corner of my eye, a dark shape looming right next to me. I screamed and jerked the wheel convulsively and felt the impact as something glanced off the corner of Bugsy's front bumper.

I slammed on the brakes, heartbeat pounding in my ears. In front of me, a motorcycle tumbled like a toy thrown by a giant and slid off the road into the bushes on the verge. Something else hurtled overhead, then slammed down into the centre of the road.

The bike's rider.

I threw the door open and stumbled out of the car in shock. Where had he come from? I hadn't heard a thing or noticed a headlight in my rear vision mirror. The first inkling I'd had that he was there was when I glanced to the side and he was right next to me in the dark, overtaking on a curve. Crazypants.

I ran to his side and dropped to my knees on the hard road. Bugsy's headlights spilled across a pale face, half turned away from me, and black wavy hair. He wasn't wearing riding leathers, just a T-shirt and jeans. In weather like this? Double crazypants.

He was in pretty bad shape. He lay on his back, arms splayed out to the sides, and I almost gagged when I saw white bone poking out of a jagged wound on his right arm. Blood was pumping out of it, too, at a terrifying rate.

I stared at him, frozen in horror for an endless moment, watching the blood spurt out of his arm and pool on the dark road, glistening in Bugsy's headlights. That was way too much blood, *way* too fast. The guy was going to bleed out.

Quickly, I snapped out of my funk, unwound my scarf, and tied it around his arm in a makeshift tourniquet.

"I'm sorry, this is going to hurt." I pulled the knot as tight as I could. "Can you hear me? What's your name?"

No response. I hadn't really expected one, but I had vague memories of first aid training at one of the many schools I'd attended. First step was to establish whether the victim was conscious or not. Mercifully for him, this guy was definitely not.

I drew in a deep, shuddering breath. I couldn't give in to the panic that was bubbling behind my breastbone. Crazy guy was depending on me and my scarf. I ran a quick, assessing glance over him. There was a lot of blood. The other arm didn't seem broken, but it was one giant graze. In any contest between human flesh and road surface, the human flesh always came off second best. His jeans were pretty torn up, too, and he'd lost one of his shoes. His bare foot was covered in blood.

I leaned over him, checking his head. I didn't know if he'd been wearing a helmet, but he wasn't wearing one now, and if he'd hit the road head first, no tourniquet was going to save him.

"Hello?" My voice wobbled, and I cleared my throat. "Hello? Can you hear me?"

His eyelids didn't flutter. He lay as still as the dead. A dark five o'clock shadow covered his firm jawline, and some distant part of me noted that he had a cleft in his stubbled chin that Superman would have been proud of. The side of his face closest to me was unmarked apart from a curious scar that severed his right eyebrow into two distinct pieces. The other side was covered in blood. Face versus gravel hadn't gone well either.

The scarf was starting to feel very wet as I fumbled for my phone. The pool had spread until I was kneeling in it, its coppery tang everywhere, mingling with the stench of burnt rubber and overused brake discs. My knees were wet, my jeans soaked through with his blood.

"I'm going to call emergency now. Help will be here soon."

My hands were shaking so hard I dropped the phone onto his chest. Damn! I'd forgotten the first rule of first aid—I should have checked his airway straight away, but I'd been too distracted by the bleeding. I grabbed my phone and punched wildly at the numbers, my fingers shaking as if I were drunk.

His uninjured hand shot up and grabbed my wrist. I screamed and dropped the phone again.

"No doctors," he growled.

I stared down at him in shock, and he stared back, defiant. His eyes in Bugsy's lights were a vivid green.

"No doctors?" I blinked at him, dumbfounded. How was he even conscious after losing so much blood? "But you need help."

He must be in shock. He had no idea how badly injured he was.

"No doctors," he repeated firmly, his grip tightening on my wrist. His fingers were strong and very warm. Was infection setting in already? There was no way he should be that warm in this weather, dressed like that. A memory of Raquel's bare arms flashed into my mind. Was he some kind of preet?

I grabbed my phone with my free hand, not prepared to give in without a fight. Preternatural or not, he needed medical attention. "Mate, there's a bone poking right out of your arm. You have to go to the hospital."

He let me go, and I thought he'd come to his senses, but the next minute he was struggling to sit up, using his unbroken arm to lever himself into a sitting position.

"What are you doing? Keep still! You could have all

sorts of injuries." After slamming into the road like that, his organs were probably all smashed to pieces.

"Rubbish. A good night's sleep is all I need."

"A good night's—" My mouth fell open. This guy wasn't just on the bus to Crazy Town, he was the mayor of the whole darn place. "Your *arm* is broken. Your arm is so very, very broken that pieces of your bone are sticking right *out* of it." I gestured at the limb in question, still unable to look at it full on. "A good night's sleep can't *possibly* fix that."

"Are you always so strident?"

I sat back on my heels. Well! Of all the stupid, ungrateful ... "If I sound a little *strident*, it's because I'm in the middle of the bush in the freezing cold, kneeling in a pool of your stupid blood, trying to save your stupid life."

He cradled the broken arm against his body with the other one and raised that odd, split eyebrow at me. It gave him a roguish Jason Momoa kind of air, but I was in no mood to appreciate it.

"You saved my life?" he asked.

I gestured wildly at the blood all around us. It was on my pants, my shirt, and my hands were sticky with it. And of course, *he* looked like an extra from The Walking Dead.

"I think you severed an artery," I said. "There was blood spurting everywhere when I got here."

"Right. So that explains my new fashion accessory." He eyed the scarf around his arm with distaste.

"That fashion accessory just saved your life, buster."

"Then I thank you for your service. I owe you a life debt." He inclined his head in a strange sort of half bow, as if he were some grand nineteenth-century nobleman rewarding a peasant for catching his horse. Then he gathered his long legs under him and got to his feet, where he stood swaying.

I scrambled up, ready to catch him if he fell. He was a lot taller than he had looked lying down. I hadn't fully appreciated how wide his shoulders were either, or how muscled his arms. Of course, I'd been more concerned with how *damaged* they were and how fast his life was leaking out onto the asphalt. How *strange* of me to be concerned about such a small thing. Certainly, *he* didn't seem to care about it at all, though he still cradled his broken arm against his chest.

"Sit down before you fall over," I begged him. Come to think of it, there wouldn't be much point trying to catch him. He was clearly way heavier than I was.

He looked around, then frowned. "I'll leave you in peace in a moment. As soon as I find my bike."

His bike? How exactly did he plan on riding it with only one working arm?

"Of course. Your *bike*. It's over there," I said airily, gesturing at the darkness under the trees. "And over there. And there. Oh, and I think some of it ended up there, too."

For the first time, he appeared agitated. "You wrecked my bike?"

"*I* wrecked your bike? Excuse *me*, but I was just driving along minding my own business. *You* were the lunatic who came out of nowhere and overtook me *on a bend*. And while we're on the subject, where the heck is your helmet and your jacket? What kind of idiot goes riding in a T-shirt? Just look at your arm! No, not that one," I snapped as he glanced down at that nasty, nasty bone sticking out of his right arm. "The one that looks like it's been attacked by a cheese grater."

His eyes narrowed. "As I recall it, I was just *riding along, minding my own business*, when some lunatic woman swerved for no reason whatsoever and clipped my front wheel."

"Oh! Of all the ungrateful—"

"I'm not ungrateful, Miss ..." That eyebrow went up again, and this time a little tingle shot through me. So maybe I'd had a crush on Jason Momoa for years. Lots of people had celebrity crushes. It wasn't my fault that that eyebrow did things to me.

I cleared my throat. "Sunday. Sunday Armitage." I waited for the usual joke about my name, but it didn't come.

"Conal Clarke," he said. "So, since my bike is going to need a smash repairer and possibly a great deal of prayer, could I ask you for another favour?"

He didn't look half so obnoxious when he smiled like that, and I felt my outrage leaking away. What a night this had been. I was exhausted and it wasn't even dinner time.

"Of course."

"Perhaps you could drive me to my motel, and we'll sort all this out in the morning."

"It's your funeral," I muttered, and led the way back to Bugsy, keeping an eye on him in case he collapsed.

I opened the passenger door for him, and he subsided into the seat, folding his long body in with a groan. "Sorry about your upholstery," he said, tipping his head back against the headrest and letting his eyelids sag closed.

I got in the driver's side and leaned over to put his seatbelt on. Not that road rules and personal safety seemed high on his list of priorities, but I wouldn't be responsible if something else happened to him. "No problem. She'll wipe clean."

Pity I couldn't say the same for my pink scarf. That had been my favourite, too, not so big and bulky that it suffocated you but warm enough to keep the chill mountain air out. I glanced down at my jeans and sighed. They weren't looking so hot either. Oh, well. I started the car and took off, driving a lot slower than I had before.

"So where are you staying?"

There was no reply. When I glanced across at him, his lips were slightly parted, his head resting against the window, and he was passed out cold.

I looked down at his hands. They were as covered in gore as the rest of him, of course, but they were good, strong hands, with long, clever fingers. The one that had been cradling his broken arm had slid into his lap in sleep.

I frowned, trying to look closer at his arm and watch where we were going at the same time. Hadn't that wound been bigger earlier? My memory was supplying gory visions of a terrible gaping wound to his arm, laid open to the bone and beyond. But it didn't look nearly as bad now.

I glanced uncertainly into his face. He was still asleep. He looked tired, filthy, and completely human.

Had his arm seemed so much worse because of the panic of the moment? But I hadn't imagined the blood spurting out of it. The evidence was all over both of us, and the car reeked like a butcher's shop. I was sure he'd been bleeding out when I found him, his lifeblood pumping out of a severed artery. Even my tourniquet probably shouldn't have been enough to save him. And yet here we were.

He had to be some kind of preet. But which one?

4

I should drive him to the hospital whether he was human or not. There was one at Katoomba, which was only fifteen minutes away. He'd been adamant that he didn't want a doctor, but he was asleep or unconscious now, which meant he didn't get a say anymore.

Taking him to his motel was out of the question. Even if I'd known where he was staying, I couldn't in good conscience abandon him like that in his current condition. So, the choices were hospital—and potentially having to deal with him freaking out about it when we got there—or taking him to my place.

Not that I would normally contemplate bringing a strange man into my home, particularly not one who was most likely a preternatural. But this one was so broken that I figured he wouldn't give me any trouble.

I wished Ariel were here—not to advise me, because *obviously* she'd say something snarky and stupid. But I needed a friend. I was still shaking, and the thought of sitting in Emergency with an uncooperative and possibly hostile patient didn't exactly appeal.

The mist slunk back under the trees as Bugsy climbed out of the hollow we'd been in. Home was only a couple of minutes away, its comfort seriously beckoning. And he *had* said no doctors. It wouldn't be my fault if he ended up with permanent damage to his arm because he refused to see a doctor.

The petrol light came on, its orange eye accusing me.

There were two kinds of people in the world: those who never let their petrol tank dip below a quarter full and liked to fill up when it was still half full, "just in case"— and then there were the people like me, who drove for days with desperately crossed fingers because they couldn't spare the money for fuel.

Well, that decided things. I *might* have enough petrol to get to Katoomba, but I definitely wouldn't have enough to get back—and I had exactly $2.35 in my account. Bugsy wouldn't be getting a drink until pay day.

"Looks like you're spending the night at my place," I told my silent passenger. "Snore once if this plan is totally fine with you."

He wasn't quite snoring, but I figured deep breathing counted. A few minutes later, I was pulling into the driveway of the optimistically named Magnolia Court, then into my own little parking spot underneath the building. I turned the motor off and let my head fall back against the headrest for a long moment, trying to relax my shoulders, which were so tight I might never move them again.

"First step is getting you inside." I touched him gently on the shoulder, trying to avoid any bits that looked too banged up. "Wake up, sleepyhead. We're here."

He didn't stir. I sighed and got out, feeling vertebrae pop all the way up my spine as I stretched. If I couldn't rouse him, this would get interesting fast, because there was no way I could move him on my own. I imagined knocking on Mr Garcia's door for assistance and grinned. Poor old Mr Garcia had enough trouble keeping upright on his own without adding six-plus feet of unconscious muscle into the mix.

I eased the passenger door open carefully, since Conal's head was leaning against it, and caught his weight before he fell straight out of the car. That would be one way to wake him up, but probably not ideal in the circumstances. I shook him more firmly, since this was the unbroken arm. "Hey, Conal. Wake up. This is the end of the line."

Thankfully, this time he stirred and opened bleary eyes. Under the harsh lights of the car park, they were a startling green against the deep tan of his skin; the light, pure green of sun-kissed sea.

"My motel?" He hung onto the door frame with his unbroken arm and levered himself out of Bugsy, looking around dazedly. It took some doing, and he swayed dangerously, so I tucked myself under his good arm.

"Kind of. It's where you're staying for the night, at least." I threw my arm around his waist as he staggered. "Easy there. Just stand still a minute till you get your balance."

"Head's spinning," he said, and I bit my lip. That could be concussion. Suddenly my decision to avoid the hospital didn't look so smart.

"Change of plan. Hop back in and I'll run you over to Katoomba." Fingers crossed Bugsy would make it. "They have a 24-hour emergency department at the hospital there." Heaven knew how I'd get back again—maybe Conal could lend me some money.

He staggered a couple of steps away from the car and leaned up against one of the concrete pillars supporting the low roof. "No. No doctors. I don't need them. Just help me get inside."

I glared at him. He was listing to one side like a drunk. Even preternaturals needed medical help sometimes. But when I glanced at his broken arm again, there was no sign of bone. He glared right back at me, and I shrugged. He was twice my size. It wasn't as if I could *force* him.

"Fine." That arm was definitely healing way faster than it should be. Hopefully, his head was just as bulletproof. I locked Bugsy's door and hauled him upright, tucking myself into his armpit for support again. "Don't say I didn't warn you."

I manoeuvred him up the stairs to the foyer. *That* was an adventure. More than once we came perilously close to tumbling right back down again. I clutched handfuls of his shirt in one hand and clung on to the rail for grim death with the other. By the time we gained the safety of the foyer, we were both soaked in sweat.

I unlocked my front door and got him inside. His eyes were half closed again, all the fight gone out of him now he'd won the battle over the hospital, and he leaned heavily on me as we staggered across the open plan lounge-slash-kitchen.

Halfway to the couch, I realised we had a problem. The couch was only a two-seater, and there was way more man than couch. I could hardly jam him in there in his current condition.

I altered course and staggered towards the bedroom instead. I wouldn't fit so well on the couch either, but better than he would.

I tried to ease him down onto the bed, but he was way past easing. All but unconscious, really. His whole weight crashed onto the mattress, taking me with him, and I ended up half sprawled across his long, lean body.

"Sorry about that," I said as I scrambled backwards, but he was so far gone he hadn't noticed. I unlaced his one remaining shoe and chucked it on the floor, then stood back and considered the rest of him doubtfully.

He was crusted in gravel and covered in blood and dirt, though most of the blood was pretty dry by now. His jeans were ripped to shreds all down the side where they'd met the road. He'd probably be more comfortable without them, but undressing him and actually getting him into the bed was a task that I wasn't prepared to attempt. Besides, my quilt was probably ruined after this. No need to destroy the sheets as well. He'd just have to sleep in his filth and we'd deal with it all tomorrow.

My gaze rested on his face, which was softened in sleep. Even without that sexy eyebrow, he had a face to tempt any red-blooded woman. His lips were full, his nose was straight, his jaw strong and almost square. Now that he wasn't arguing with me anymore it didn't make him look stubborn, just ridiculously handsome. And that cleft in his chin ... I'd always had a thing for those. It was the Superman Look, and virtually irresistible. The only thing that could possibly make him *more* handsome would be a dimple when he smiled.

And that just wouldn't be fair. Conal Clarke was already way more good-looking than any one person had a right to be. My fingers itched to sketch that handsome face.

Fascinated, I moved my attention to his broken arm— only now it wasn't broken. There was no sign of bone anymore. The wound was still there, but it was half the size it had been before.

So—obviously a preternatural. One of the ones that could pass as human, which didn't narrow it down that much. But they were all trouble.

I left him there and shut the bedroom door behind me.

"Wow," I told my empty apartment. Years of talking to Ariel had given me the habit of speaking aloud, even if I was alone. "Tonight has been a literal car crash. Luckily, Strong, Independent Women can handle anything."

That was one of Ivy's favourite sayings. She was all about the girl power. She'd been reminding me what Strong, Independent Women could achieve since I was six years old.

First, this Strong, Independent Woman needed something to eat, stat. And that was Ling's influence. A good meal could fix almost anything—and if it wasn't fixed, well, at least you faced your problems with a full stomach.

There was no sign of Ariel as I made myself a cup of soup from a packet and popped a couple of slices of bread in the toaster to go with it. Even if there'd been anything more closely resembling a nutritious dinner in my house at this point in the pay cycle, I couldn't have been bothered to prepare it. I yawned so hard while I waited for the toast that my jaw popped.

The toast launched itself at warp speed, as usual. I caught it and slathered it with butter. At least there was still plenty of that. The soup was warm, and I felt my whole body relax as warmth sank into me. Ling was definitely on to something—a bit of food in your stomach really did help.

While I thought of it, I poured some milk into a bowl and set it beside the front door. I did that every night—I hadn't given up hope that a brownie would one day decide to take up residence. It would sure save me a lot of cleaning. Even Ling couldn't find any fault with a brownie's work.

It probably came from spending the last twenty years living in a tiny motorhome, but Ling was very firm on *a place for everything and everything in its place*. A mere pile of books on the coffee table had made her shudder last time she visited, so heaven knew what she would make of the current state of barely controlled chaos.

Probably best if we never found out.

I collapsed into a dining chair, soup cradled in my cold hands. If Conal Clarke decided to sue me over his busted bike, I was in serious trouble.

My gaze fell on the bookcase. The cards called to me, as they usually did when I felt a need for guidance.

Oh, not my own deck, with all its limitations. I hesitated for a moment. After all, Conal was in the next room. But the door was shut, and he'd probably be out for hours. I pulled *The Lord of the Rings* off the shelf. It had been my mother's favourite book, and I actually owned two copies. One to read and one to hold my greatest treasure, my last connection to Mum.

I brought it to the table and munched absently on my toast as I opened the book to reveal its secret—the pages had been painstakingly glued together and a neat rectangle cut out of the middle of them so that the book formed a sneaky little box to hide something in.

And the something, in this case, was my mother's deck of cards.

Every cartomancer drew or painted her own deck— that was part of the magic. I tipped them out into my hands, the feel of their worn edges as familiar to me as my own deck. I couldn't use these cards for magic, because they would only answer to my mother, but just holding them in my hands made me feel less alone. And they still worked just fine as a Tarot deck.

My fingers tingled with power. Mum had been a much stronger cartomancer than I was. Even after all these years, magic lingered in her cards. I started shuffling, keeping one ear open for any sound from the bedroom. I was sure Conal wouldn't wake up, considering what bad shape he was in, but you could never be too careful.

Traditional Tarot decks were very similar to the decks

we used, although no one now was sure which had come first—too much had been lost over the centuries. Some cartomancers even read Tarot for a living, although to me that seemed like asking for trouble.

A traditional Tarot deck had seventy-eight cards, fifty-six minor arcana and twenty-two major arcana. The fifty-six cards of the minor arcana resembled a regular deck of playing cards in the way they were divided into four suits which ran Ace to 10, followed by four court cards. The major arcana had names like Death, the Tower, the Lovers, or the Empress. They represented big things like life events and major changes.

A cartomancer's deck only held as many cards as she could work with. In my case, that wasn't so many. I didn't have a single one of the majors. But Mum's deck was nearly full. It was also gorgeous. I'd inherited my artistic talents from Mum, but I was nowhere near her level of skill yet and maybe never would be. She was a true artist, each card lovingly drawn in a free-flowing, joyful style and full of the bright colours she'd loved so much.

Ariel popped into existence in the chair opposite me, making me jump. You'd think after all these years I'd be used to it, but it had been a stressful night.

"Where have you been?" I asked. "I was starting to get worried."

"I'm a big girl, Mum, you don't have to worry about me."

I fanned the cards out on the table in front of me, letting my fingers wander over the familiar pictures lovingly. When I looked at the gentle half smile on the face of the Empress or saw the light in the laughing eyes of the Fool, Mum's face became clearer in my mind. I had very few actual memories of her since I'd been so young when she died. Most of what I knew of her had been learned from the Dynamic Duo or from long hours spent gazing at the few photos of her that they possessed.

"You're looking better," I said. "Not so see-through. How are you feeling?"

"Fine." She shrugged. "Did I miss anything?"

"Nah. Just the part where I nearly killed a guy."

I picked up Mum's cards again and started shuffling, letting the familiar comfort wash over me. This time I drew a card. I did this whenever I felt unsettled or needed some motherly advice. In a strange way, I felt as if Mum still spoke to me through her cards.

"That's it? That's all you're going to tell me?" Ariel asked, incredulous. "No way. Spill!"

I grinned at her, a laugh bubbling up inside. Ariel often disappeared without warning, sometimes for days at a time, and she never told me where she'd been. In fact, sometimes it seemed as if she wasn't even aware that she'd been gone. She picked right up where we'd left off as if the space of hours or days had never happened. It was fun to have a big secret to taunt *her* with for a change.

I shrugged. "Knocked him off his bike. He was really cute, too."

"Before or after you knocked him off his bike?"

"Both, actually."

I flipped over my card and found that I'd drawn the Fool. In Mum's deck, the Fool was a girl with sun-bronzed bare legs, wearing a dress patterned with daisies. She laughed up at the sun, spinning around as she danced perilously close to the edge of a cliff.

But if you looked carefully, that cliff was like nothing that had ever existed in reality, strangely crystalline and glittering, as if it were encrusted with jewels. The joyful dancer didn't look entirely human either, her face unnaturally long, her eyes unusually large, and her hair spinning around her like cobwebs, light as air. There was even a suggestion of something behind her that might have been wings.

In traditional Tarot, the Fool was often a warning against impulsiveness. Something new was beginning, but you had to take care not to leap into it without looking first. But of course, a cartomancer could make it mean many things. And why would a winged girl have to look before she leapt? She seemed lighter than air already, and the cliff was no looming danger but a beautiful fairy landscape for her to dance into.

Ariel made an impatient noise. "What happened to him?"

I nodded at the bedroom door. "He's in there."

Her eyes widened. "What, did you run him over so you could abduct him and he wouldn't fight back?"

"Well," I said, pretending to consider it, "he *was* pretty weak when I got him into the bedroom."

"Nooooo."

I laughed at the outrage on her face.

She disappeared, and I knew she'd gone to check him out. I got up and peeked into the bedroom. As expected,

Conal was out like a light, and Ariel stood next to the bed, frowning down at him.

"He *is* pretty cute. But what's that on his arm?"

He'd shifted in his sleep, and his sleeve had ridden up, exposing a well-defined bicep. My breath caught in my throat. He had a tattoo there. Only the bottom was visible, but my pulse was racing as I entered the room and pushed up his sleeve.

Oh, son of a mother trucker. A stylised flame bloomed from a cross in the centre of a circle.

That was a Soldier of the Light tattoo. My fingers recoiled automatically.

Suddenly he didn't look so delicious. He was a wolf, one of the enemy. Men like him had been hunting and killing women like me for centuries.

And now I had one in my home. In my *bed*. This was like my worst nightmare come true.

Horrified, I met Ariel's gaze. "He's one of *them*."

"Stay calm," she said. "Who's afraid of the Big Bad Wolf?"

"Are you kidding? *I* am." There was a time for self-confidence and there was a time for facing facts.

My stomach churned as I stared down at him. My first instinct was to run and keep on running until Conal Clarke was a distant memory—but I was done with that. That had been my life for too long. I was taking a stand in Kurranderra. No more running. I had a life that I liked, and I wasn't giving it up without a fight.

"Then we just have to get rid of him as fast as possible," Ariel said.

"Yeah."

"So, I'm guessing you *didn't* make the beast with two backs with him?"

I choked back a laugh. However bad the situation, Ariel could always make me laugh. "Beast with two backs? Where on earth did you get that from?"

She shrugged. "I dunno. I think it's Shakespeare, from when I was watching that series of plays last year." Ariel watched way more TV than I did because she spent so much time at home with the TV for company while I went to work. She was practically addicted to daytime soaps. "So did you?"

"Of course I didn't. The man's a *wolf*. Not a simple werewolf. One of *them*."

"Yeah, I got that. But you didn't know that until now, did you?" She shook her head. "Shame. Another opportunity wasted. But you'd have slept with him if he wasn't, right?"

I threw my hands up. "Does it matter? He's a Soldier! He'd rather burn me than bonk me."

And here I was with Mum's cards casually on display in the next room. I rushed back to the dining table and began gathering them up with shaking hands. At least my own deck was safely tucked away at the back of the wardrobe.

"But he doesn't know about your magic, does he?" Ariel asked.

"No." And unless he caught me actually casting a spell, he wouldn't.

"Are you scared?"

"Of course I am! Do I *look* stupid?"

The Two of Air slipped out and fell on the table. I picked it up, wondering, as I always did when I saw this card, what the missing Three of Air looked like.

Because there were two cards missing from Mum's deck: the Three and the Queen of Air. I'd always wondered if they were missing because she'd had them with her when she died.

"He's probably only here to search for the elder," Ariel said, trying to be encouraging.

"Yeah." That was their job, after all, and the only thing these supposed "Soldiers" were good for. They were meant to keep humans safe by hunting down any preternaturals that crossed the line.

"So, you just need to keep your head down until he leaves. Shouldn't be a problem."

I nodded. She was right. I could do this. "I'll tell Ethan I can't help him out anymore. Hopefully they'll find the elder soon and he'll be gone."

Which reminded me, I hadn't called Ethan to tell him about the monster lurking behind the shop. Too late now. It would be long gone.

The Fool stared up at me as I shut the book on her face. I glanced toward the closed bedroom door. New beginnings? No way, José. Not with that guy.

However pretty his sea-green eyes, Conal Clarke was a stone-cold killer.

5

_____

The next morning, I woke to the sizzle of something frying and the delicious smell of bacon wafting through my tiny apartment. I sat bolt upright on the couch, completely disoriented for a moment, and gazed wildly around. There was a strange man in my kitchen and he was cooking _my_ bacon.

I leapt off the couch—well, at least, that was the intention. What actually happened was that my back complained about being crammed into a tiny two-seater sofa for the night at the same time my foot got caught in the blanket that had been wrapped around me, and I half fell, half staggered off the couch and crashed into the dining chairs.

The strange man in my kitchen turned to look at me about the same time as my brain finally came online. Right. Conal Clarke, witch hunter. And also, apparently, a cook.

"You look ... a lot better than you did last night." I had

to make a conscious effort to close my mouth, because it wanted to hang open in astonishment.

A lot better was only the understatement of the century. He'd obviously showered, because his dark hair curled damply against his neck, but showering couldn't have cleaned his clothes or fixed the giant rents in his T-shirt and jeans.

He smiled, crow's feet appearing at the corners of those amazing green eyes. "I told you I didn't need the doctor."

I staggered over to him, unhappily aware that I had slept in my bloodstained clothes and my hair probably looked like a bird's nest from being stuffed into a corner of the couch. *He* was the one who'd been injured, so how was it fair that he looked like he was getting ready for a model shoot and I looked like something the cat wouldn't even bother to drag in?

The closer I got to him, the more outraged I became. He smelled *divine*, and there wasn't a mark on him. No wounds, no gravel rash—not even a paper cut. Even his clothes looked like they'd just come off the rack, and that T-shirt had been a bloody, torn mess last night.

"Are you hungry?" He turned back to the stove. "I cooked everything you had."

There was definite disapproval in his voice, as if everything I had was nowhere near enough. He had my four precious rashers of bacon frying in one pan, and the four eggs in the other. Guess I wouldn't be having a cooked breakfast tomorrow.

"Well, your motel might have provided a better menu,

but you checked out on me before you could tell me the name of it, so beggars can't be choosers."

The toaster popped as I finished speaking, and two slices of toast launched skyward. Faster than thought, his hand shot out and snatched them out of the air, then he fed another two slices of bread into the mouth of the monster.

"You should eat more." He glanced at me long enough to run a critical eye over me. "You look like you could use a decent feed."

I put my hands on my hips. He might be a psycho killer, but there were limits. "Anything else you'd like to criticise while you're at it? Was the bed entirely to Sir's liking last night?"

He actually appeared to give the question some thought. "Your driving," he said after a moment.

"Sorry?"

He served two slices of sizzling bacon onto each plate. "You asked if there was anything else I'd like to criticise. Your driving. You could be living your blissful, practically food-free existence without ever having met me if only you were a better driver."

"Oh, that's rich. You were the idiot overtaking me out of nowhere on a bend. Did you get your licence out of a cereal box?"

He cocked that scarred eyebrow, momentarily distracting me. How did one little scar make a man look so hot? Although, come to think of it, it wasn't just the scar. There were those amazing eyes, too, and that little smile that tugged at the corner of his mouth. *Don't forget the psycho killer part*, I reminded myself before I got too carried away.

"Are you always this full of sweetness and light in the morning?" he asked.

I gave him a syrupy smile. "Do you always ride like a crackhead?"

"I won the Australian Crackhead Championships three years running," he deadpanned.

The toaster chose that moment to eject the next two slices of bread at warp speed. He caught them as deftly as he'd caught the first two, laying them on the plates next to the bacon. Then he served the eggs, one on top of each slice of toast. Sunny side up, just the way I liked them.

I leaned across the bench and poked him hard in the arm as the last egg nestled into its toasty bed.

"What was that for?"

"Checking if you're real. If all of this"—I gestured, indicating his whole body—"is real. You didn't even flinch when I poked your arm, and last night it had a *bone* sticking out of it. I'm guessing you're some kind of preternatural."

Let him think I was some clueless human. I'd decided last night, as I lay awake worrying, that that would be the best plan. Keep it casual, as if I had nothing to hide, then get rid of him as fast as possible.

He carried the plates to the table and set them down opposite each other. "Why don't we eat first?"

I grabbed some cutlery and sat down. He made a good point. No use letting that bacon get cold. I figured if he knew what I was, he would have attacked by now—and if he killed me later, at least I'd go with a full stomach.

He ate fast, like a man who hadn't seen food in a week. His miraculous healing powers must take a lot of fuel. By the time I'd eaten my two rashers of bacon, his plate had been scraped totally clean, and from the way he was staring at it, I had the impression that if I hadn't been there, he would have picked it up and licked off the last vestiges of egg yolk. Then he eyed my eggs with such obvious interest that it was like having a golden retriever watch me eat.

At least he wasn't drooling. I picked up one of the egg-topped pieces of toast and dumped it on his plate.

"I'm not hungry," I lied. "Go ahead."

I'd half expected him to do the usual polite dance of insisting that he couldn't and me having to insist that he could, but he took me at my word and the egg went to join its brethren in record time. He still finished eating before me.

When I was done, I put my knife and fork together neatly on my plate. "So."

He leaned back in his chair, one arm hooked over the back of it. "So."

"Oh, come on," I said when he stopped there. "I've housed you, fed you, and now I think you owe me some answers."

"That's one way of looking at it," he said, that little half-smile playing around his mouth again. I really wished I had a pencil in hand. That expression just begged to be sketched.

"What other way is there?"

"You ran me off the road and very nearly killed me, and in the *anguish* of your repentance, you brought me back here and did what *little* you could to make it up to me." He eyed the empty plates and sighed. Clearly, the feeding part of the deal hadn't measured up to his expectations. "I'd say there's a very good argument that you're still deeply in my debt and I owe you nothing."

"Maybe you'd say that if you were a *complete jerk*." Was there some kind of *don't ask, don't tell* code among the wolves? "You don't have to be shy with me. My ex-boyfriend is a vampire. I'm not going to come over all faint when you tell me what you are—because clearly you're *something*. Look at that arm. Not a trace of gravel rash, not a broken bone in sight. You're not human."

"I think we can agree on that," he said. "Do the details really matter?"

"Are you kidding? Super healing is all well and good, but if you've got some magic that can get bloodstains out of clothes and stitch them back together so they're as good as new, I'd love to hear about it." I gestured at my own blood-stained shirt. "Because I've got some prime material right here that you could work your magic on."

He threw his head back, showing the strong, tanned column of his throat, and laughed in delight. "That's a new one. Most people get excited by the super healing, but Sunday Armitage thinks a great laundry trick is far more interesting."

"You can laugh, but if you had to try scrubbing the stains out, you'd be pretty excited, too." He'd remembered my name, despite the state he'd been in last night. That made me feel oddly warm inside.

"Sorry to burst your bubble, Sunny— May I call you Sunny?"

I opened my mouth to say all my friends did, then nodded instead. I was pretty sure he wasn't going to be one of my friends. Even without the whole witch-hunting thing, there was still the little problem of a wrecked motor-bike to be sorted out, and I didn't have any insurance.

"Shame," Ariel said, appearing on the kitchen bench, feet swinging lazily. "Are you sure you don't want to bonk him? He washes up *real* nice."

Will you cut that out? I hate it when you read my mind. And of course I'm not going to bonk him. Are you insane?

"Unfortunately, that trick only works on my own clothes," Conal said. "And I have to be wearing them at the time. Although, you'll be pleased to know that hideous scarf you tied around my arm last night is back to its blood-free state."

"That scarf is *not* hideous."

His eyes lingered on my blood-soaked T-shirt. I was glumly certain that even Sard's Wonder Soap wouldn't be up to the challenge of fixing it. And this had been one of my favourite shirts, too. "How did you get so much blood on you?" Concern warmed his eyes. "You weren't hurt, too, were you?"

"Nope. This is all yours, and I got it trying to save your ungrateful life."

"I'm not ungrateful. I believe I thanked you for saving me last night."

I shrugged, toying with the knife handle on my plate. "I'm not so sure I did anything. Your A-plus super-secret healing powers probably would have done the job without me."

He shook his head. "I saw the amount of blood on the road. I would have bled out before my body had time to heal itself if you hadn't been there. I owe you a life debt."

"That sounds serious."

"It is. I'll protect you with my life." He said it lightly, as if it were no big deal, but something in his taut stillness suggested he wasn't joking. "Pinkie promise."

I opened my mouth to say something scathing about the promises of Soldiers of the Light, but luckily caught myself in time.

"Fine. I saved you. So how about showing some of that gratitude and answering my questions?"

"Such a fierce negotiator," he said, a smile lurking in those green eyes. In the sunlight coming through the kitchen windows, they sparkled like peridots. "Are you a lawyer?"

I snorted. "You think I'd be living in a place like this if I were a lawyer?"

He glanced around my apartment, and I knew how it must look to him. Bare wooden floors; a single cramped couch; the tiny table at which we were sitting, with its mismatched dining chairs; and a not-quite-level set of bookshelves, their cheerful yellow paint peeling. *Behold my elaborate furnishings.*

"I figured you were going for the minimalist look. I hear it's very in these days."

He looked at me, and there was something in his eyes —not quite pity, but close enough that I looked down at my empty plate. I didn't need anyone's pity. All I needed was pay day to come a little faster and for no one to demand I pay the cost of their wrecked motorbike.

Oh, and for this annoying Soldier to get out of my life.

"I like him," Ariel said. "He's sassy."

Don't get too cuddly. This wolf has teeth.

"Should I be worried that I have an unidentified preternatural in my home?" I was still thinking about teeth. "I mean, you still look hungry. You're not going to eat me, are you?"

"Are you offering?" Ariel asked. "You just told *me* not to get cuddly!"

Wow, I was doing well today. *You have a filthy mind.*

Fortunately, I didn't blush like Bethany, but I leapt up all the same and gathered the plates with unnecessary enthusiasm so that I wouldn't have to look at the smile spreading across his face.

"There's not enough meat on your bones to tempt any self-respecting preternatural," he said. "I don't suppose you have anything else to eat, do you?"

I rinsed the plates off in the sink then started the hot water running to wash them properly. Spending so many years living in cramped quarters with the Dynamic Duo had given me an appreciation for washing up after every meal and packing things away.

"There's plenty of bread in the freezer if you want some more toast, and jam in the fridge."

I probably hadn't needed to add that bit about the jam.

He could hardly have missed it when he got out the eggs and bacon, since there was barely anything else in there.

Again, I half-expected him to politely refuse the offer, but again I was surprised. He came into the kitchen and took a pile of bread out of the packet. There were only a couple of slices left when he put it back in the freezer.

I squirted some dishwashing liquid into the sink and breathed in its lemony scent as bubbles foamed up. "You're really going to eat all that?" He had six—no, seven—slices there.

He put two slices in the toaster and eyed me in confusion. "Yes? Why, do you want some?"

I could tell he was looking for a *no*. Clearly, witch-hunting worked up an appetite.

"It must take a lot to fuel muscles like that," Ariel said, studying the way his T-shirt clung to his back with naked interest.

Let's focus on what's important here, shall we? We can't afford to be distracted by a pretty face.

"Who said anything about his face? Are you sure *you're* not the one who needs to focus?"

I blamed those astonishing green eyes. And that sexy, sexy eyebrow. I turned my attention to the sink full of dishes. My gravestone was *not* going to say *Killed due to an unfortunate obsession with Jason Momoa's eyebrow*. I needed to take my own advice and focus on getting rid of this guy, pronto.

He loitered by the toaster, not offering to help with the washing up. That was probably fair enough, given the idiosyncrasies of my toaster. He had to stay close and be prepared to catch if he didn't want his snack ending up drowning in the sink.

"Are you going grocery shopping today?" he asked casually. Maybe a little too casually. I shot him a sidelong glance, but his expression was bland, as if he were just making conversation. "I'll give you some money to make up for all this food I'm eating."

"You don't need to do that." The habit of hospitality had been ingrained in me from an early age. Ling had a fondness for feeding people that bordered on an obsession —and guests were never expected to contribute anything. "You should probably save your money for your motel and, you know, the bike."

I cleared my throat nervously. I had no idea how much motorbikes cost, but I was absolutely certain it was more than I could afford. My best hope lay in convincing him that the accident had been his fault.

"Which it totally was," Ariel said.

I appreciated the loyalty, so I didn't point out that she hadn't actually been there.

The toast leapt up, and he caught it without even looking. "Ah, yes. The bike. Where exactly did you say it was?"

He turned away and began to slather his toast with jam, and I let my breath out in a rush. "It's on Ridge Road up near the old Rogerson place." *You idiot, Sunday. He doesn't know where that is.* "It's a big white building that looks like a Spanish hacienda with a circular driveway and lots of fruit trees. You can't miss it. It was on the bend just before that, going from here to there. I'm afraid it's in a few pieces."

He shrugged. "It's probably not as bad as it looked last night."

I wasn't so sure about that, but it had been dark and I hadn't been paying that much attention to the bike. Maybe he was right. That would be good. He could get on his bike and ride off into the sunset as far as I was concerned.

The two slices of toast and jam disappeared in a few bites, and he was all ready when the next two popped out. His capacity for food was amazing. I stopped washing up to watch him eat. It gave me a curious satisfaction to see him devouring my food with such obvious relish. At least he couldn't complain that I had starved him.

A guest should always leave your home richer than when she arrived, Ivy always said. She meant for the experience, but Ling usually added, *and stuffed to their eyeballs with food*.

"I hope you're right." I took a deep breath. "I don't have car insurance."

I mean, I had third-party insurance, because it was compulsory, but I was pretty sure that didn't cover this kind of damage to property. It was only for injury to people.

"Shouldn't be a problem," he said between bites.

Excellent. The last thing I needed was protracted contact with a Soldier over fixing a stupid bike. I needed this guy out of my life *yesterday*. I went back to scrubbing dried egg off the tines of a fork.

In no time at all, it seemed, the toast was all gone and he was passing me the plate and knife to wash.

"Guess I'd better head out there and assess the

damage," he said. He was walking away from me as he spoke, back into the bedroom, giving me a nice view of broad shoulders tapering to a narrow waist and a cute butt.

He reappeared almost immediately, and I wondered what he'd been doing in there.

"Do you want me to give you a lift?" I asked. Bugsy had enough petrol left for that.

A mocking light danced in his eyes. "What, and give you another chance to kill me with your terrible driving? I don't think so."

I was still staring in outrage, fumbling for a good come-back, when the door closed behind him.

6

*M*onday started off great. I sang along to the radio on the way to the supermarket before work, high on sugar after a breakfast of chocolate croissants. It turned out that Conal had left some money behind despite my telling him not to, and I'd spent it all first thing Saturday morning.

When I walked into my bedroom after he'd left, it had been the first thing I'd seen. Snuggled up next to my clean scarf, a little pile of twenties stacked up on my pillow. Five of them.

He deserved a way better breakfast than I'd given him for a hundred bucks. I'd stood there, holding the money in my hand, actually physically feeling a weight lift off my shoulders. I could buy petrol and restock the fridge and pantry. With that sort of money, I could even afford a few treats.

I had kind of mixed feelings about it—but not mixed enough that I refused to spend his cash. And it wasn't as if

I could give it back, was it? I had no idea where to find him, and I was unlikely to see him again, as long as I kept my head down while he was in town.

It was probably his way of apologising for the dirt and bloodstains he'd left all over my quilt and pillowcase. And if I'd felt any guilt when I handed it to the cashier, well, I'd just looked at the tray of mini cheesecakes *with berry-licious topping* in my basket and the guilt had disappeared like magic.

My phone rang as I pulled up in the car park behind Second Chances. *Ling the Merciless* popped up on the screen.

"Hi, Ling! How are you?"

"A rogue has killed two people in that town." That was Ling for you—straight to business.

"I'm good, thanks for asking. How are you?"

"Sunday Armitage, don't sass your aunt."

"What Ling means to say is *hi, darling, we're worried about you*." That was Ivy. Ling had put it on loudspeaker.

"Hi, Ivy. I miss you guys. Where are you at the moment?"

Ivy started to reply, but Ling cut her off. "Don't let her distract you with small talk. Sunny, you need to leave before the Soldiers arrive."

"I'll be fine." No need to tell her that at least one Soldier was already in town—much less that he'd been right there in my home. Ivy would panic and Ling would get mad, and we'd have another one of those fights like we'd had when I first said I was staying in Kurranderra. And no one had time for that.

"It's too big a risk," Ling said firmly.

Ling said everything firmly. She lived in the absolute certainty that she was always right. It was just as well I loved her.

"It's not that big a deal. We've had rogues in the mountains before, and it looks like an elder. I'm sure the hive will shut it down. There's no need to run."

"But wouldn't you like to hit the road with us again?" Ivy asked hopefully. "You've been there a year."

"Yes, I have. Isn't that great?" I said brightly. Surely she wasn't serious? I knew she was worried, but I was a little too old to be tagging along with my aunties. I liked my independence. "I've made some friends here. I've got a job and a place to live. I'm happy."

"But there are always new people to meet and new places to explore," Ivy said in a wheedling tone. "Think of what you could be missing out on just around the bend."

I shook my head. "I'm not like you two. You love the road. Always have."

"You used to enjoy going on the road with us when you were small," Ivy said, her voice softening as if she were thinking back to earlier times with that little Sunday.

Had I? Maybe they remembered it differently than I did. They were thinking of the excitement of exploring new places. Sure, some of it had been fun. Discovering where to buy the best milkshake in town had always been the first priority for ten-year-old Sunday when we arrived somewhere new. But perhaps their memories glossed over the parts where I cried every time we left another set of friends behind and hit the road again.

"Well, maybe I've changed. I want to see how normal people live."

"Normal is boring," Ling said.

"Then maybe I'm boring."

"You definitely are," Ariel said, popping into being in the passenger seat.

Go stick your head in the toilet. I got out of the car and locked it.

"Is normal worth dying for?" Ling asked.

"You can't risk it," Ivy said. "You can't let the Soldiers find you."

"They won't find me," I said patiently. Conal had been right there in my house and his charming behaviour proved that he'd had no idea I was a cartomancer. He wouldn't have been happily vowing to protect the life of a sworn enemy. "As long as I don't use magic, I'll be fine."

"That's what your mother thought, too," Ling said darkly.

I sighed. We had no actual proof that the Soldiers had killed Mum, but nothing short of death would have stopped her coming home, leaving her six-year-old daughter to be brought up by her best friends.

"I have to go, or I'll be late for work."

"Think about it," Ling said. "Think about what you're risking."

I said I would and hung up, but my happy mood was gone. They meant well, but I wasn't stupid—and I wasn't prepared to spend my life on the road as they did.

"Thank goodness you're here," Cheryl said as I walked in. Her thick brown hair was already escaping its ponytail and she looked more tired than usual. She was a fit forty-something but never seemed to get enough sleep. "I just had a call from the school. Mikey's sick. He said he had a tummy ache this morning, but I thought he was just trying to get out of school. They have to do their speeches today, and he hates public speaking."

She had her bag over her shoulder already, her keys in her hand. Cheryl was a single mum to twin boys, and her life seemed to be one long series of domestic disasters, but she handled them all with ruthless efficiency.

"Does that mean Ryan's going to get it, too?"

She grimaced. "Probably. They share everything, even the germs. Can you handle things here by yourself until Bethany comes in this afternoon?"

"Of course." Monday was our busiest day, but I was an old hand by now. "You look a bit pale. Are you sure you're not coming down with it, too?"

"I'm fine. Just tired." She smiled. "Story of my life, but I wouldn't have it any other way. See you tomorrow, I hope! I'll let you know."

Of course, the minute she was out the door, the shop filled up with people, all needing my attention. Half of them were grumpy and the other half were rude. It was a plague of Mondayitis.

One woman ranted at me for a solid five minutes about a stain on the hem of a dress that was so tiny you almost needed a magnifying glass to find it, and yet she insisted on getting the dress at half price because it was "ruined".

"If it's ruined, what does she want it for?" Ariel said, scowling.

It was only ten dollars anyway, but I gave in and let her have it for five and watched her sail out of the shop with a smug, self-righteous expression on her face. Sometimes I wished I could be like Ariel and blurt out whatever I was feeling. Still, Ariel wasn't the one who had to hold down a job.

I'd barely got rid of her when a middle-aged guy with a buzz cut and a hard, military look about him came in and stalked all over the shop, sniffing as though he found everything in it, including me, personally offensive. After the third time I'd caught him glaring at me, I was almost ready to lash out, Ariel-style, but thankfully he left before I said something I might regret later.

On top of all that, Bethany was half an hour late for her afternoon shift and seemed to have a serious dose of Mondayitis herself. She barely even perked up when I told her about the accident and meeting Conal. By the time we closed up, I was ready to write off the whole day.

I walked swiftly through the car park, with only a little frisson of fear down my spine as I glanced into the darkness behind the dumpsters. Thankfully, there was nothing there tonight. Someone had even cleaned up all the mess and sat the broken lid back on top of the dumpster that had flown open.

I got into Bugsy and locked the door behind me. No point taking risks. But when I put the key into the ignition and turned it, a deathly silence greeted me.

Great. I turned the key again. Still nothing. This wasn't Bugsy's usual coughing reluctance to start—there was nothing more than a click as I turned the key in the ignition over and over again.

I let my head fall back against the headrest and closed my eyes. Of course Bugsy would pick tonight to stand me up. It was the perfect crappy ending to a crappy day. Mondays sucked.

She probably needed a new battery. Pay day was tomorrow, so I could get one then, but what was I supposed to live on for the next two weeks if half my pay went on a new battery? Tears of frustration pricked at my eyes, but I refused to give in to them. At least I wouldn't have to worry about anyone stealing Bugsy overnight. See? There was always an upside if you looked hard enough.

Unfortunately, I'd just missed the last bus that went out past my place, so I rang Bethany, who'd left ten minutes before me, but she didn't pick up. Cheryl was at home with a sick kid, so I couldn't ask her for a lift. Time to ring Ethan. He'd said he would see me home safely if I needed him.

When his phone went straight to voicemail, I sighed. Of course. That was just the kind of day I was having. I got out of the car, slamming the door behind me.

I settled my bag more comfortably over my shoulder and set off down Main Street. Home was only a five-minute drive away, but it would take me a good half-hour to get there on foot. Luckily, I'd worn my running shoes to work this morning instead of my boots, otherwise my feet would have been one big blister by the time I got there.

The smell of pizza from Johnny's Pizzeria next door to Second Chances followed me halfway down the first block, making my stomach rumble. I passed the community centre and the post office, crossed the bridge over the railway line, and went past the little antique shop on the corner of Bentley Street.

Ten minutes later, I had left the streetlights behind and was out on the empty, tree-lined roads where properties were few and far between.

It was cold, though not as cold as it had been the night I bumped into Conal. I hadn't seen him again, and I wondered whether his bike had been repairable or not. At least that wasn't my problem.

If only he hadn't been a Soldier of the Light. I pictured those brilliant green eyes and that cleft in his chin. I'd never even asked where he'd gotten that delectable scar through his eyebrow, and now I'd never know. I entertained myself for the next five minutes with speculation instead, watching my breath form clouds in front of my face as I huffed up a hill. Dense bushland lined both sides of the road here, though the fires last summer had burned out a lot of the undergrowth.

"What are you doing out here on your own?" Ariel demanded, making me jump as she materialised beside me.

"Walking home, obviously."

"You haven't had another accident, have you? Maybe Conal was right about your driving."

I glared at her. "That was clearly a baseless insult. I'm a perfectly good driver, but I can't drive without a working car."

"Oh, so Bugsy finally gave up the ghost, did she?"

I sighed. "I sure hope not, I think she just needs a—"

I broke off, my mouth suddenly dry with fear as something stepped out of the trees onto the road ahead of us. It was dark, but the moon would be full in a few nights, and there was enough light to see the monster.

If it was a dog, it was the biggest dog I had ever seen. I'm talking, like, Guinness World Record-sized. It looked as though it would come up to my shoulders if it were standing right next to me, but my devoutest wish at that moment was to *never* experience that thing standing anywhere near me. It looked like a grey German Shepherd, if German Shepherds had come the size of small ponies. Its shoulders were massive, its neck thick with powerful muscles.

It took a step toward me, and I almost forgot to breathe.

"Head back down the road," Ariel said urgently. "There's a house on the corner at the turn-off to the falls."

I took a step back and then another, my eyes never leaving the menacing creature in front of us. "That's half a kilometre back. Your faith in my athletic abilities is touching, but look at that thing." I had no doubt it would run me down long, long before I got anywhere near the house on the turn-off.

My cards were at home, hidden safely away at the back of a drawer. I'd always thought it was safer not to carry them around unless I was actually planning to use them. But even if I'd had them on me, I doubted the wolf would hang around while I crafted a defensive spell. Maybe it was time to buy a gun.

If I lived.

There was something chilling about the slow way the huge wolf paced down the road toward me, as if it wanted me to see it, *wanted* me to know what was coming for me. There was a human intelligence behind those eyes.

Which glowed yellow, as if I had needed any other hint that this beast was a preet. Was it a Soldier of the Light? I'd never seen one in wolf form, though I'd heard plenty of stories.

Was it *Conal*?

"Conal? Is that you?"

The wolf snarled and gathered itself to spring. Guess not, then. Conal had said he would defend me with his life. This one seemed more interested in ending mine.

"Get out of here," Ariel urged. "What is *with* you lately? You're always standing around doing nothing when things are trying to eat you." She stepped in front of me, and a wind sprang up around her.

My best hope now was that it was a regular werewolf, not a Soldier. At least a werewolf *might* leave me alive. I kept backing down the road, my feet like lead weights. Running would be worse than useless down the long straight road behind me. On the flat like that, it would be on me in seconds.

Ariel turned transparent and then dissolved into the air, a mini tornado appearing where she had stood. Its top stretched up into the trees overhanging the road and dragged branches down. They broke off with cracks like gunshots, and the tornado lashed them in the beast's direction.

I turned and ran.

Logic had lost its hold on me. Pure instinct set my feet in motion as adrenaline coursed through my body. Ariel would hold it off. She *had* to. My feet pounded on the road, and I ran faster than I'd ever run before in my life. Behind me, the noise swelled. Branches crashed down, while others creaked and swayed in the wind that tore through their leaves. The wolf howled, giving wings to my feet.

I stumbled. Caught myself. Risked a glance over my shoulder. Damn. That was a bad idea. The wolf surged straight through the tornado, ducking falling branches, and powered after me.

What should I do? Panic threatened to overwhelm me, rising in my throat and seizing my lungs in an iron grip. I darted off the road into the trees. Maybe I could dodge it long enough to find a tree to climb.

Bushes tore at my clothes as I passed, reaching out to snare me. Branches lashed my face. I could barely see where I was going. The trees blocked too much of the thin moonlight. The wind roared through the treetops above me, tossing their branches around like matchsticks and picking up whatever it could to throw at the wolf that was bearing down on me.

I didn't dare look behind me again. I stumbled and slammed my hands against the rough bark of a tree trunk to catch myself. I barely felt the sting of scraped skin as I drove myself onward, fearing every moment that my foot would go down into a hole or I would trip on a tree root and end up sprawled among the bushes, easy prey for the death that chased me through the trees.

"Get back onto the road!" Ariel yelled at me. "The trees are sheltering it. I can't hit it hard enough."

A massive branch crashed down virtually on my heels, and I screamed for the first time. "Watch it! You're going to knock me out with one of those. Are you trying to turn me into instant wolf snacks?"

My right foot landed badly, and my ankle twisted. I crashed to the ground. This was it.

I looked back, my hand scrabbling through the leaf litter for a weapon. The night was a pattern of black and silver. Mostly black. I strained into the darkness, searching for any sign of the beast.

My hand closed on a branch as thick as a baseball bat, and I staggered to my feet. My right foot wouldn't take my weight properly. A whimper of pain escaped me when I tried.

Ariel's wind still roared desperately through the trees, whipping leaves and small sticks into my face. One of the patches of darkness moved, and yellow eyes blinked at me.

My hands tightened on the stick.

The thing stalked towards me, taking its time, as if it were enjoying the moment.

"Don't come any closer," I shouted into the roar of the wind, trying to look threatening as I brandished the stick. "I'll bash your brains out."

The creature stepped into a shaft of moonlight. Its mouth opened so that it seemed to be laughing at me. Twigs and bits of leaf were stuck in its fur, but it didn't appear hurt, despite Ariel's best efforts.

The attack came so fast that I almost missed it, despite

the fact that my world had narrowed to this moment, my whole being focused on watching the wolf. One minute it was standing there, grinning derisively at my puny defence; the next its powerful hind legs had launched it into the air.

I got my stick up just in time and swung as if all the bases were full and the game was hanging on a home run.

The shock reverberated up my arms as stick met wolf. I'd aimed for its head, but it was hard to see in the dark what I'd hit. I went down, borne to the ground by the weight of the massive beast, and its teeth closed on my arm.

7

$\mathcal{I}$ screamed. The pain was unbelievable, a searing hot fire that burst through my arm, blasting nerve endings with sick agony.

I'd lost my stick. I couldn't breathe; the wolf was too heavy. Its hot, fetid breath was in my face.

I was about to die.

Something slammed into the beast and tore it free from my arm. It was too dark to see. I couldn't understand what was happening. Vicious snarls rang in the air.

Another wolf? Cradling my bleeding arm, I staggered to my feet.

"Get out of there!" Ariel screamed. Her voice was high and frightened. "Now, while they're distracted with each other."

I couldn't see her—I could barely make out anything in the darkness. There was a flash of fur as two wolves rolled through a patch of moonlight, snarling and snapping at each other. The newcomer was completely black. Blood leaked between my fingers, and I realised I was shivering.

"Can't," I said. "I've twisted my ankle."

Even now, with the fighting wolves almost close enough to touch, I couldn't put any weight on that foot. Weren't people supposed to be capable of amazing feats in the heat of the moment? Not this little black duck. I sagged against the nearest tree.

The first wolf yelped, and the other's snarls changed to a note of victory. Moments later, they both streaked out of sight between the trees, the black one chasing the grey one. It was only as I listened to the crashing sounds of their flight and pursuit that I realised the wind had died away completely.

Dizziness swept over me as I leaned against the tree trunk. Was I safe? Why had the black wolf chased off the first one? Did it want me for its own snack? Were they just two toddlers fighting over the last Cheezel in the bag? Or had that been Conal, honouring his life debt to me?

I drew in a deep, shuddering breath. I had to get out of here. I couldn't wait around to find out the answer.

The world spun dangerously as I bent down and groped around on the ground for my stick. It had been nearly as tall as me. Maybe I could use it to help me get back to the road. I didn't know what would happen after that, but I couldn't afford to think too far ahead. Finally, my hand closed around the stick's comforting weight, and I used it to lever myself back upright.

That was good. That was a start. I took a tentative step

with my bad foot, leaning heavily on the stick. Pain shot up my leg, and I gritted my teeth. *This is fine. I can do this.*

The road wasn't as far away as I'd thought, but Ariel's trail of destruction made it hard going. There were branches down everywhere, getting in my way or even stopping me entirely. I had to circle around a place where a huge branch had come down from a gum tree, its many smaller branches forming an impenetrable wall between me and the road.

After hobbling and grunting forever, the trees thinned, and I stepped back on to the tarred surface. My arm was still bleeding, though not as heavily, but it burned as if someone had lit a fire in my veins. My other hand, which clutched my makeshift walking stick, was slippery with sweat, despite the fact that I was shaking with cold. Or maybe shock.

Probably shock, actually. Being attacked by a werewolf was a first for me. I took a step down the road, then another.

"That's it," Ariel said. I could see her again, but she was barely there, translucent as glass in the moonlight. "You can do it. One foot in front of the other."

"I know how walking works, thanks." My arm and leg both burned with the fire of a thousand suns, and my head felt light. "This would be easier if you hadn't left half a forest scattered in my way."

"Sorry." A wind stirred again, rustling the leaves on the branches that lay across the road but doing nothing to shift the heavier limbs. Beside me, Ariel winked out of existence. Guess she'd drained her battery.

I let out a shaky sigh as the wind died away. My own battery was pretty near empty, too. If only a car would appear on the deserted road. I needed help. Home was probably only ten minutes away at my normal walking pace, but at this rate I wouldn't be there until dawn.

Still, if wishes were horses beggars would ride, as Ivy liked to say. I'd have to get home under my own steam. Determinedly, I picked my way through the debris scattered across the road, feeling a sense of achievement when I eventually made it out the other side.

I plodded on, leaning into the climb when the road started to rise on the approach to the old Rogerson place. Right up on the next bend was where I had knocked Conal off his bike.

A rustle in the undergrowth by the road froze me in place. I broke out in a cold sweat. Were the wolves back? This was so unfair. I just wanted to get home without being eaten—was that so much to ask?

I squeaked when a man appeared in the darkness under the trees, then relaxed as I recognised him. Oh, this wasn't suspicious *at all*. He must be the black wolf—but where was the grey one?

"What are *you* doing here?" I'd keep up my *clueless human* act as long as I could. "This is a funny time of night for a bushwalk, isn't it?"

Conal strolled out onto the road. "I could say the same thing to you. Do you need a hand?"

"I need more than a hand," I said, suddenly dizzy with relief. If he'd known I was a cartomancer, he wouldn't be acting so casual. I was safe—for now, anyway. "At least a whole arm."

I don't remember fainting, but the next minute, I was waking up cradled in Conal's strong arms, my head lolling on his shoulder.

"What are you doing?" I asked.

"Taking you home," he said. He was striding down the middle of the road, not even puffing at having to carry my weight.

"You don't know the way," I objected. He'd been passed out when I'd driven him to my place on Friday night.

"Relax," he said. "I've gotten to know this neighbourhood quite well over the weekend."

My head flopped back onto his shoulder. For some reason, it felt very heavy. I closed my eyes, letting the rhythm of his steady stride lull me.

"Wait." I forced my eyes open again as a thought occurred to me. What if he wasn't the black wolf, and him turning up was just a freaky coincidence? "There's a wolf around. A werewolf. Two of them, in fact."

A laugh rumbled deep in his chest. I felt it where my body pressed against his. "Relax," he said again. "It's fine."

I felt certain that he ought to be taking my news more seriously, but somehow I didn't have the energy to insist. On the bright side, if they *were* just regular werewolves, and one of them came back, maybe I'd get lucky and it would be so busy eating Conal that I'd be able to limp to safety. Stranger things had happened.

I must have lost some time again, because it seemed like only a moment later that I opened my eyes and found myself lying on my own bed. Or, if it wasn't my bed, someone else's which had that exact same patch of flaky paint on the ceiling above it, the one that was shaped like a map of Tasmania. I considered it for a moment, until a tug on my arm distracted me.

"Ouch." I stopped examining the ceiling and checked out what Conal was doing.

He was sitting on the bed next to me, wrapping my forearm in a roll of gauze bandage. The ouch had come as he fastened the bandage with one of those stretchy things with the grabby teeth on each end. My brain couldn't come up with the word for it, if I'd ever known it.

"How did we get in?" My house keys were somewhere with my handbag, lost in the mad flight through the forest and the tussle with the wolf. A sudden suspicion seized me, and I frowned at him. "You didn't bust my door, did you?"

Amusement lit those sea-green eyes. "I promise you there was no breaking and entering. I used your front door key." He nodded at the bedside table.

When I turned my head, I found my keys lying there next to my phone, with my handbag on the floor propped against the wall. "Where did that come from?"

"What do you mean? You had it with you."

I was pretty sure I hadn't, but I couldn't be bothered arguing. My whole body ached—my arm with a bright, fiery pain, and my ankle with a duller throb.

I watched him for a moment as he turned my hands over and smoothed a cream that smelled antiseptic over the stinging scrapes on my palms. "Shouldn't I be in hospital?"

"What is your obsession with hospital?" he asked mildly, his attention on my hands. "You're so busy trying to drum up business for them, anyone would think you had shares in the place."

"I'm not obsessed! Any normal person would go to hospital after an attack like that."

"Any normal person would go to hospital for a sprained ankle and a few scratches?" He raised that scarred eyebrow at me mockingly. "Normal people must be pretty pathetic, then."

Hey, I should introduce him to Ling. They'd get along like a house on fire.

I pulled my hands away grumpily. "Sure, make light of the fact that I almost *died*. I was attacked by a werewolf. It's a wonder I wasn't torn to shreds."

And what do you have to say to that, *Mr Soldier?* Would he drop the mysterious act and tell me straight up what he was?

Gently, he recaptured my hands. "Keep still. You are the worst patient ever. I bet they'd throw you out of your precious hospital for lack of cooperation." He covered the big scrape on the heel of my left hand with a couple of oversized Band-Aids and surveyed his work critically. "There. That should do it. Do you have any painkillers in the house?"

"There's some in the top of the cupboard over the kettle," I said, and he got up and left the room. I could hear him moving around in my tiny kitchen, followed by the sound of the water running as he filled the kettle and switched it on.

He came back into the room with two Panadol in one hand and a glass of water in the other. "Take these. They'll take the edge off the pain."

Obediently, I swallowed the painkillers and drained the glass of water. I hadn't realised until it touched my lips how thirsty I was. "Thanks. What are you boiling the kettle for?"

"I thought I'd make you a cup of tea," he said as he left the room again. "Isn't that what people like when they've had a bad day?"

"A bad day!" I raised my voice to be heard above the bubbling kettle and the sound of him banging around opening cupboards as he looked for tea and cups. "Is that what you call it? I'm telling you, I was attacked by a *werewolf*. That's a little more than just a bad day. That's a *nightmare*."

I heard him open the fridge, muttering to himself.

"Why is there never any food in your house?" he called.

"What are you talking about? There's lots of food." I'd bought plenty of stuff with the money he'd left me. "Why? Are you hungry?"

"Fortunately not, or I'd be doomed to starvation." In a moment, he was back, bearing a cup of peppermint tea and two of the mini cheesecakes on a plate, which he put on the bedside table. Then he helped me sit up and arranged the pillows behind me.

"I made the tea black," he said. "I didn't know how you liked it."

I raised an eyebrow in disbelief. "It's herbal tea. You don't put milk in herbal tea."

He shrugged and leaned against the wall, shoving his hands into the pockets of his jeans. "Don't you?" Clearly, he was supremely indifferent. "I'm not much of a tea drinker."

I'd thought I wasn't hungry, but once I'd eaten the first cheesecake, I felt so much better that the second one quickly followed it into oblivion. He watched me eat with a critical eye.

"You should probably have more than that. You had quite a shock."

Well, at least he was admitting it now. The way he'd carried on earlier, you would think I had said I'd been attacked by a kitten, not a werewolf. I paused, cup halfway to my mouth as a thrill of horror shot through me. I'd been so distracted by the night's events that I'd missed something *big*.

He straightened, sensing the change in my mood. "What's wrong?"

The teacup trembled in my hands as I stared at him in horror. "I just had the most terrible thought. I've been bitten—I'm going to turn into a werewolf."

He pushed off the wall and retrieved the teacup from my shaking hands, setting it down on the bedside table before I spilled anything. "You are *not* going to turn into a werewolf," he said firmly.

"How do you know?"

"You're missing a vital part."

"What?"

He gestured at his crotch, grinning.

"A *penis*? What do you mean? I'm sure there must be female werewolves."

"Nope. Lycanthropy's a mutation on the Y chromosome."

"How is that relevant? I'm not talking about being *born* a werewolf." Did he think this was funny? "People get turned into werewolves all the time after they get bitten."

"Sure," he agreed affably. "As long as they're male-type people. Women just get a cool scar to show their friends."

Really? I *had* heard that only men could become Soldiers, and Conal's certainty that I wasn't about to grow fur reassured me.

"How do you know all this?"

"I know about these things."

"*How*?" Could I get him to admit what he was? "Are *you* a werewolf?"

He laughed. "You should see your face right now. You're full of questions for someone who should be resting and recovering. Trust me, you'll be just fine."

Typical. Soldiers preferred to fly under the radar. Humans knew they existed but rarely saw them—especially not in werewolf form. The Soldiers said secrecy made their job easier. Ling said it was because if they'd gone public, people might enquire more closely into their activities. Coming out as an organisation that had spent years persecuting women wouldn't be a good look in modern society.

He headed for the door. "I'll come back tomorrow to check on you."

The thought of facing the grey wolf again on my own made me uneasy. "Don't leave! What if that thing finds me?"

"It won't," he said without hesitation. "Don't make such a fuss. I have things to do. I can't babysit you all night."

Any gratitude I'd been feeling promptly disappeared. I glared at him.

"I don't need babysitting," I said, revolted. "Especially not by a person who doesn't even know that you don't put milk in peppermint tea."

"Good," he said, unmoved by my disapproval of his tea-making knowledge. "Get some sleep. You'll feel better tomorrow."

"But I might get rabies. Maybe I'm not going to turn into a werewolf, but I've still been bitten by an animal. I need a rabies shot! What if I die of rabies because you wouldn't take me to the hospital?"

He sighed. "You won't get rabies. No self-respecting raby would dare infect you."

"That makes absolutely no sense."

"See you tomorrow." He headed for the door, clearly in a hurry to get wherever he was going.

"Wait." I cast around for a way to make him stay. He was infuriating and *clearly* misguided, but I didn't want to be alone right now.

He quirked that eyebrow at me impatiently.

"Tell me how you got that scar across your eyebrow."

"In a bar fight with two Swedish grandmothers."

"Really?" My own eyebrows shot up, but he was

through the bedroom door already and striding across the lounge room towards the front door.

"Tomorrow, Sunday," he called.

Then the door shut behind him, leaving me alone. It wasn't until then that it occurred to me that he hadn't asked a single question about the attack, as if he already knew what had happened.

That settled it. He was *definitely* the black wolf.

8

I tossed and turned for most of the night. Partly it was pain keeping me awake, but mostly I was worried that Ling was right, and I'd have to leave town. The likelihood of that grey wolf being just a random werewolf and not an actual Soldier was vanishingly small. Not with Conal here too. Most likely they were a hunting pair, here to track down our rogue. Which was bad news for me.

Ah, the glamorous life of a cartomancer, always running, always weighing up one danger over another. Good times.

I mean, danger was part of the deal, regardless of the Soldiers. Cartomancers helped protect humanity too—just not as aggressively as Soldiers. If we found a preternatural monster causing trouble, we had our own ways of dealing with them. I still helped out the coven with that occasionally, but honestly? With my lack of power, there often wasn't a lot I could do to help. So why not try to live more like a regular person?

I did *not* want to go back to that roving life. I'd put down roots in Kurranderra. I *liked* it here. And I felt a weird sense of responsibility to this place and the people who'd made me feel so welcome. Was I just going to leave them to the elder's mercy because some stupid Soldier had decided to take a bite out of me?

Surely I was safe. How could it have known I was a cartomancer? It couldn't, unless it had seen me work the cards. I hadn't even used magic in weeks, except for hunting the elder the other night.

Uneasily, I recalled the thing growling at me from the bushes, not long after I'd worked my tracking spell. I'd assumed it was the elder, but if it had been this wolf instead ...

But it couldn't have been. I'd set my magic to hunt the elder, and it had led me straight there. And then fizzled out, of course, as my magic so often did. But *Conal* didn't know what I was, and *he* was a Soldier. If they were a hunting pair they'd be working together.

Maybe the *wolf* was our rogue monster, and we'd all been assuming the attacks had been made by an elder.

No, that didn't make sense. A wolf couldn't drain a person's blood—at least not without leaving one ginormous mess behind. But then, what did make sense about this?

I woke up with no clearer idea of what I should do than I had when I fell asleep. At least my ankle was feeling better. I gingerly put my foot to the floor and was happy to find that it would bear my weight this morning. My arm felt better, too—so much better that I winced when I remembered the fuss I'd made about rabies the night before.

I carefully unwound the bandage around my forearm to have a look, since I hadn't gotten a proper look at it last night. I'd been too distracted with the pain and fear, and by the time I'd found myself back in my own bed, Conal had already wrapped it up.

Conal must have cleaned and disinfected the wounds, too, because they were looking pretty good this morning. It was an impressive series of puncture wounds—the size of that thing's mouth was *horrifying*—but scabs were forming already. My arm didn't look half as bad as my imagination had painted it in the dark, when the blood had been dripping between my fingers. In fact, it didn't look anywhere near as bad as the pain I was in last night had suggested, which made me feel like a bit of a wuss.

I wrapped it back up again, though my work wasn't as neat as Conal's had been. I wouldn't tell *him* it was feeling better. That man didn't need his ego stroked by being told he was right. But I was happy there was no sign of infection.

I hobbled into the bathroom. My ankle was still sore, but at least I could walk. I wouldn't have to call in sick to work, which I'd been dreading. Poor Cheryl probably still had at least one sick twin on her hands. I flushed the toilet then went to the sink to wash my hands.

"Son of a beech tree!" My mouth dropped open as I caught sight of my reflection in the mirror over the sink.

I touched my hair, hardly able to believe what I saw in the mirror. It made no sense at all. But that was my hair, still in yesterday's loose ponytail. I watched my fingers slide down the long strands in the reflection, and then— just to be sure—I pulled some around in front of me and inspected it in real life.

There was no mistake. Overnight, my hair had turned completely white.

Five minutes of contorting myself and taking selfies with my back to the mirror proved that every last strand on my head had changed colour. Yesterday, my hair had been the colour of rich dark chocolate. Today I looked like a grandma.

A sudden thought struck me, and I yanked my jeans down again to inspect my, er, lower hair. Yep. That was all snow-white, too.

Ling had a single lock of white hair at the back, underneath the rest of her hair, which she chopped so short that no one knew it was there. Ivy supposedly had a white streak at her temple, but since she was constantly dyeing her hair in bright colours, I'd never seen it.

A white lock was a sign of a cartomancer's power, which explained why I'd never had one. My magic wasn't strong enough to make a difference. But that's all it ever was—a single lock. No one had more than a strand or two. So even if my magic had suddenly decided to get off its lazy butt and start earning its keep, there was no way it could have made every hair on my body turn white.

I hobbled back to the bed and sank down onto the mattress. What did I do now? I stared at the phone in my hand until inspiration struck.

"Come on, come on. Pick up." At this time of day, she

was probably still asleep, ignoring her three alarms as usual. *Please God, don't let her have her phone on silent.* I breathed a gusty sigh of relief when she answered, sounding half asleep.

"Hello?"

"Bethany! Thank goodness. I need your help."

"At seven-thirty in the morning?" She yawned hugely. "Someone better have died."

"It's worse than that. I've got a situation here."

Oh?" She sounded a little more awake at the prospect of drama. "What kind of situation? Did you wake up in a strange man's bed?"

"Worse."

"There's *two* strange men in the bed?" Now she sounded *really* awake.

"No! Get your mind out of the gutter. Something terrible has happened." I didn't know how to explain it—I *couldn't* explain it. So I just blurted it out. "My hair has gone white."

I didn't get the shocked reaction I was expecting.

"What do you mean, your hair has gone white? Did you bleach it before you went to bed or something?"

"No, I swear I didn't touch it. I don't understand what's happening."

"Are you *drunk*?"

"Of course I'm not drunk! Wait, let me send you a photo."

I sent her one of the five million selfies I'd just taken. I could tell when the text arrived, because there was a sharp intake of breath on the other end of the line.

"Oh, wow. Your hair is *white!*"

I bounced impatiently on the bed. "I *know*, Bethany. That's what I've been trying to tell you."

"You look so *cool*," she breathed.

"I do *not*. I look like a grandma. I can't go to work like this! I can't even leave the *house* like this. Can you come over and help me dye my hair? *Please*?"

"Sure. Have you got any dye there?"

"No." I'd never changed my hair colour in my life.

"That's okay, I'll bring some. Give me fifteen minutes. I'll be there soon." She hung up.

It was the longest fifteen minutes of my life. I would have paced up and down in impatience, but my ankle wasn't up to pacing, so I settled for changing my clothes, which were looking a little worse for wear from last night's adventures, and obsessively brushing my newly white hair. Maybe I could brush the white back out?

I knew that didn't make sense, but what about this *did*? Nobody's hair just turned white overnight. I mean, it did sometimes in stories, when someone had had a terrible shock, like all their family dying when the *Titanic* went down or something. I was pretty sure that on the scale of one to *sudden complete loss of hair colour*, a little run-in with a werewolf didn't even rate.

At last, Bethany knocked on the door, and I hobbled over to open it. She actually screamed when she caught sight of me, one hand flying to her mouth. "Oh, girlfriend, that is *rad*. Are you sure you want to change it? You look *amazing*."

"I look bizarre," I said, shutting the door firmly behind her. "Have you got the dye with you?"

"Sure." She pulled a box out of her carry bag and showed it to me.

My eyes met hers in disbelief. "Pink? Are you kidding?"

"It's all I had," she said. "Take it or leave it."

"I guess I'll take it, then."

"It'll look fantastic against your skin colour," she assured me, taking my arm and steering me toward the bathroom. Then she noticed the way I was walking. "Hey—are you all right? Why are you limping? And what's that bandage for?"

"I ran into Conal again last night."

She squealed again. "Are you *kidding* me? You had another car accident?"

We made it as far as the bathroom, and I grabbed an old towel to protect my clothes from spills. "No, I didn't *literally* run into him. I saw him on Ridge Road when I was walking home. Bugsy broke down," I added when she opened her mouth to ask another question. "I couldn't get her started after work, and no one I called was picking up, so I walked. And then this thing attacked me in the forest and Conal saved me—"

"Whoa, whoa, hang on there. Back it up a bit." She stared at me, wide-eyed. "Something attacked you? Was it the elder?"

I filled her in on the events of the evening—most of them, anyway. I left out Ariel's part and my assumption that Conal was the black wolf. To take the weight off my ankle, I sat down on the toilet seat while I talked, and

Bethany perched on the edge of the bath opposite me, taking it all in with avid interest.

"Wow. That is quite some night," she said when I was finished. "No wonder your hair turned white. That sounds really stressful."

"No, but seriously, Beth. Nobody's hair turns white because of stress. We're not living in a Dickens novel. Do you think there was some kind of poison in that monster's bite?"

It was the only thing I could think of. Maybe werewolf spit reacted badly with cartomancy.

She looked sceptical. "A special hair-colour-changing poison? You could ask Ethan, I guess, but I doubt it. I've never heard of anything like that." She brightened and arranged the towel around my shoulders. "Anyway, let's get started. Time for your makeover!"

It *was* kind of fun. Beth had brought a whole bunch of stuff with her as well as the dye—clearly, she was a pro. She had rubber gloves and a shower cap to keep my wet hair out of the way while the dye was processing. We spent the waiting time on the couch together, drinking tea and chatting until it was time to rinse off.

When it was all done and the dye rinsed out, I straightened up, my hair dripping, and stared at the stranger in the mirror.

"I look like a walking stick of bubble gum."

Bethany stood next to me, examining my image in the mirror. "You do not. You look great. You look like a party searching for somewhere to happen."

I raised a pink eyebrow at her. "I'm not really a party person."

"Why not? You're twenty-three, not forty-three. You should be out there having fun. This is the best time of our lives!"

I leaned my wet, pink head against her dark one briefly. "Thanks, Beth. You always know how to put a positive spin on things."

She smiled back at me. "Don't look so serious. It's just hair." She tugged on a wet lock in a friendly way. "I know it's a shock to have it change so quickly, but its colour means nothing. It doesn't change who you are inside. Have fun with it. Try purple next time!"

I grinned. "Ivy would like that."

"She's right," Ariel said, appearing on my other side. "You should—"

Bethany shrieked and dropped the towel.

I turned quickly to her. "What's wrong?"

She was still staring in the mirror, her face drained of colour. "There's someone else in the room with us."

Then she bolted out of the bathroom.

I exchanged a shocked look with Ariel. No one *ever* saw Ariel except me.

"She was staring right at me in the mirror," she said.

I hurried after Bethany and stopped her at the front door. "Don't go! There's no one else there."

"I saw it," she insisted, casting a fearful look over my shoulder towards the bathroom. "A ghostly figure in the mirror."

"What did it look like?"

"Like ... like a girl, about our age. Her hair was floating around her head. I don't know; I didn't get a good look before I ran." She grabbed my hands. "Let's get out of here! You have a *ghost* in your house."

"I really don't—do you think I wouldn't have noticed by now if this place was haunted?" I held her hands tightly. I had the feeling that she'd bolt if I let her go. She really *had* seen Ariel. The floating hair thing was a dead give-away. "It was probably just a funny trick of the light. Do you want to sit down?"

"Should I come out and give her a proper scare?" Ariel asked.

Don't you dare! Scaring the crap out of our friends is no way to repay them for helping us.

"I'd better go," Bethany said, edging towards the door.

"Don't go without your stuff."

"I'm not going back in there to get it."

"I'll get it. Really, Beth, there's nothing to be scared of. Stay there." I glanced back at her as I headed for the bathroom. "I mean it. No running away the minute my back is turned."

She had her arms wrapped around herself. "Don't go back in there. It might get you."

"Woooooooh," Ariel said, making pretend-ghost noises.

Shut up.

At least Bethany couldn't seem to hear her.

"It's fine, Beth, honest. There's nothing there." I packed Bethany's equipment into her carry bag and brought it out to her. "Here you go. Thanks again for your help. What are you doing for the rest of the day?"

"Um ... going shopping, I guess." She gave me a weak smile. "Now that someone has dragged me out of bed so early on my day off, I may as well make the most of the day. Do you want to come?"

"I'd love to, but I've got work." And also no money to spend. Still, even window-shopping would be fun with Beth.

"Oh. I thought you would have called in sick after the night you had." She glanced at her watch. "You're running a bit late, aren't you? Cheryl will have a cow."

"I texted her earlier and told her I'd be late. But I'd better get going. See you at work tomorrow."

"Sure." And with a last fearful glance in the direction of the bathroom, she made her escape.

After she'd gone, I pulled out Mum's Tarot cards. Something screwy was going on, and I needed counsel.

"Can you see me?" Ariel asked, zipping around the room.

"Of course."

"What about now?" She took the form of a white cat and leapt up onto the kitchen counter. "Or now?"

"Would you sit still? I'm trying to centre myself here." The familiar feel of the cards in my hands as I shuffled normally calmed me, but today they weren't working their usual magic.

"You're not even looking at me," she complained.

My hands stilled, and I stared pointedly at her. She sat down and started licking her butt.

"You are *gross*."

"What? Cats do it all the time, and everyone thinks they're adorable."

"Not *because* they lick themselves. In *spite* of it. And you are not a cat."

She shimmered back into her usual form, and I started shuffling again. "But I'm not a real person either, am I? Only now Baby Goth can see me." There was a pause, and then she added in a small voice, "Do you think I might be *turning* real?"

There was such a world of yearning in her tone that I looked down at the cards. I wasn't used to seeing emotion laid bare on Ariel's face like that. Everything with her was jokes and sarcasm.

But there was a reason *Pinocchio* was her favourite fairy tale. The story of the little wooden puppet who wanted to be a real boy really resonated with her.

It had started when we were young, and she'd wanted to be able to touch the dolls I played with or move the game pieces on the board. I always did everything for her, but I'd known it frustrated her. She hadn't mentioned it much since we'd grown up, and I never brought it up either. If she wanted to watch TV, I turned it on for her. It was just the way things were. She didn't complain ... much ... that she couldn't turn on the TV, and I didn't complain that I had to go to work while she lay on the couch watching it.

"I don't know, Ariel. Maybe it was just a fluke thing."

Her face closed down again. "Sure. Queen of the fluke, that's me."

She winked out of existence, and I finally pulled a card. The Five of Earth. I stared down at the bowed figure in the snow, dread gnawing at me.

Isolation and loss.

Yippee.

9

I had to catch the bus to work, of course, since Bugsy was still stranded in the car park behind the shop. But my pay had landed in my bank account this morning, so I could get someone to fit a new battery when I was on my lunch break.

I joined Nicole at the bus stop just as the bus pulled up. Nicole was a short, smiley woman with the curliest hair I'd ever seen. She lived upstairs, across the landing from Mr Garcia, and always waved in a friendly way when she saw me, though her work kept her so busy that I didn't see her often. She was a silversmith and created the most beautiful jewellery, which she sold from her gallery in town, around the corner from Second Chances.

"Good morning!" she said cheerily as we climbed aboard. "Love the hair! Is that new?"

I twisted a bright pink lock around my finger self-consciously. "Yeah."

"It suits you! You don't usually catch the bus. Where's your car?"

I told her about Bugsy's troubles as I squeezed into the seat next to her. Her glasses made her brown eyes look enormous as she listened, nodding intently.

"I could take a look at it if you like. I'm good with cars."

"That's okay. I'm pretty sure it's the battery. I'll get a new one today. But thank you."

As the bus trundled along Ridge Road, I shivered, even though the sun was shining now and lorikeets scolded each other in the trees, flitting across the road in bright rainbow explosions of colour. I watched the bushes, but nothing emerged from them today, man or wolf.

We got off the bus in Main Street, and I said goodbye to Nicole. My ankle twinged as I stepped down. I realised that was the first time it had bothered me since I'd gotten up this morning. By the time I arrived at Second Chances, it felt good again, as if the exercise had worked all the kinks out. It mustn't have been sprained after all, just twisted a little.

"Good heavens, your hair!" Cheryl said as I walked in. But her usual smile was missing.

I tugged self-consciously at a bright pink lock. "Yeah, I felt like a change. Sorry I'm late. How's Mikey today?"

"He's fine. Back at school." Her eyes were red, as if she'd been crying.

"Are you okay? You look upset."

"Oh, honey, the most terrible thing has happened." She ran a hand through her thick brown hair distractedly. From the way it was standing up all over the place, this wasn't the first time she'd done it. "I don't think we can stay open today. I should have rung you, but I've been so busy with the police. They've only just left."

"The police?" I looked around, scanning for damage, but everything looked as it should. "Did we have a break-in?"

"No." She pressed a hand to her mouth for a moment. "I found a body."

I stared at her. Did she mean a human body?

Don't be stupid, Sunday, of course she does. Nobody says *I found a body* because they stumbled across a dead kangaroo on the side of the road. "A *body*? Where?"

She waved her hand toward the rear of the shop. "Out the back. I got here early this morning. First car in the car park. There was a strange smell when I got out of the car. Like meat." Her hand was shaking, and she folded her arms, tucking her hands tightly into her armpits. "A couple of crows flew up when I slammed the door, and I looked over, and there he was. Just lying on the ground."

"Who was?"

"That boy who delivers for Johnny's."

"Toby?" He was even younger than me. He couldn't be dead.

But she was nodding, a sick look on her face, and it turned out that he *could* be dead, even if I'd only spoken to him last week when he'd told me all about his indoor soccer team and how he was going to have to take up running again, because he hadn't exercised since he'd left school, and, man, he was getting seriously unfit.

And nineteen was way too young to be unfit.

"Do you need to sit down?" Cheryl asked. "You've gone all pale. You're not going to faint, are you?"

I shook my head.

"Let's both sit down," Cheryl said.

"This is awful." I eased myself onto one of the stools behind the counter, and Cheryl took the other. "I can't believe it. What ... what happened?"

"The police said it looked like a preternatural attack. I didn't ... I mean, after that first look ... I didn't look at him properly." She shuddered. "I had to throw up."

She was looking pretty green again just talking about it. I grabbed her hand, and she squeezed mine gratefully. Cheryl and I weren't super close—not like Bethany and me. She was in her forties and her crazy, twin-filled life was nothing like mine. Plus, she was my boss.

But we were friends, and she sure looked as though she could use a hug, so I put my arms around her.

"That must have been horrible."

She nodded against my shoulder. "Not as bad as when his parents turned up. Imagine finding your baby like that. Completely drained of blood. Left lying in a car park all night, like he was just a meal and not a person." She drew back, her eyes hardening. "They ought to lock up all those filthy preets and throw away the key."

"I can't believe it," I said again, hardly listening to her. I was thinking of the wolf that had attacked me—but wolves didn't drain their victims of blood. This was the work of the rogue elder. The thing that had been lurking behind the dumpsters on Friday night. What were the vampires *doing*? Why hadn't they caught it yet? "He was so young."

If I'd remembered to tell Ethan on Friday night about the rogue appearing behind the shop, would Toby still be alive?

She nodded, her eyes shadowed, perhaps thinking of her own kids. "I'm still shaking. I don't think I can work today. Johnny's is closed, of course. Alf is beside himself."

Alf was the owner of Johnny's Pizzeria, which was as much of an institution in Kurranderra as the post office. The original Johnny had moved on to the great pizzeria in the sky long ago, but his shop had persisted.

"You should head home," she added. "I saw your car in the car park this morning. Everything all right?"

"She wouldn't start last night," I said. "I need to get someone to come out and replace the battery."

"Why don't you get that organised while I close up?"

So I got on the phone, a feeling of unreality gripping me as I went through the mundane process of arranging a new battery. Someone was dead, and yet here I was, dealing with such an ordinary thing. It didn't seem right.

And it was testing my resolve to stay out of the hunt for the elder, since *clearly* the vampires were incapable of finding their butts with both hands. I just hoped Conal was better at elder-hunting than they were.

The alley between our shop and Johnny's was blocked by police tape, so I had to walk around the block to get to Bugsy. That whole section of the car park around the dumpsters was blocked off with police tape, too, and a couple of men were still there taking photos and scouring the area, though thankfully there was no sign of Toby's body. There were some splashes of dull red on the side of one of the dumpsters, though, and I turned away with a sick feeling in my stomach to wait for my battery to arrive.

It turned out that Bugsy didn't need a new battery after all. One of the connections to the terminals was loose. I managed to smile and nod as the nice man explained it to me, but inside a sick feeling was growing. Was it just a coincidence? Or had someone set me up so that I'd have to walk home last night?

Dip me in feathers and call me a rooster. That grey wolf had ambushed me.

No, wait.

I shook my head as I got into the car to head home. I was being paranoid. If that wolf had sabotaged my car, how could he be sure I'd be walking? Normally, I would have gotten a ride with Cheryl or Bethany. It had just been bad luck that neither of them had been available. Or was I imagining that the wolf somehow had the power to make Cheryl's kids sick?

No, I was jumping at shadows. Perfectly understand-able with a pair of Soldiers in town. Nevertheless, I rang Ethan on the way.

"Ciao, bella," he said lightly. "What's up?"

"Did you hear about Toby?" I asked.

His tone sharpened immediately. "Yes."

"It sounds like the elder, right?" *Completely drained of blood*, Cheryl had said.

"It does. Why?"

"It's just ... I saw something there the other night."

"Where?"

"The place where Toby was killed. There was something lurking behind the dumpsters when I left work on Friday night. I meant to tell you, but ... something came up and I forgot. Oh, Ethan." My voice cracked. "Maybe Toby would still be alive if I'd remembered."

"Don't blame yourself," he said immediately. "This thing is wily. Even if we'd set up a twenty-four-hour watch outside your work, I doubt we would have caught it. It's evaded all our attempts to pin it down so far."

"But Toby might still be alive."

"And someone else would be dead instead. Or it might have got him somewhere else. Don't beat yourself up with might-have-beens."

I sighed. "How are you going to stop it?"

"We'll find a way. Don't you worry about it."

"I have to worry about it. I'm involved. Last night I was attacked—"

"What? Are you all right?"

"Yes, I'm fine." I turned into my driveway and parked in my usual spot.

"You were attacked by an elder and you're *fine*?"

"It wasn't an elder. It was a Soldier."

"*What*? Why am I only hearing about this now?" There was a rustling sound on the other end of the line. "Where are you?"

"At home. I just arrived." I got out of the car and locked it, giving Bugsy a little pat on the roof. It was good to have her back. The garbage bins had been emptied, so I brought them all in. I wasn't having Mr Garcia drag his bin around at his age, and there were only Nicole's and the Chapmans' besides ours. It seemed rude to bring two in and leave the other two behind.

"Stay there," Ethan said. "I'm coming over."

"You don't have to do that."

"You got attacked by a *Soldier*. Believe me, I have to. Why are you even still there? Do you need a place to hide?"

"Conal didn't know I was a cartomancer."

There was a hiss of breath. "Who the heck is Conal? And what's he got to do with it?"

"He's ..." The guy I knocked off his bike on Friday night. The guy with that Jason Momoa-style scar and the mocking light in his sea-green eyes. The guy with more secrets than answers, who could turn into a black wolf. "He's the one who saved me from the Soldier."

"Okay. Start at the beginning. What happened, exactly? The queen will need to know if there are Soldiers running around the mountains."

"Conal said—"

"I don't care what this Conal person said." There was a note of hostility in his voice, and more than a little posses- siveness. "Tell me what happened."

I sighed as I let myself into the apartment. Ethan had taken the end of our relationship surprisingly well, but he remained pretty invested in my welfare for some reason. As if he'd decided that I wasn't capable of looking after myself without him keeping a watchful eye on me. As if I were his pet project. Maybe he felt guilty about the glamour thing, and the fact that I'd inadvertently revealed the fact that I was a cartomancer under its influence.

I settled on the couch while I gave him a brief recap of all my dealings with Conal Clarke, from the moment I'd knocked him off his bike—which was *totally* not my fault—until he'd left last night, promising to return to check up on me. Ethan listened without interrupting, and a heavy silence fell when I finished my story.

"So, to summarise," he said at last, sounding very serious, "we have two Soldiers in town—a hunting pair, in effect. One of them knows you're a witch—"

"Cartomancer," I said firmly. "And that's only if he *was* the thing growling at me in the bushes the night we were hunting the elder. It's more likely that it was actually the elder."

"But then how do you explain someone sabotaging your battery? That sounds like something a Soldier would do."

"True, but it could have been a coincidence. The battery guy said the connections can work themselves loose sometimes, and it's not exactly unusual for Bugsy to break down." I chewed my lip, thinking. "Did you sense anything watching that night when I was casting the spell?"

"No, but that doesn't mean it wasn't. Or that it couldn't smell the after-effects of the magic or something."

"That's not how it works," I said impatiently.

"Enlighten me, then. How *does* it work?"

"When we cast a spell, at the moment that the spell takes form, a portal opens to the elemental plane."

"I always thought the elemental plane was just another word for magic."

"No, it's an actual place. Very different to the human world, of course. It's the source of all magic—and magical beings. Some are elementals, made purely of Air, or Water. Others are preternaturals. Your vampire ancestors probably flew out of a belfry somewhere there and entered our world when the first cartomancers started casting spells."

That was one theory, anyway. The other was that all the human-based preternaturals were the result of elemental magic warping humans. I generally preferred the latter theory, but it was fun to taunt Ethan.

"Just for your information, I've never turned into a bat in my life."

"Whatever. The point is, when the portal opens to allow the magic through, Soldiers can sense that, if they're close enough."

"Okay, so this Soldier is out hunting the elder, and he senses the portal opening, has a look around, and finds *you*. Only thanks to your fearsome vampire protectors, he can't attack you at the time."

"Fearsome shmearsome." He was probably right, and his presence that night had saved me, but his head was already big enough.

"So, he spends some time hunting for you and finds you last night, conveniently alone on the open road. Or he sets you up to be alone. Either way, we need to talk about your survival instincts, but first—"

"My survival instincts are fine," I protested.

"But *first*," he powered on, ignoring the interruption, "we need to get you out of that house, before he talks to his buddy—*who now knows where you live*, due to your regrettable Good Samaritan instincts."

I didn't think it counted as being a Good Samaritan if you had *caused* the injury in the first place, but I could tell that Ethan wouldn't react well to that kind of argument. Besides which, I was pretty keen on staying alive.

"But why haven't they talked already? Why did Conal fight the other one in the first place?"

"I have no idea." Ethan sighed. "Maybe they *have* talked, and this Conal is playing a longer game. Maybe he wants to use you for something."

I couldn't help a snort of derision. "Come off it— Soldiers only have one game, and it's called *Kill the Witch*. There's no way he'd be playing nice with me if he knew."

"He was playing nice?" Suspicion coloured his tone. "What was he doing?"

"Nothing," I said hastily. "I just meant he was friendly."

"Fine. I'll talk to the queen. We can take you to one of our safe houses."

"You can't tell her I'm a cartomancer! At the rate you're going, soon the whole *hive* will know." It was bad enough that he and Raquel knew. Ling and Ivy would be horrified.

"The queen knows how to be discreet."

"Unlike you."

"Keeping it from her now will do more harm than good. She can help you."

"I don't want to be indebted to the hive."

"We're not your enemies," he said gently. "And now that there's a hunting pair in town, you need all the friends you can get. The Soldiers like to strike first and ask questions later. Or not at all. And there's no court of appeal from their decisions."

"Great." I eyed my front door. Would it stand up against a determined Soldier? What about the windows? *Conal knew where I lived.*

"I'm coming over," he said. "I'll talk to the queen on the way. Sit tight until I get there. Do *not* let anyone else in."

He hung up, and I sat there, hugging my knees. Now I knew how the three little pigs must have felt when the wolf came knocking. *Little pig, little pig, let me in.*

No way, José. And I didn't even have any hairs on my chinny-chin-chin.

10

*a*riel materialised on the couch next to me. "Hey, why aren't you at work? You're sitting in my spot."

"Change of plans," I said glumly. "What do you want first: the bad news or the bad news?"

"Sterling choice." She eyed me more carefully. "You look upset. Fine, hit me with the bad news."

"Toby's dead."

Her eyebrows shot up. "The pizza kid with the proto-moustache?"

"Yes." Toby's efforts to grow facial hair had amused her no end, no matter how often I'd explained he was only trying to look a little older than his baby face suggested and she should really give him a break. "He was drained last night by the elder."

"Oh, wow. Poor kid." She digested that for a moment. "And what's the other bad news?"

"We have to leave town."

Conal knew where I lived. How had I thought I could

carry on with normal life? I blamed the stress of the attack and its aftermath. I hadn't been thinking straight. The grey wolf knew what I was, and Conal knew where to find me. All they had to do was pool their information and I was toast. His fine talk of promises and life debts would go up in smoke as soon as he heard the word *witch*.

"Ouch. That *is* bad news." She turned into a fluffy white cat and scampered across the room to leap up on the countertop that separated the tiny kitchen from the rest of the living space. "You look miserable. Why don't you make yourself a tea? That's what you usually do when you need cheering up."

I glared at her. "I don't think a cup of tea is going to cheer me up when there's a Soldier out there who wants to kill me."

"You won't know until you try," she said, then turned to smoke and disappeared into the spout of the teapot. A moment later, she burst forth again. "Hey, look, I'm a genie!"

"What is *wrong* with you today?" I grumbled, coming into the kitchen. Now that she'd mentioned tea, I had a craving for a cup of Earl Grey. I'd make one and then I'd start packing. "Stay out of my teapot. I don't want to be drinking Ariel cooties in my tea."

She took her usual form and perched herself on the countertop next to me. There was a suppressed excitement about her that caught my attention, as if she were vibrating too fast for the human eye to see, like hummingbird wings.

"What's changed about you? Why could Bethany see you before?"

"I don't know." She shrugged, but her nonchalant act wasn't fooling me. "I feel different somehow."

Great. That was all I needed—for Ariel to go all screwy on me. She was my best friend, the one constant in my life.

Too much was happening at once. Kurranderra was meant to be my peaceful little backwater. Now people were being killed, something weird was happening with Ariel, and some Soldier might be preparing to blow my house down.

As days went, this one was pretty crap already, and it wasn't even eleven o'clock yet.

"Different good?" I asked cautiously as I spooned tea into the pot that she'd just left. Mostly I used teabags, but Earl Grey was my tea-as-soothing-ritual tea. Strictly loose-leaf in the pot, just the way that Ivy used to make it when I came home from yet another new school, crying because none of the kids would play with the new girl.

"Different." She shrugged again, the movement shivering through her whole body. It was like watching the picture fizz on an old TV. "Just different. But it's got to be good, right? Bethany saw me!" She couldn't contain her excitement any longer and went zipping around the ceiling, no more than a spark of light, like a tiny firefly bouncing off the cornices. "I'm a *real* boy!"

I sighed. I hoped she wasn't in for a disappointment.

"Don't get too excited," I cautioned. I knew that it chafed her that I was the only one who could see her. She wanted to talk to other people, but most of all, she longed to experience the world as I did, to be able to touch and feel everything for herself. I'd figured out long ago that the rude comments and outrageous behaviour were the armour she hid her sadness behind. "Just because Bethany glimpsed you in the mirror doesn't mean that everything's going to change. She might be the only one. Maybe she's just become attuned to you because we all spend a lot of time together."

She stopped zipping and floated back down to the kitchen like a deflated balloon. "Maybe. But we spent years with Ivy and Ling, and *they* don't see me." She perked up again as she considered this. "I'm going to go walk down Main Street and see if anyone else does. Maybe I can scare a few people into believing in ghosts."

"Ariel, don't—"

But it was too late. She was gone already, disappearing in a little eddy of wind that stirred the edge of the electricity bill, which I'd tucked under the fruit bowl.

I should probably ring the company, since I was home anyway, and see about setting up a payment plan. Going on the run would be bad enough with the wolves after me. I didn't need the debt collectors as well.

I poured boiling water into the teapot and breathed in the perfumed scent of Earl Grey. Maybe later. I wouldn't be able to focus on such everyday tasks until I'd spoken to Ethan and figured out the next steps.

There was a knock at the door. Perfect timing. I hurried over and threw it open.

"Jesus, Mary, and Joseph," Conal said. "What have you done to your hair?"

He was taller than I'd remembered, filling the doorway with his presence. Today, he had on a shirt in a deep green that brought out the green in his eyes even more strongly. He looked like a dream come true, when in fact he was a nightmare.

"Never mind my hair," I said, suddenly angry. My life had been so simple before he'd crashed into it—literally. He had no right to stand there looking so ... so *delicious* and sure of his welcome when my life was falling apart around me. My heart was still hammering from the shock of finding a mortal enemy on my doorstep. "What do you want?"

He raised that ridiculously sexy eyebrow at me. "I said I'd be back today, remember? I wanted to check on you."

"I'm fine, as you can see." He was a Soldier, and I'd just opened the door to him like a fool, though he seemed friendly enough. I wasn't getting any *burn the witch* vibes from him. He seemed no different than he had last night. Still hadn't had that chat with his buddy, then. Not that it really mattered—the other Soldier would track me down eventually—but it meant I had a little more time. I started to shut the door, but he stopped it with one muscled arm.

"Aren't you going to invite me in?" And then he stepped in anyway, making the point moot.

"Why? Are you a vampire?" I scowled at him—but not before I scooted backwards. Up close, his size and aura of strength was overwhelming. If he *did* decide to kill me, there wouldn't be a lot I could do about it. "If I rescind my invitation, will you fly out the nearest window?"

"Did you get out of bed on the wrong side this morning? I don't remember you being this tetchy—or this ungrateful—before."

"Fine. But you'd better start talking, because I have a *lot* of questions." I went back into the kitchen and got a mug for my tea. After a moment, I got one for him, too. He might be the enemy, but manners had been ingrained in me from an early age. I poured the tea, then glanced back at him as he opened the fridge. "What are you doing?"

"It's breakfast time." He got out the bacon. I'd bought a huge packet of it with his money, and most of it was still there.

"Correction: it's closer to lunch time. And I've already had breakfast."

"Lucky you. I haven't." He pushed past me, and I caught a whiff of his scent—something that conjured visions of cool pine forests and snowy mountain tops. "And who ever said no to a second breakfast?"

"What are you, a hobbit?"

"No hairy feet here." He pulled the two frypans out of the drawer under the microwave and put them on the stove top.

"Just make yourself right at home," I said pointedly.

"Thanks. Don't mind if I do." He flashed me an unrepentant smile, and my heart did a quick backflip in my chest. That smile lit his face and made me forget I was supposed to be angry with him. Or scared of him. In fact, I almost forgot how to breathe.

I watched him hunting around for oil in the cupboard, then shoved on his shoulder. It was like trying to move a boulder with a toothpick. "Get out of the way and let me do it. It is *my* kitchen."

"Such gracious hospitality," he said, but he moved. "Is this for me?" He indicated the second cup of tea.

"Knock yourself out." I carefully didn't look at him, annoyed that a stupid smile could have such an effect on me. He was the *enemy*. Why should I care if he smelled like forests or had a smile that could stop traffic? "I figured you'd need a drink to lubricate your throat for all the talking you'll have to do."

He picked up the cup and took a cautious sip while I heated the frypans and got bread out of the freezer for toast.

"Is there something different about you this morning?" he asked, eyeing me over the rim of his cup. "Apart from the travesty you've made of your hair, I mean."

My hand went to the long pink waves curling around my shoulders before I could stop myself. Travesty? I'd give him *travesty*. "Stop trying to change the subject. You owe me an explanation, buddy, so start talking. What was that thing that attacked me last night? *Why* did it attack me? And how did *you* happen to be there just in the nick of time to save me?"

If I could get him to admit he was a Soldier, I might be able to find out what he knew, and figure out why the other wolf wasn't sharing info with him. There was still a faint hope that the other wolf was just a regular werewolf gone rogue and not a Soldier. He might have just grabbed an opportunity to attack someone who was vulnerable, and he actually had no idea I was a cartomancer. I wasn't too proud to grasp at straws.

"That's a lot of questions," he said. "A man would need

a lot more than a cup of tea to keep him going to answer all those."

"I'm *getting* you your breakfast."

"That oil is smoking. Better hurry up."

I slapped a few rashers into the smoking pan, then shot him a look of pure frustration. "This town is under attack. Toby Macfarlane *died* last night. All I want is information —is that so much to ask? You owe me." Conal Clarke was Trouble with a capital T. Everything had gone south from the moment we'd met. If I were smart, I'd kick him out of my house and leave town, just as my aunties wanted.

"I *owe* you? Saving your life doesn't count for much in this little equation of yours."

"My life didn't *need* saving until you showed up. You and your werewolf friend."

"Not a werewolf." He paused. "A Soldier of the Light."

Finally. Now we were getting somewhere. I was glad I had my back to him, though, because it took me a minute to get my expression under control. I forced myself to continue as if I'd never heard of the Soldiers. "See, that wasn't so hard. What's a Soldier of the Light? You're one, too, aren't you?"

I risked a glance at him. He nodded, watching me carefully, and I let out a shaky breath. Far out, Brussels sprout. I had a *Soldier* in my kitchen. How was I still alive?

"The Soldiers are an ancient league of guardians, meant to keep the human world safe from preternatural threats."

Ha. He'd conveniently left out the bit about burning innocent women. He made it sound almost *noble*.

"And you can turn into a giant wolf. Sounds like a werewolf to me."

"There are some significant differences."

"Such as?"

"Werewolves lose their higher reasoning when they change. They become little more than animals. We don't."

"So a normal werewolf can't just join up and become a Soldier?"

"No. Not unless he was bitten by a Soldier. Werewolf bites make werewolves; Soldier bites make Soldiers. It's like the difference between—I don't know—cats and dogs. We're completely separate things. Another difference is that we have superior healing powers."

"Including for your clothes."

"Yes. Including for our clothes. You're still obsessed with that?"

I ignored that. "So you're like a preternatural super-hero? Dedicated to truth, justice, and saving the helpless humans?" Wow, I even managed to say that without choking on the irony. Go me.

"No capes," he said drily.

"Fine. So your cover's blown, now. You might as well tell me everything. Stop acting like everything's a riddle wrapped in—"

"Bacon?"

"Sorry, what?"

"A riddle wrapped in bacon." He eyed the bacon the way another man might have looked at a naked woman. "Then fried in bacon fat. With maybe a big helping of bacon on the side."

The sound of bacon fat popping in the frypan behind me was the only sound for a moment as I stared at him, non-plussed.

"I was *going* to say a riddle wrapped in a mystery, inside an enigma."

He blinked, coming back from whatever bacon-filled heaven he'd been in, and frowned at me. "That doesn't make any sense."

"It's a famous quote from Winston Churchill. I think he was talking about Russia at the time."

He shrugged dismissively. "I like my version better. What's Russia got to do with anything?"

"It's got more to do with it than *bacon*. What is wrong with you? Don't you ever stop thinking about food?"

"Not when I'm hungry," he said pointedly.

"Calm your farm. This will be ready in a minute." The scent of bacon frying filled the air, making my stomach growl even though I'd already eaten. I gave in and got out a second plate for myself.

"Are you sure you have enough there?"

He treated me to that heart stopping smile again. I firmly repressed the urge to sigh like a schoolgirl and serve him whatever his carnivorous heart desired. He really was gorgeous when he smiled. But didn't he know it. Women all across the country had probably given him whatever he wanted when he flashed that smile. But I was made of stronger stuff. I knew what he was.

"Positive. We need to leave room for the vegetables— and you'd better eat those, mister." I sliced a couple of tomatoes in half and laid them, cut side down, in the frypan next to the bacon. I had some baby spinach in the fridge, too. "You're not getting scurvy on my watch."

He eyed me doubtfully. Even doubtful was a good look on him. In the morning light streaming through the kitchen window, his green eyes were the colour of a sunlit wave. He had his sleeves rolled to the elbows, showing strong, tanned forearms but conveniently hiding that hateful tattoo. His jeans were a faded blue. With his black hair tumbled carelessly to his shoulders, he looked like a model from a Levi's commercial.

"Scurvy doesn't come on that fast," he said.

"Yeah? Do you really want to risk having all your teeth fall out? You'd make a pretty crappy werewolf with no teeth."

"I'm not a werewolf," he said with exaggerated patience. "I told you, I'm a Soldier. It's a different thing altogether."

"Potato, potahto." I cracked three eggs into the second pan, then reconsidered. It probably took a lot to fuel a werewolf. I added two more. "You're a guy who turns into a wolf." And *that* was a sentence I'd never imagined coming out of my mouth. "If it walks like a duck and quacks like a duck …"

He grinned in genuine amusement, those sea-green eyes lighting up from within. "I promise you, I've never turned into a duck."

When the food was ready, I brought it to the table. He sat down opposite and tucked in, focusing on his plate. I sneaked glances at him as I ate. It wasn't that he gulped it down or stuffed huge amounts in at a time, but he certainly applied himself to the task with enthusiasm. He had two or three times as much on his plate as I did, but he finished when my plate was still half full.

"So," I said when he leaned back in his chair and picked up his tea again. "Tell me more about these Soldiers."

"How much do you know?"

"Assume I know nothing and start at the beginning."

He grinned. "Way, way back at the dawn of time, when the first preternatural crawled out of its lair and decided that humans were good to snack on ..."

"Not that close to the beginning. I meant the part that affects me. You say the Soldiers are supposed to protect humanity. So why did that other one attack me?"

"I don't know," he said. "I haven't been able to find him."

Maybe he'd been run over by a semi-trailer. A girl could hope.

"And you saved me because ...?"

"Because I promised to." He leaned forward, green eyes intense. "I'm a man of my word, Sunday. I said I would protect you with my life, and I will. Even from my own brethren."

"I'm just a boring, normal person." I looked away, unnerved by the shiver that ran through me at the intensity in his eyes. It wasn't a shiver of fear. "There's no reason the werewolf police would be interested in me." *And if you believe that, I have a bridge I could sell you.*

"*Not* werewolves," he said firmly. "And not really police. More like executioners."

11

————

I winced. "Wow, you need to work on your reassurance game."

"Sorry. Liam and I arrived a week ago—"

"Liam?"

"The guy who attacked you. He's—"

Someone knocked on the door, and he lost the lazy grin and came instantly alert.

"Are you expecting someone?"

"Yes. It's only Ethan." I got up to open the door, but he was there before me. "Oh, no, you go right ahead. Treat the place like your own. Let my guests in, by all means."

He ignored my sarcasm and actually sniffed the air. His face darkened into a scowl. "It's a vampire."

"I *know*. Let him in."

"Sunday?" Ethan called through the door, concern in his voice. "Are you all right? Who's that with you?"

"No one important," I said, scowling at Conal.

"Why is there a vampire at your door?" Conal demanded.

"He's a friend of mine." I tried to reach past him, but he blocked me. "Get out of the way."

"Sunday, open the door," Ethan said, and there was such a tug in his voice that my feet carried me closer without my even deciding to move. Only Conal's grip on my arm held me back.

"He's glamouring you," Conal said. "And it's a vampire that we're hunting."

There was no sparkle in those green eyes now, and, for the first time since he'd walked in, I felt a frisson of fear up my spine. Seeing that hard look on his face, I could well believe he'd been sent to hunt and kill. *More like executioners*, indeed.

"Ethan is no elder," I snapped, shaking off my fear. Conal owed me his life; he wasn't going to attack me. He'd just said so. I wasn't sure now who I was more annoyed with—Conal for blocking the door, or Ethan for glamouring me again, after he'd promised he never would. "Let him in."

He opened the door. They stood there, bristling at each other, like two dogs trying to decide if they would fight.

"Invite me in, Sunday," Ethan said tightly.

Oops. I'd forgotten I'd rescinded his invitation after the last glamouring incident. While many of the myths about vampires had turned out not to be true when they came out of the coffin, that one was. They had to be invited into someone's home, at least the first time they visited. Or after a peeved ex-girlfriend withdrew their invitation.

"Only if you promise not to use your glamour on me again. Though I'm not sure what your promise is worth, since you've promised that before."

"I'm sorry. I know I promised, but I thought you were in danger." He gave me a significant look. He certainly hadn't expected to find me fraternising with the enemy.

"Come in, Ethan." I glared at Conal until he stepped back to allow him over the threshold.

"Who is this?" Ethan asked without taking his eyes off Conal. The hostility emanating off him in waves was so thick I could have cut it with a knife. Conal returned his glare with a flat, cold stare of his own.

"This is Conal Clarke. He's a Soldier of the Light."

Some of the hostility went out of Ethan's stare but none of the wariness.

"You're the one who saved her?"

"That's right."

"She wouldn't have needed saving if your buddy hadn't attacked her. What kind of guardian attacks the very humans he's supposed to be guarding?"

"What kind of vampire uses his glamour on his human friends?"

I sighed. "Guys, a little less testosterone, if you please. We have bigger problems here."

Ethan flicked a glance at me. "I don't consider someone trying to kill you a small problem, Sunday."

"Neither do I, quite frankly, but we're not going to solve anything by standing around here glaring at each other, are we? Why don't we all sit down?"

Since the table was the only place with enough room

for us all, the two men settled there while I whisked the empty plates out to the kitchen.

"What is your interest in Sunday?" Conal asked.

"She's my friend," Ethan said. "I'm *interested* in keeping her alive. Unlike your buddy, apparently."

Conal sighed. "If it makes you feel any better, I don't understand why he attacked her either. We're supposed to be hunting a rogue elder."

"But this guy is your partner, isn't he?"

A flicker of distaste crossed Conal's handsome face before being smoothed away. "Not my partner. We both happened to be assigned to this case, that's all."

"But no one told him to go around attacking innocent humans, did they?" Ethan said, a challenge in his voice.

"No."

"So why did he?" I asked.

Conal shrugged. "Beats me. I can't find him. Haven't seen him since I chased him off last night. We don't exactly work that closely together—there's a lot of ground to cover up here, as you may have noticed."

"There's this marvellous human invention called the telephone," I said. "You might try it."

"Unfortunately, some madwoman knocked me off my bike the other night and my phone got busted up. I bought a new one this morning, but he's not answering. After I left you last night, I went looking for him, but he'd disappeared, and I lost his trail in the stench of vampire around the back of your shop."

He knew where I worked? I couldn't remember telling him. That made me a little uncomfortable.

"So, you're here to hunt the elder?" Ethan repeated, obviously annoyed by the mention of vampire stench.

"That's right."

"The queen won't like it. The hive prefers to take care of its own business."

Conal smiled slightly. "The hive might want to get on with it, then. This thing has killed five people now. When was the queen planning to step in?"

Five people? I'd only heard of three. This was worse than I'd thought.

"We'll handle this ourselves," Ethan insisted. "We don't need the help of Soldiers who can't tell the difference between an elder vampire and a human."

Conal sighed. "I assure you Sunday doesn't smell like an elder vampire. I don't know what got into Liam, but normally he's one of our best, even if he is an ass. We're here to do the job right, and we won't be taking orders from your queen."

"For goodness' sake," I said. "Does it matter who gives the orders? The point is to stop the killings. Surely you can agree on that, at least." I turned to Ethan. "If Conal wants to hunt down this thing, let him." *And then I wouldn't have to feel so bad about leaving all my friends behind. At least I'd know they were safe. Take the hint, Ethan.*

"The hive prefers to handle its own problems," Ethan repeated.

"But it's not just your problem, is it? It's everyone's problem now, and it seems to me that the hive hasn't been doing a very good job of handling it so far. Personally, I don't care who fixes it, as long as it gets fixed. It's stupid for you two to be arguing over who gets the glory of killing the thing. If you really care about protecting the people of Kurranderra, you should be working together."

"It's not that simple," Ethan said.

"Of course it is. The hive needs to stop this elder before all of you get tarred with the same brush and people start hunting vampires again. Conal is here to hunt the elder. *Clearly* you need to cooperate." Kurranderra was in danger and the vampires wanted to quibble about status, or who got to claim the honours, or whatever they were doing? "It's in the queen's best interest."

"The queen makes her own judgements about what's in her best interest," Ethan said, a little bite in his voice.

"Not when I'm in town, she doesn't," Conal said. "But Sunday's right. We'll get this thing done faster if we work together. I could use the hive's assistance."

Ethan glanced at me as if to say *look at what you made me do* then nodded at him with a sigh. "Fine. I'll arrange for you to meet with the queen."

"Me, too," I said. If Ethan and Conal could barely be civil to each other, could I trust them to sort this out with the queen unsupervised? I was thinking that was a big fat *no*. This could be the last thing I could do for Kurranderra before I left.

"Good idea," Conal said. "Until I find out what Liam's up to, I'm not leaving you alone."

Ethan bristled at that, and I did, too.

"You can't stay here," I said.

"You needn't sound so horrified," Conal said. "Would

you rather Liam tried to kill you again and succeeded this time?"

"Of course not, but ..."

"You could come and stay in my motel room instead, if you like."

"Absolutely not," I said. The less time spent with Conal Clarke the better. "I could stay with Bethany."

"You need someone to protect you. I doubt this Bethany's up to the job."

"You shouldn't drag Bethany into this," Ethan added. Interesting. Was that concern for her? Maybe her crush wasn't completely one-sided. "But you have options. The queen is prepared to extend the protection of the hive to you."

I bit my lip, considering. Obviously being torn apart by Liam wasn't high on my list of preferred options, but how much protection would Conal be if he knew the truth? I'd be gambling my life on the strength of his honour. Ling would throw a fit at the very thought.

On the other hand, there was Ethan's offer, which sounded about as appealing as jumping into a pool of sharks to escape the wolves chasing you. I liked Ethan, but I didn't *entirely* trust him. And the rest of his hive was an unknown quantity. Vampires were nowhere near the monsters that fiction had painted them—but still. Vampires. They weren't exactly anyone's first thought when looking for selfless protectors.

"I have a life," I said. "A job." But I could find no solutions to my dilemma. None that appealed, anyway. Much as

I hated the thought, I'd probably have to take the aunties' advice and skip town, at least for a few months until the hunt died down. Was there any way to save my job?

"Work should be pretty safe," Conal said. "He won't do anything in such a public setting. And I have work of my own, which I can do when you're there. But you can't be here alone."

"The hive could supply guards," Ethan said.

"You're making pretty free with the hive's resources," Conal said. "Shouldn't they all be out searching for this elder of yours?"

Ethan stood up, his chair scraping loudly over the floorboards. "Let me just step outside and talk to the queen now. I'm sure she'll support me in this. It's not in the interest of the hive to leave humans vulnerable to attack, with all the publicity this elder is getting."

"You do that," Conal said as Ethan headed for the door. "Let me know how that goes for you."

Ethan gave him a dark look as he left.

"You can't stay," I said to Conal as soon as the door closed.

In the end, the sheer insanity of a cartomancer having a Soldier in the house decided it. He said he still owed me a life debt, and if I were a regular human, I would trust him to protect me. But I wasn't, and I couldn't take the risk of having him around.

"Why not?"

"Because ..." Because you'd turn into a monster if you knew the truth. "Because there's only one bed!"

"Are you worried I'll be so snared by your womanly wiles I won't be able to control myself?"

I drew myself up. "Are you knocking my womanly wiles?"

He moved closer, and I got a whiff of that wild, foresty scent of his. His eyes sparked with humour and something else—something that looked a lot like desire. My mouth went suddenly dry.

"Not at all." His gaze dropped from my eyes to my lips. When he spoke again, his voice was husky. "Wile away. I promise not to resist."

I swallowed hard. He was so close I could feel the heat of his body. His mouth was a mere breath away.

I stepped back abruptly, before I got lost in the depths of those sea-green eyes. "You're not my type."

Liar, liar, pants on fire.

His mouth quirked into a smile that was almost as devastating as that stupid eyebrow and my knees went weak. "Shame. However—" His tone was suddenly all business. "This is about protecting you. It's stupid to risk your safety because of sleeping arrangements. I can sleep on the floor."

I shook my head. "*Really* not a good idea."

He stared at me for a long time, frowning. "Fine. But I'm keeping an eye on you. I'll go see if Liam has been back while your vampire friend's still here to keep an eye on you. His bed wasn't slept in last night, but his clothes were still there. Maybe I can sort this mess out straight away."

"That would be nice."

"I'll give you my phone number," he said. "Lock the

door behind me and call immediately if anything disturbs you. Anything at all."

I dutifully entered his number into my contacts, and he left. The apartment seemed very quiet with both of them out. It felt bigger, too, without their two big personalities posturing all over it. I sat down at the table with my half-empty cup of tea. It had gone cold, but I couldn't be bothered making another one.

I looked around my small home, feeling desolate. I'd been happy here. But it was time to say goodbye. I'd go to this meeting with the queen, to make sure that Kurranderra would be protected, and then I'd leave.

As always, I sought refuge in Mum's cards. Shuffling calmed me, and I focused on the feel of the cards in my hands, blocking out any thoughts of wolves and vampires and bloodstains on the ground. Gradually, my breathing slowed.

A card leapt from the pack as I shuffled. I smiled. I called those "jumpers". They often seemed like gifts from the universe, as if Mum were especially impatient with me and couldn't wait to impart the wisdom I needed at that moment.

I turned it over. It was the Fool. Again.

New beginnings, huh? Mum seemed pretty insistent on that one. I sighed. I'd *made* a new beginning, right here in Kurranderra, and I didn't want to start over again. At least the card implied that I wasn't about to become wolf chow in the near future.

I gazed at the card's familiar artwork. The dancing girl with her luminous inhuman eyes. The way her skirt swirled around her and the suggestion of wings rising from her shoulders. The strange, crystalline landscape stretching away from the cliff. It was foreign, but still as familiar to me as breathing. I could probably draw each of these cards from memory, after having spent so many years staring at them and tracing the lines of each drawing with my fingertips.

The Fool gazed out of the card, up and to the right, as if she were looking over my shoulder, a dreamy smile on her face. Glimpsing that great new future she kept promising me, maybe? How much of Conal Clarke was in it?

Now there was a face I'd like to draw. And paint. The contrast of light green eyes against tanned skin drew my eye every time I saw him. That straight nose and cleft in his chin were classically handsome, but the scar through his eyebrow ruined the perfection of his features, giving him personality. And all of it was framed so beautifully by the tumble of black hair to his broad shoulders.

There was something so alluring about that face. He would be a great model for the Devil card, if I were strong enough to use the major arcana. It was a face designed to lead any woman into temptation.

Not that I would be giving in to temptation. I could never forget that he was the enemy. The sooner he was gone, the better.

The sooner *I* was gone, the better.

I glanced down again at the dancing Fool. She might be able to leap off her ledge, secure in the knowledge that her wings would save her from the drop, but I had no such protection. How could I stay here with the wolves circling?

It was too big a risk. I hated to admit defeat and leave, but the aunties were right. I should leave hunting the rogue to the Soldiers. That was their job, after all.

But they've been here a week and not found anything. And I'd been so close the other night in the bush with Ethan and Raquel. My magic had definitely latched onto something before it had cut out so abruptly. It was a risk—but what if one more try was all I needed to finish this whole thing? Then I could leave with a clear conscience.

My eyes blurred, and I blinked rapidly to clear them. I had the strangest feeling that I was falling forward. I jerked in my seat, but I hadn't actually moved. The card in my hand tugged at my gaze, compelling my attention.

All at once, it seemed I was there on that crystalline cliff. The wind of another world stirred my hair, bringing the brooding scent of a building storm with it. I stared into the card, and it was like looking out a window. I could see the trail that had brought the dancing girl to this place, leading down into the distance. Strange triangular buildings that I'd never been able to see before clustered there.

My fingers tingled, and warmth rushed through my hand and up my arm. A fizzing sense of anticipation filled me, like that moment when you hover at the top of a roller-coaster, right before you dive into the dizzying swoop and your stomach drops out of your body. Suddenly, my body felt bigger on the inside than the outside as pressure built within me, threatening to explode out of my veins.

And then the dancing girl turned her head and stared straight into my eyes.

12

$\mathcal{I}$ hurled the card away from me with a shout. What the *fluff*?

I stood up so fast that my chair tipped and crashed to the floor behind me. The Fool's card landed facedown and slid across the floorboards, disappearing under the bookcase. I stared at the darkness there, my whole body shaking, watching it as if it might sprout teeth and bite me, but nothing else happened.

Ethan burst back in, phone still in hand. "What's wrong?"

"I—I—" I couldn't tell him. He'd think I was crazy. "A cockroach just ran across my foot."

"Right." He tucked the phone in his pocket.

I flipped the empty book over the deck to hide it from Ethan's sight, trying to make the movement casual. He knew I owned a deck of cards, of course, since he'd seen me use them. But *this* deck was different, not for anyone's eyes but my own.

Then I retreated to the kitchen and switched the kettle on. If ever a moment called for a soothing cup of tea, this was it. The cards lay quietly under the book, just regular pieces of cardboard. But something had changed. My fingers still tingled, as if sparks were bursting under my skin, and I tucked my hands into my armpits while I waited for the kettle to boil. I could tell myself until I was blue in the face that I'd imagined the whole thing—I was tired, the last few days had been a shock, yada, yada, yada —but I wasn't buying it. That had been real, and I knew it.

"Where did the Soldier go?" Ethan asked.

"To see if he can find this Liam guy. The other Soldier."

"The queen's sending a car. She wants to see you both this afternoon." He picked up the downed chair and set it back on its legs. "Can you be ready about two o'clock?"

"Sure." I brought my tea back to the table. I tried to focus on Ethan, but my gaze kept darting to the shadows under the bookcase that hid the Fool.

"Do you want me to stay until the car gets here?"

"No, I'm fine. I'll be *fine*."

"Okay, then. I'll see you later. Wear something nice."

He let himself out, and this time I locked the door. Hesitantly, I returned to the table and rested my fingertips lightly on top of the deck, ready to snatch them back at a moment's notice. The cards vibrated lightly under my touch.

Okay, this was too much. Moving quickly, I jammed the deck back into its hidey hole inside the *Lord of the Rings* and replaced the book on the shelf. I didn't go near the Fool. I'd deal with that later. Snatching up my bag and keys, I left the house, taking the stairs down to the car park two at a time. I had a couple of hours to kill, and I didn't want to spend time alone.

Halfway to town, I finally relaxed, forcing my fingers to release their death grip on Bugsy's steering wheel and letting out a big breath. I'd go to the coffee shop—that should be safe enough. Conal had said Liam wouldn't attack me in a public place. It was pay day, and I'd fluffing well earned a treat. One peppermint mocha latte coming up.

There was even a parking spot just outside the door. The parking gods were smiling on me. I went inside and ordered, then snagged one of the booths in the window where I could keep an eye on the people walking up and down the street. I felt as jumpy as a cat on a hot tin roof.

On the other side of the road, Nicole came out of her shop Gems and Jewels, flipping a sign on the door to *Back in Five Minutes* before locking the door behind her. It seemed like a hundred years since I'd chatted with her on the bus this morning. So much had happened.

She crossed the road and came into the coffee shop, still wearing the heavy leather apron that she wore for smithing. She had a little workshop in the back of her shop, and she spent so much time there designing and making jewellery that I sometimes thought it would be cheaper for her just to sleep there as well.

Once she'd ordered a coffee to go, she turned away from the counter and saw me. I waved and she came over to plonk herself in the seat opposite me.

"Hi, Sunny. Did you get your car going again?" She was very short, no taller than Ling, and today her wild brown curls were tied back from her round, smiling face.

"Yep. Turned out it wasn't the battery after all. I probably should have taken you up on that offer to look at it," I said. "Did you realise you still have your apron on?"

She laughed. "I'm not *that* absentminded. I only popped in to grab a coffee to go." Then she peered at me a little closer. "Are you okay? I thought you were working today."

I sucked in a breath. She hadn't heard the news, even though Second Chances and Johnny's were just around the corner. She'd probably been engrossed in her workshop. "The shop's closed today. Toby Macfarlane ... he was killed last night out in the car park."

"*What?* What happened?"

"It looks like that elder has struck again."

"Poor Toby. That's awful." She looked as shellshocked as I had been when Cheryl told me.

"I know, right? Sorry to drop it on you like that." I shook my head. "His poor family."

"My goodness. Those vampires need to hurry up and find that rogue. This is getting out of hand. Oh, here's your coffee."

The waitress, a middle-aged woman with a kindly smile, offered a steaming cup. "One peppermint mocha latte?"

"Yes, please." She set it down in front of me. "Thanks."

"Nicole," the barista called.

"And there's mine," Nicole said, getting up. She paused beside the table. "Are you all right? Come upstairs tonight if you need someone to talk to."

"I'm okay. But thank you."

I really admired Nicole. She didn't look that much older than thirty, but she had a thriving business and was truly talented at what she did. She worked hard, and it was nice of her to offer to spend some of her rare downtime with me. There was a caring heart underneath that leather apron.

I toyed with my phone as I sipped my coffee. What a day. My hair had gone white, poor Toby was dead, and I had a Soldier of the Light trying to move in with me. The world had gone crazy.

Craziest of all—Bethany had seen Ariel in the mirror. All these years, I'd been the only one who could see her.

And that had caused *so* many problems. All the conversations I'd checked out of, distracted by her; all the times people had caught me talking to thin air and decided I was crazy—and how much anxiety my aunties had suffered before I'd learned to keep quiet about my friend. They'd spoken in worried voices about therapy when they thought I wasn't listening. There'd been all those too-casual questions about whether my imaginary friend had come to play today. Kids at school had outright called me a liar and shunned me. I'd quickly learned that I wasn't acceptable to anyone if Ariel came as part of the package.

So I'd kept her hidden, like a shameful secret, all the while wondering what was wrong with me. Were my aunts' whispers right and Ariel was a strange coping mechanism, a way for a small child to handle the grief of her mother's death? Or was I just plain old crazy, like the kids at school said?

Of course, I'd eventually realised she was real. The other night in the forest wasn't the first time she'd called the wind to protect me. I'd tried to tell Ling and Ivy about that, but they hadn't listened. I'd even pointed out that no one would imagine themselves a friend who was so *annoying*, thinking they would see the logic in that, but it made no difference.

Maybe now they'd listen.

I dialled Ling's number.

"Hello, darling," Ling said after a couple of rings. "What's up?"

"Is this a good time to talk?"

Suspicion immediately entered her voice. "What's wrong?"

I opened my mouth to say *nothing*, then reconsidered. Ling could smell a lie a mile off.

"Sunday?" Ling prompted as the silence lengthened. "Ivy, get over here. Sunday's on the phone. I'm putting you on loudspeaker, honey."

"Sunny?" Ivy sounded breathless. "What's the matter?"

"Can't I ring my two favourite aunties without something being the matter?" I asked weakly.

"No," they said in unison.

"I know that tone in your voice," Ling said. "Don't try to hide it now. What did you ring me for? Spit it out."

Okay, then. Here went nothing. "Remember when I was little and I used to play with that imaginary friend?"

"Why?" Ling asked. "You're not seeing things again, are you?"

I took a deep breath. "No, I'm not seeing things *again*. I'm seeing the same things I have seen all my life, only now other people are seeing them, too."

"What do you mean?" Ivy sounded puzzled.

"I mean Ariel isn't a figment of my imagination. Bethany saw her in the mirror this morning. It's like I always told you. She's real. I'm not crazy."

"Oh, honey," Ivy soothed. "We never thought you were crazy."

"And that's not all, either." I had to tell someone about what had happened with the cards before I really *did* go crazy. "I was looking at the Fool this morning—"

"I thought you couldn't work with the majors?" Ivy asked. "Have you had a breakthrough?"

"I wasn't working. Just looking." I braced myself for the next part. "And it wasn't my deck, it was Mum's."

There was a gasp on the other end of the line, though I couldn't tell which aunt it was.

"You have Dana's cards?" Ling asked.

She sounded bewildered, even a little hurt, and guilt made me wince. It hadn't been easy to hide them from my aunts all these years, but Mum had made me promise that if anything ever happened to her, I would never show them to anyone.

Nobody, do you understand, sweetheart? I had very few memories of my mother, but that was one of them. The earnest look on her face as she held my hands and stared into my eyes. *You must promise me, darling. Only ever take them out when you're alone. They're very special. No one else can know you have them.*

Not even Auntie Ling or Aunt Ivy?

She'd shaken her head. *Not even them. Better to get into the habit of always making sure you're alone before you take them out. You don't want to make a mistake one day.*

Why, Mummy? What would happen if someone saw me with them? Would I get into trouble?

That depends on who it was. Her expression had been grim. *If it was the wrong person, you could get into terrible trouble.*

"Yes." It was a relief to have the secret out. "Not the whole deck, but most of them."

"I thought they'd been lost with Dana," Ivy said, almost to herself. "To think she had them all this time."

"Why on earth didn't you tell us?" Ling asked.

"Does it really matter?"

I should have. They weren't actually related to me at all, these aunties of mine, but they'd loved my Mum like a sister. And I'd figured out, when I was thirteen and came into my magic, why Mum hadn't wanted to trust six-year-old me with the truth. Maybe I wouldn't have magic in my blood, and I'd never have to know about cartomancy. But in the meantime, she had to say something to stop me flashing her cards around where unfriendly eyes might see them.

"The point is, when I touched them today, I felt this tingling in my hand, and it was as if I could see a real world on the other side of the card. Like it was a window I was looking through. And then the girl in the picture—she ..." I felt like an idiot saying it out loud, but I ploughed on. "She turned her head and looked at me."

The two of them went so quiet I thought the line must have dropped out. I couldn't even hear them breathing.

And then Ling said, with her usual decisiveness. "That's it, we're coming back."

"You can't," I said without thinking.

"Oh?" Ling asked, and there was a world of menace in her polite tone. "And why is that?"

Wow, you really botched that one. I shook my head at my own stupidity. It was never a good idea to tell Ling she couldn't do something. She always took it as a personal challenge.

And now I'd have to tell her.

"There's been ... that is, there's a couple of Soldiers in town."

"*What?*" they yelled in unison.

"It's fine," I said quickly. "One of them owes me a life debt. He thinks I'm a regular human." No need to worry them by telling them about the other one.

"He owes you a *life* debt?" Ling asked, still in that dangerously polite voice. "Sunday Armitage, what on earth have you been up to?"

"It doesn't matter," Ivy cut in. "You can't trust a Soldier's word."

"True," Ling agreed. "Pack your bags. We're coming to get you."

"No! Don't do that. There's no sense endangering yourselves."

"Oh, so you *are* in danger?"

Oops. "It's under control."

"Nonsense. We'll be there tomorrow night."

And then she hung up.

13
———

I stared at myself in the bathroom mirror. I was wearing my best dress—an emerald-green halterneck with a twirly skater skirt. Ethan had warned me that the queen would expect more than jeans and T-shirt as a gesture of respect, and I didn't want to make a bad impression. Silver hoops dangled from my ears, and I wore strappy black heels that showed off my long, tanned legs. Great for dressing up. Not so great for running.

There had better not be any running. Ethan had promised I'd be an honoured guest of the vampires, but ... vampires. Any flesh-and-blood person—especially blood—had a right to feel a teensy bit nervous about visiting a hive.

The only question was what to do with my newly pink hair. It made quite a statement against the shimmering emerald green of the dress. I couldn't help feeling that I had looked better with my own natural dark brown, but I straightened my shoulders. I could work with this. At least pink and green went together, right?

I had brushed my hair until it shone, and now I pulled it up into a loose bun and secured it with a few bobby pins. I surveyed the effect in the mirror. Not too shabby. With the dangling earrings, it certainly looked more formal than my usual everyday ponytail, but I liked the effortless chic of the messy bun, as if I rolled out of bed looking this good every morning.

Blue eyes stared back at me, outlined in a little more makeup than I normally wore. Their expression was worried, and I practised a smile, consciously forcing my forehead to relax its anxious lines. It would be *fine*. Humans went to the vampire hive *all the time* and made it out again safe and sound. Vampires were way more civilised than popular fiction suggested. I was in no more danger in the middle of the hive than I would be walking down Main Street. Maybe less, since there wouldn't be tourists haphazardly parking all over the place and trying to drive and sightsee at the same time.

I added a touch of pink lipstick. I usually preferred redder shades, but they didn't look so good against the pink hair. The bandage around my forearm caught my eye as I applied the lipstick, and I frowned again.

Maybe it wasn't such a good idea to walk into the hive wearing a bloodstained bandage. However civilised its inhabitants, that seemed like asking for trouble. Quickly, I unwound the bandage and threw it into the bin under the sink.

My arm was looking good—scabby, but good. I dug out

a packet of large Band-Aids from the bathroom cabinet and stuck a few of them over the scabs instead.

There. That was better. Much more discreet than the ugly bandage. Waterproof, too.

Conal looked up as I came into the living room, and a smile lit his sea-green eyes. "You look good."

I smoothed the skirt of my dress, torn between pleasure at the compliment and the constant background hum of anxiety at being this close to a Soldier. Keeping my game face on was wearing me out. "Ethan said I should dress up."

He stood up. "The queen has sent a limo for us." He'd dressed up for the occasion, too. He wore a dark blue jacket over a white T-shirt that smelled so new I suspected he'd just bought it in Katoomba. He probably hadn't packed anything fancy for his little hunting trip. A pair of cream chinos completed the look. He could have stepped out of the pages of the menswear catalogue, all ready to go boating on his yacht or to a champagne occasion at the Opera House.

"A limo? That's flashy."

He shrugged. "Nessa likes making it clear that she could buy and sell the rest of us on the street corner by raiding her petty cash. Vampires are into power plays. Will you be warm enough?"

My shoulders were bare, and the dress had a low scoop at the back. I went into the bedroom and grabbed a black suede jacket that I'd picked up from Second Chances. Not quite as fancy as the dress, but better than freezing.

"Okay, I'm ready now." I came out, swinging the jacket around my shoulders.

He opened the front door for me and gestured that I should lead the way. A white stretch limo was idling at the curb outside.

"Is someone else coming with us? That seems like a lot of car to transport two people."

"Nope." He strode down the steps and opened the back door of the limo for me. "The queen is demonstrating her hospitality with a grandiose gesture." I noticed he didn't call her Nessa again within earshot of the driver. As I passed him to get into the car, he whispered, "There will almost certainly be cameras, so don't say anything you don't want the vampires to hear."

I nodded. What did he think I would say? *Get your free blood here?* I slid into the car and greeted the driver.

The interior was enormous. Ten people could have ridden in comfort. There was a small TV and a minibar containing champagne and several bottles of spirits.

"Good evening, sir, ma'am," the driver said as Conal climbed in beside me and shut the door. "Help yourself to anything, with the queen's compliments."

I thanked him, wondering if he was a vampire, too. He wore a uniform, complete with a cap, so perhaps he was just a human employee. It didn't seem polite to ask, so I busied myself checking out the bar as he closed the glass screen between us. The champagne was French and most likely cost more than my week's rent.

"You want something to drink?" I asked Conal.

"Probably best not to turn up at the vampires' lair smashed and legless, don't you think?"

I saw the driver's eyes flick toward him in the rear vision mirror before he turned his attention back to the road. He could still hear us, then, despite the screen.

"There's quite a range of options between pleasantly buzzed and completely legless, you know. But whatever." I had no stomach for alcohol anyway. I was too nervous about the upcoming meeting and my own imminent departure.

Music was playing, something full of weeping violins and soaring crescendos that I didn't recognise. Being chauffeured through the streets as the music swirled around us was quite an experience. There was no sound from outside—the limo must have been soundproofed. It was as if we were caught in our own little bubble in time, cut off from the real world that slipped past the windows.

It was a long drive. We wound down the mountainside, the limo taking the curves in style, and onto the motorway, which took us halfway or more across Sydney, never stopping or slowing.

We didn't talk much. I passed the time staring out the window, torn between nerves at the coming meeting and an uncomfortable awareness of Conal's presence beside me. All my senses were tuned to him. I wanted to drink him in, and I had to force myself not to sneak little glances in his direction every five minutes.

After more than an hour, the huge car slipped silently off the motorway. I couldn't tell where we were, although the occasional glimpses of a vast expanse of water suggested we were somewhere around the harbour. We drove through quiet, leafy streets, where the trees were so old that their branches almost met over the top of the road. The houses were large, set at the top of long driveways on expansive blocks. Most of them were protected by high stone walls and wrought-iron gates. Nothing looked as though it had been built in the current century. This was old money.

It wasn't an area of Sydney I'd been to before. Not the kind of place where motorhomes were a regular feature. Everyone who lived here probably drove Mercs or BMWs —or even had their own private limousine.

Our car turned into the driveway of an especially impressive house. Its wrought-iron gates slid open soundlessly as the car approached but, despite that modern touch, the house itself looked like it belonged in another century. Three stories tall, with gable windows in its steep roofs and mullioned windowpanes, it could have been an English nobleman's residence, or perhaps a school for the rich and privileged. Ancient ivy crept across the whole front of the house, clothing it in green leaves that shivered in a slight wind. The car swept up the long driveway and stopped under a sheltered portico.

The front door opened as we got out, and Ethan appeared. He wore a jacket and tie with carefully pressed pants, and he looked more like an accountant than a vampire. A far cry from the casual guy I'd once gone out with.

"I hope you enjoyed the ride," he said, leaning forward to drop a swift kiss on my cheek. "Welcome to the hive."

"Thanks. It's bigger than I expected."

He led the way inside, chatting over his shoulder. "This is only part of it. The bulk of the hive is underground."

My eyebrows flew up. "Really? It must be huge."

"Like an iceberg," Conal commented.

"Precisely." Ethan led us to the foot of a massive staircase that swept up from the foyer then divided into two before it reached the next level high above. "I must ask you to submit to a search," he said to Conal as two large and very serious-looking men came out of a doorway half hidden behind the stairs.

"I'm not carrying any weapons," Conal said.

"Nevertheless ..."

"Hands against the wall, please, sir," one of the enormous newcomers said.

Conal sighed and did as he was asked, spreading his long legs wide. The man patted him down quickly and professionally, while his partner stood back, watching the proceedings with an unblinking stare. I wondered what his job was, apart from making the whole thing twice as uncomfortable as it needed to be. Maybe he was just on standby in case someone objected to the search too strenuously.

"And your handbag too, please, miss," the first guy said when he'd finished with Conal.

Wordlessly, I handed him my bag. All I had in there was my phone, wallet, keys, and pink lipstick. He checked each item without comment, then handed the bag back to me.

"The queen needn't feel threatened by me," Conal said as we followed Ethan up the staircase.

"It's standard procedure."

Standard procedure for all visitors or just for Soldiers and their companions? I didn't quite see the point of frisking Conal—he was a weapon all by himself. Who needed to bring knives or guns when you could turn into a giant freaking wolf and rip someone's throat out? As for me, I was clearly nothing to be afraid of—had they just checked my bag for the sake of appearances, so it wouldn't look as though they were singling Conal out?

Surely a hive full of vampires had nothing to fear from the teeth of a lone Soldier? Vampires weren't exactly defenceless—they were pretty well endowed in the teeth department themselves. It was probably just posturing, to prove they could make Conal submit to their will.

"Here we are," Ethan said, stopping in front of a carved wooden door at least twice his height. The ceilings were ridiculous in here. I'd hate to be the one who had to change the light bulbs. "Are you ready?"

"Sure," I said. He was making me more nervous with his obvious caution. *Let's get it over with already.* Conal nodded, and Ethan opened the door.

He cleared his throat. "Soldier of the Light Conal Clarke and Miss Sunday Armitage, Majesty."

We entered a room twice the size of my whole apartment. Gilt panels stretched to the elaborately carved ceiling, and floor-to-ceiling drapes in deep blue velvet framed windows all along one wall. Armchairs stood in small groups around the room, in a variety of styles from carved

Louis XIV-type ones with brocade seats to more modern leather upholstery.

In one of these groupings, two women sat, one on either side of a smallish table that held wine glasses full of a deep red liquid, as well as a tea set decorated with tiny blue flowers. Three men were ranged behind them, standing in a loose knot, and another couple sat together on a small gold sofa to one side of the women. Almost all of them wore evening dress, despite the fact that it was only four o'clock in the afternoon.

One of the seated women had long red hair cascading down her back and curling about her pale, pretty face. Her eyes were as green as Conal's, and her lips made a blood-red slash across her face. She wore a black sheath dress with a huge slit up the side and had gold bracelets stacked up one arm almost to her elbow.

The other woman must have been quite old when she was turned. Her hair was pure white, and she wore it pulled up into a severe bun. White lace frothed at the neck of a sky-blue gown that brought out the blue of her eyes. She was knitting a scarf out of bright red wool, and the sound of her wooden needles clacking together was the only sound in the room.

The elderly vampire was the only one who wasn't in evening dress, apart from Conal and me. I stared at the queen in her beautiful black gown and immediately felt under-dressed for the occasion. She stared back, her gaze assessing, and I dropped my eyes, suddenly remembering how dangerous a vampire's gaze could be.

I could hear myself breathing, faster than I would have

liked, so I took a deep, calming breath. Could the vampires hear my heart beating? Or the blood coursing through my veins? I'd never been in a room with so many vampires at once before, and I was feeling very uncomfortable under the weight of their unblinking stares. Less like a guest and *way* too much like dinner.

Conal strode forward and bowed to the old lady. "Your Majesty."

Wait, what? *She* was the queen? The redhead smiled at my confusion and crossed one slender leg over the other, baring it to the thigh.

The queen nodded pleasantly at him. "Soldier. Ethan tells me your search isn't going any better than ours."

He shrugged. "The rogue can't evade us forever. We've narrowed his—or her—location to the bushland around the town of Kurranderra." He cocked that scarred eyebrow at her. "Do you know the identity of the elder?"

"You can be sure it's not one of our hive," the redhead snapped, abruptly swinging her foot to the ground again and sitting forward in an aggressive stance.

"Hush, Victoria," the queen said. "No one suggested it was."

"It doesn't matter," Conal said. "We'll find them either way."

"But assuming it is an elder—and we haven't established that yet for certain—it would be easier if you knew something of their former personality," the queen suggested, "so that you could guess where they might go, or find some pattern in their attacks."

"Yes."

"The same thought had occurred to me, but unfortunately not every vampire in Sydney owes allegiance to our hive. And there is nothing to stop outsiders moving in." I must have made a surprised sound, because she smiled at me before turning her attention back to her knitting. "You have heard something different, Miss Armitage?"

"Only that all the vampires in an area have to join a hive," I said, trying very hard not to look as though as I were arguing with the queen.

"That's true," she said. "But ours isn't the only option in the area, and new arrivals have a grace period while they decide which to join. Most of them are aware of the wisdom of a quick decision, but some have to be persuaded."

Her needles darted busily through the wool, and nothing about her pleasant expression changed, but I got the distinct impression that the persuasion would be of the *offer you can't refuse* variety.

"But we are leaving our guests standing," she added suddenly, addressing Victoria as if it were the redhaired vampire's fault. "Pour some tea, Victoria. Sit down, both of you."

Ethan somehow got between us and bundled me into a seat next to him on a couch that was barely big enough for two, leaving Conal alone in an armchair facing Queen Nessa. Conal sat back and crossed his legs, looking remarkably at ease for a man surrounded by vampires. He accepted the tea Victoria offered him but didn't drink, merely balancing the cup on his knee.

I took my own cup and tasted the tea. It was a flowery

blend, like an Earl Grey but stronger. A sweetness like mango lurked in the aftertaste. "This is lovely," I said, surprised. I hadn't expected vampires, who only cared for blood, to provide something so tasty.

"It's my own blend," the queen said. "I enjoy experimenting, though nothing tastes as good as I remember it. Sometimes, as I brew my little recipes, I feel like Beethoven, writing his symphonies on the memory of sound."

I wondered if she had actually known Beethoven. There was no telling how old a vampire was, of course, since they stopped ageing once they were turned. She cast a wistful look at the teapot before taking a sip from her glass. I was a hundred per cent sure that red liquid wasn't wine.

"Are we to stand around discussing tea all night?" one of the men behind her said, impatience in his voice.

"Peace, Miguel. All in good time."

Miguel folded his arms, his nostrils flaring as he exhaled in a heavy sigh. He was wearing the old-fashioned kind of dinner suit, where the shirt front is nothing but layers of ruffles. Lace cuffs peeked out of the sleeves of his velvet jacket, covering half his hands. In a get-up like that, he could have been Beethoven's best friend.

Victoria shifted in her seat as if she, too, were impatient. "What is your interest in this girl?" she asked Conal, ignoring me completely.

I would have told her how rude she was, except I was even more interested to hear the answer than she was.

"My interest is personal," Conal said, "and need not concern you."

Every eye in the room turned to me, and my cheeks warmed a little under the attention.

"He doesn't mean *personal* personal," I said hurriedly. "He's made it sound like we're dating. Which we totally aren't."

"Oh?" Queen Nessa looked amused. "There is another kind of personal? The *im*personal personal, perhaps?"

I felt myself growing hotter. Even worse than being stared at by a roomful of people was having them laugh at you. I shot an imploring glance at Conal, but he was grinning, too, the jerk, those green eyes full of mischief.

"I assure Your Majesty my interest is extremely *personal* personal."

It was? That was news to me. I took another sip of tea to cover my embarrassment.

"We are not interested in your love life, Soldier," Miguel snapped. "We heard she was attacked by one of your colleagues." He turned to the queen. "Why are we persisting with this farce? We don't need a Soldier's help to bring down an elder, especially if they can't even be trusted to uphold their sacred duty to protect humanity. Next thing we know, they'll be turning on *us*."

At least Ethan hadn't blabbed to the entire hive that I was a cartomancer—unless they were all just pretending in front of Conal.

"And yet Miss Armitage doesn't seem to have taken that *personally*," the queen said. She looked directly at me for the first time, and those big blue eyes were like a laser target, drilling into mine. "Ethan tells me you argued quite strongly for our cooperation."

Finally, someone was talking *to* me instead of *about* me.

"Of course I did. We all want this elder stopped, right?"

"Does she understand what she's asking?" Miguel snapped.

Okay, that was enough. "I'm right here," I pointed out acidly. "You can ask me yourself."

"Miguel," the queen said.

Her tone was mild, but the vampire swallowed whatever he'd been about to say and stepped back with a huffy little bow.

"What Miguel means is that Soldiers are friends to humankind. Not to other preternaturals. When Soldiers arrive, preternaturals tend to die."

Trust me, lady, I know all *about that.*

"*Humans* are dying right now," I said. "Five of them, at last count. And your hive hasn't been able to stop it yet."

Miguel actually hissed at me, as if he were a cobra instead of a person. Maybe it hadn't been the most diplomatic thing to suggest the queen was incapable of handling her own business, but sometimes there was no benefit in sugar-coating things. People were dying— people Conal was here to protect—and the vampires wanted to throw up roadblocks? I couldn't see what they were so afraid of. It wasn't as if any of *them* were the rogue.

Or a cartomancer, for that matter. If anyone here should be scared of Conal, it should be me. He wasn't about to start killing vampires at random.

Was he?

He certainly didn't look like a crazed killer, sitting there in his chinos with his cup of tea balanced on his knee. Sure, he didn't look exactly *harmless*—there was a quiet watchfulness to him and a sense of underlying strength. I'd seen his wolf form, however briefly, and I had no doubt he would kill without hesitation if he thought it was necessary. But if these vampires hadn't done anything wrong, they shouldn't have any reason to be afraid. Soldiers reserved their senseless vendettas for people like me.

"It's only a matter of time before we find the elder," Victoria said, scowling at me.

I shrugged. "So why not join forces and shorten the time, before more people die?" *And get Conal and his psycho mate out of town before I become a wolf chew toy again.*

"Do you have nothing to say for yourself, Soldier?" Miguel asked, a red light burning in his eyes.

Ooh, that wasn't good. I'd never actually seen a vampire's eyes turn red before, but it wasn't smart to hang around when they did, unless you wanted to become an unwilling blood donor. I shifted uneasily in my seat, remembering the red eyes of the rogue in the darkness behind the dumpsters, and Ethan patted my knee in a reassuring way.

"Are you going to let this human do all your talking?" Victoria added.

Conal shrugged, setting his untouched tea down on the nearest table. "She's doing a pretty good job so far. I don't need the hive's help, but I'm happy to accept it. She's right; this business will go quicker if we work together."

"You owe the human a life bond," the queen said.

Conal flicked a glance at Ethan. "Word spreads fast."

"If we agree to pool our resources, will you swear on that bond not to harm any member of this hive?"

The silence stretched, the only sound the tap-tap-tapping of the queen's knitting needles. I rolled my eyes. *What's the hold-up here? Just say yes, Conal.*

"There is too much talk," Miguel growled.

Then he exploded into motion, so fast I swear I didn't even see him move until he'd dragged me out of my seat and had me in a vice-like grip, his breath hot on my neck. My heart nearly pounded its way right out of my chest. Everyone else leapt up, too, except for the queen.

"You have five seconds to let her go," Conal said, his eyes glowing an uncanny yellow, "before I rip your heart out."

"Stand down, Soldier," Miguel said. "We'll keep your little human toy as insurance for your good behaviour. If one hair of a vampire's head is harmed while you are hunting this elder, you might get her back a little broken."

"Three seconds." Conal stood unmoving, those yellow eyes boring into the vampire. He was like a coiled spring, taut with the promise of violence. The black wolf was very close to the surface.

"This is not the way we treat our guests, Miguel," the queen said, her knitting needles stilling again. "Release Miss Armitage. We promised no harm would come to her here."

"And it won't," Miguel said. "As long as the Soldier behaves himself."

He shoved me behind himself, and the vampires who'd

been standing with him closed in on either side. I cast a frightened glance at Ethan, but he hadn't moved. He was staring at the queen with an odd look on his face.

She stood up, letting the long piece she'd been knitting spool to the floor. "Relax, Miguel. Sit down, please, everyone. Let me see if my scarf is long enough yet."

She approached the angry vampire and looped her knitting around his neck while he stood stiffly, glaring at Conal. The vampires around me stepped back, and I quickly moved to Conal's side. His arm snaked out and clamped me to him.

Queen Nessa stood back, admiring her handiwork, then drove her free knitting needle into Miguel's chest.

14

$\mathcal{M}$iguel imploded in a shower of dust, and I screamed. The sudden savagery was shocking.

"Let's go," Conal said, backing toward the door and tugging me with him. "Your Majesty, I will coordinate with Ethan."

"Excellent," she said. There was a smudge of Miguel-dust on her pale cheek, and the point of the needle was as dark as if she'd dipped it in charcoal. She smiled at us with the air of a woman who had never enjoyed a tea party more. "But it appears Miss Armitage needs more protection. Raquel will meet you in the foyer. She will make an excellent bodyguard."

"That won't be necessary," I said hurriedly. "I don't need ..."

I trailed off as Conal's grip tightened warningly. Right. Probably not the best idea to look a gift vampire in the mouth, even if said vampire was a pain in the butt and not someone I wanted to get to know any better. The queen might not take ingratitude well.

"Umm ... I mean, thank you."

As the door closed behind us, Victoria was carefully wiping off the smudge on the queen's face with a lace-edged handkerchief, and one of the male vampires was brushing at the knitted scarf in a futile effort to remove all traces of his former hive member.

Conal hurried me down the stairs, his hand never leaving my arm. As the queen had promised, Raquel waited in the grand foyer.

"Apparently, you need a nursemaid," she said coolly. "Should I pack baby wipes?"

Wow. Spending time with her was going to be so much fun.

"Just your coffin," I said, but my heart wasn't in it. I was still shaking.

Outside, the limo was waiting where we'd left it. Conal bundled me inside and got in next to me, sitting so close I felt the heat of his body all down my side. Raquel took the seat opposite. I sagged against my seat in relief as we drove down the long driveway and back onto the street.

I'd just seen a vampire staked in front of my eyes. What was I, Van Helsing?

"That was ... intense."

"Yes." Conal pressed against me, as if determined to get between me and any danger. "Don't be fooled by Nessa's grandma act. She's as ruthless as they come."

"Yeah, thanks, I figured that one out for myself. Right about the time she shoved a knitting needle into a guy's heart and he kasploded into vampire dust." I shuddered, grateful for Conal's warmth as my frantic heartbeat finally started to return to normal. "A warning *before* we went in might have been helpful."

"She staked someone?" Raquel asked, looking only mildly interested. "Let me guess—Miguel?"

I nodded. "How did you know?"

"I would have done it months ago. He's always pushing, testing her authority." She snorted. "As if he could run a hive without a queen. Some of the older males don't deal well with accepting female authority." She gave Conal the side-eye. "A bit like Soldiers."

"I'm fine with women on top," Conal said flippantly.

Raquel and I rolled our eyes at the same time, and I felt an unexpected moment of solidarity with her.

He took a bottle of scotch from the bar and poured a glass with a steady hand. "Drink up. You'll feel better."

"I highly doubt that."

He shoved the glass towards me. "Trust me."

Ha. It would be a cold day in Hell before I trusted a Soldier of the Light. But I took the glass.

"I guess you've seen a vampire staked before." I sipped, then coughed as the fiery alcohol burned its way down my throat.

"Once or twice. Never with a knitting needle, though." He actually sounded impressed. "That's a first."

"I can't believe she did that," I said. "He was part of her own hive."

Conal shrugged. "He disgraced her by attacking you.

He signed his own death warrant the minute he touched you."

I digested that for a moment while the scotch warmed me from within. Conal was right, it did make me feel better. Or maybe I had Raquel's words to thank. From what she said, it sounded as though Miguel had had it coming —my visit had only advanced the date of his demise.

"The queen said we hadn't established yet that the thing you're all hunting is an elder," I told Raquel. "Why would you be hunting it if it's not one of yours?"

Vampires usually only took action if they were directly involved. Soldiers were the main force that hunted and killed dangerous preternaturals. We cartomancers did our bit, too, with smaller threats. Our way of removing threats was more humane than the Soldiers'—we opened a portal to the elemental plane and ejected rogues from the human world. But I'd only helped the coven with that a couple of times since I'd been in Kurranderra.

Conal glanced at Raquel, who was watching the road and didn't answer, apparently bored by our conversation. "She was just covering her butt," he said. "She wouldn't be offering the hive's cooperation if she thought it was a banshee or something else. That offer is basically admitting she's at fault. I bet they've been trying to catch it for weeks. You have, haven't you?" he asked Raquel.

"You don't know as much as you think you do," she replied without turning from the window. "Which is also typical of Soldiers."

She seemed to dislike Soldiers almost as much as I did. At this rate, we'd have so much in common that the next step would be slumber parties and doing each other's nails.

"What I *know* is that the hives all keep tabs on their elders, and they talk to one another," he said. "Nessa would have known there was a threat before it started its killing spree, so to pretend she was somehow caught by surprise is pure fiction."

"Why would she lie about that?" I asked.

He threw a challenging glance at Raquel, who was still ignoring him. "Because she can? Vampires have elevated lying to an artform. You know how to tell when a vampire is lying?"

"How?"

"Their lips are moving."

I snorted. "Thanks for the tip."

"Any time. How's that drink going? Do you need a top-up?"

I raised an eyebrow. "Are you trying to get me drunk?"

"No? But I could be persuaded."

"No, thanks. I'm a sloppy drunk. You wouldn't like it."

He turned sideways in the seat to face me, stretching his arm across the back of it. "Do you get all maudlin and tell your friends over and over again how much you love them?"

"Every time. And I cry. Right up until the part where I end up on the bathroom floor driving the porcelain bus."

"O-kaaay, then." He removed the half-empty glass from my grasp. "That's enough scotch for you."

The drive back seemed shorter than the one out had been. Conal kept me entertained with vampire stories.

Some of them were quite funny and seemed designed to goad a reaction out of Raquel, who merely yawned ostentatiously and stared out the window. He was a good storyteller, and the scotch plus the sheer relief of escaping the vampire hive in one piece relaxed me. Before I knew it, the limo was pulling up outside my apartment block.

"Come in," I said to Raquel, remembering that she would need an invitation.

While Conal and Raquel said goodnight to the driver, I fumbled the keys out of my bag and started up the front steps without them. The porch light was out again—it had to be a faulty fitting, because no matter how many times we changed the globe, it burnt out in a matter of days. But the moon was heading towards full and there was plenty of light to see my way.

Inside, the foyer light was a welcoming glow, and I shoved my key in the front door of my unit as Conal came in the foyer door behind me.

"Sunday, wait—"

I'd already stepped through the door and was reaching for the light switch before my brain caught up with what he'd said. He burst through the door on my heels as something massive surged out of the dark of my apartment.

I went flying, knocked aside as Conal tackled the monster. My shoulder slammed into the floor, and I skidded up against my couch. My head rang as I lay there squinting into the dark.

It was a confusion of shapes, glimpses of furred limbs and yellow eyes. There were two wolves now, who snarled and snapped at each other, spittle flying from vicious white fangs. I scrambled back as far out of the way as I could, my heart pounding.

They were too alike in the dark—just a blur of motion. I couldn't tell which one was Conal. One of them shook the other off and leapt at me, its snarling face a vision out of a nightmare.

I screamed, sure I was about to die, until someone snatched me off the floor as if I weighed no more than a doll. Raquel.

"Stop!" I cried as she carried me toward the door. "Conal needs help!"

"He looks fine to me," she said. He had landed on the other wolf's back, snapping furiously at its neck. They went rolling away again. "Maybe they'll kill each other and the world will have two less Soldiers in it. I don't see a problem."

But she set me down by the front door and placed herself between me and the brawling wolves. A moment later, one of the beasts rolled onto its back. The other stood over it, fangs buried in its neck, until a kind of shiver rolled over the defeated wolf and it turned back into a man. Then the victor stepped back.

I flicked the light on with a shaking hand just as Conal changed back, too. The guy on the floor was bleeding profusely, but he scrambled to his feet as if he hadn't just almost had his throat ripped out. He spat on the floor between them. Charming.

"Hey, I know you!" I cried in outrage as I recognised the grey hair and hard face. "You came into Second Chances on Monday and spent ten minutes roaming around glaring at me. Did *you* kill Toby?"

He ignored me. "Thou shalt not suffer a witch to live," he snarled at Conal.

"Have you completely *lost* it, Liam? What happened to protect and serve?"

Liam shoved his face right up into Conal's, his fists clenched. "Protect and serve *humans*. Not witches!"

Conal didn't back down. He was taller, and glowered down at the shorter man, though his tone was even. "Sunday's not a witch."

A gloating look spread over Liam's face. "Oh, I see how it is. Madden was a fool to recruit outsiders. Better we died out than pollute our ranks with the likes of *you*."

"Sunday's *not a witch*," Conal repeated through gritted teeth. "And I owe her my life."

"Keep going," Liam jeered. "Every word you say digs a deeper hole. You think because you're the Grand Master's golden boy you can get away with fraternising with the enemy? I thought you were smarter than that, Clarke."

He started to circle around Conal, as if itching to start the fight again.

Conal blocked him with a single step to the side. "Where's your proof?"

Liam growled—actually growled, as if he were still in wolf form. "My proof will be presented to Grand Master Madden. I will *end* you, Clarke."

He shoved roughly past Conal, leaving a smear of blood on the sleeve of Conal's jacket.

He glared at me as he approached the doorway, and I

glared right back. Stuff *him*. This was the second time he'd tried to kill me. Stupid wolves and their stupid vendetta. What had I ever done to him?

Admittedly, having a vampire between me and him made me feel a lot braver. That growl had been all too familiar. He slammed out of the apartment, and I heard the foyer door bang shut behind him.

I was right. *Liam* had been the one growling in the bushes the night I'd gone elder-hunting with the vampires—not the elder. He must have been out hunting the elder himself and been close enough when I'd cast my spell to realise there was a cartomancer around. If Ethan hadn't come back when he did, Liam probably would have attacked me then and there.

Instead, he'd bided his time. He must have searched all over town until he picked up my scent again. That explained all the sniffing when he'd come into the shop yesterday.

"Nice friend you've got there," I muttered in Conal's direction.

I was shaking again, all that lovely whiskey gone to waste. He'd come right out and told Conal I was a witch. Would Conal still honour his life debt to me if he knew the truth?

At least he didn't seem inclined to believe it. Might as well brazen it out and try playing the clueless human card one more time. Raquel wouldn't give me away.

"What was all that about witches?" I asked.

Conal ran a hand through his dark hair, his eyes troubled. "I don't know. Do you happen to have a black cat and a broomstick tucked away somewhere?"

"They're in my gingerbread house in the woods," I said. "I have no idea how he found them."

Humour sparked in the depths of those green eyes. "That's what all the witches say."

15

————

*C*onal left. If he was hoping to catch up with Liam, that was bad news for me. Once the door had closed behind him, Raquel turned to me with a challenging look in her eye.

"Right," she said. "We need to have a chat."

I flopped onto the lounge. "Stick a fork in me and call me done. What a nightmare of a day."

She pulled one of the dining chairs over and sat, arms folded across her chest. "You think *this* is a nightmare? Wait until he comes back with a whole bunch of his buddies. How long do you think it will be before he realises the truth?" She shook her head. "I knew the Soldiers had a thing about witches, but I never realised it was *this* bad."

I let my head drop back against the cushions and closed my eyes. I didn't even tell her to call us cartomancers. *That* was how tired and wrung out I was. "Yeah. It's a real obsession with them."

"Why? What did witches ever do to them?"

"According to them, we're the ones who let in all the other monsters—the vampires, werewolves, banshees, ghouls, et cetera, et cetera. All our fault."

"So I'm a monster?"

Her tone was so frosty that I opened one eye to peer at her. "No offence, but you *are* kind of scary."

"But how is my existence your fault? Vampires have been around forever."

"Don't they teach you anything at vampire school?" Ariel asked, appearing on the couch beside me.

"Who's this?" Raquel didn't even bat an eyelid. Wow. Nerves of steel. My estimation of her went up another notch.

A wide grin broke across Ariel's face at this proof she was visible, and she bounced a couple of times in her seat.

"Raquel, meet Ariel." I waved a tired hand. "Ariel, Raquel."

"And what are you?" Raquel asked.

Ariel changed shape in the blink of an eye to an almost exact replica of Ethan. She even tossed the hair out of her eyes the same way he did. "I'm anything you want me to be, baby."

She sounded like him, too.

Raquel raised an eyebrow at me, and I sighed, currently incapable of mustering any shock at Ariel's corporealness. "There's no point asking; she has no idea and neither do I. But back to your original question: why do the wolves blame us for the existence of preternaturals? It's because of the way magic works."

Raquel assumed an expression of polite interest, and Ariel wriggled around until her legs were in my lap, as eager as a kid at story time, even though none of this was news to her. I could actually *feel* the lightest pressure from her legs, as if a silk scarf rested on me. That was new.

"Cartomancers are born with an unusual ability," I went on, "though it doesn't usually manifest until puberty. That ability allows us to open a portal to the elemental plane and manipulate the magical elements there. That's all a spell really is—opening a portal and pulling through the right pieces of magic to get the desired effect."

"And the cards?"

"A way to help us focus our ability. Blending the elements to create a successful spell is challenging even with them. It would be chaos without them."

"And how does this have anything to do with preternaturals?"

"Because sometimes when we call the magic through the portal, something else comes through, too. Sometimes that's an elemental—the creatures who live there. They're bad news, but fortunately they can't survive long in this world without a host."

"And an elemental is ...?" Raquel raised an eyebrow, inviting me to finish the sentence.

"Just what it sounds like. A being of fire, air, earth, or water that lives on the magic of the elemental plane."

She digested that for a minute. "Okay. You said 'sometimes' it's an elemental that comes through. What about the other times?"

"Sometimes it's a magic creature that originated in the

elemental plane, like a basilisk. But more often it's just some stray wisp of magic—and legend says that's where the trouble started."

She tilted her head to one side. "Go on."

"Loose magic can have unintended consequences, and early cartomancers weren't as careful as we are today. Uncontrolled magic started affecting a human or two and changing them into other things. So the Soldiers are right that the existence of preternaturals is partly our fault. But it's not as if we did it on purpose."

Raquel looked offended. "You're saying that witches accidentally created the first vampires with bits of *loose magic*?"

Ariel laughed. "Not a very sexy origin story, is it?"

"We're very careful these days," I assured her. "That kind of thing rarely happens anymore, because the cards help focus our spells. The first witches either didn't use cards or only had a basic system. We're not sure, since most of our early records have been lost."

"But that means witches must have created the Soldiers, too, because they're preternaturals, same as the rest of us."

"I know. Talk about ungrateful."

"And illogical. I hate crusaders. They don't *think*."

I guess vampires knew a bit about crusaders. They'd suffered more organised attempts to make them extinct over the centuries than any other type of preternatural. Other than cartomancers, of course.

"It's even more stupid when you realise that the Soldiers used to work directly with the cartomancers," I continued. "They acted as a team, with us providing the magic force and them providing the muscle, guarding us while we worked."

"I'd heard rumours to that effect," Raquel said. "How long ago was this?"

"A long time ago. Centuries."

"So, what would Conal do if he knew you were a witch?" she asked.

I shrugged. "Normally, he'd kill me, no questions asked. But he owes me a life debt, so I'm not sure."

"He's still a Soldier," Ariel said. "He'd probably wrestle with his conscience for a few minutes first, *then* kill you."

"Then you have no choice," Raquel said. "You have to get out of here before they come back in force. If Conal doesn't do it, Liam will." She stood up. "And I'm not going up against a Hunt for you. That would be a quick way to commit suicide, and not in the hive's best interest. We should go back to the hive. Kurranderra isn't safe for you anymore."

I hauled myself out of the soft depths of the couch. She was right. Every minute I stayed was a gamble—a gamble that Liam wouldn't come back with a bunch of his Soldier buddies, that Conal wouldn't find out, or that he'd honour his vow if he did—and my life was the stakes.

Saying goodbye was going to be unbearable. I'd really thought I could stay here forever, and I'd let myself put down roots. I'd made friends. Cheryl. Ethan. Bethany. Even Mr Garcia and Nicole.

What if the elder attacked them? Oh, Ethan could take

care of himself, but the others—they were human. They'd end up like poor Toby.

The thought of Bethany lying dead and drained somewhere made me clench my fists. No. I couldn't just run away and leave her in danger. I'd never forgive myself if something happened to her when I could have done something to prevent it.

"No," I said. "Not yet. First let's try one more time to find the elder."

"Us?" Raquel quirked that supercilious eyebrow again. "As in, you and me?"

"Why not?" Ariel asked. "Are you scared?"

The vampire threw her a withering look. "Half the hive is already out there searching. The wolves probably are, too. I don't think they need our help."

"But they don't have my magic," I said.

"Your magic wasn't much use last time." She shuddered. "A perfectly good night wasted wandering around the bush."

"Something weird happened to that spell. I can do it again and make it stronger." I rushed into the bedroom, feeling a surge of energy at the prospect of doing something useful, and grabbed my cards and a jacket. Raquel was waiting with a bored expression on her face when I came back out. "Let's get something good out of this horrible day."

She sighed. "You look like a little kid getting ready to go to the playground. Your positivity is sickening."

"Come on." I swiped my keys and phone from the bench and headed for the garage. "We can do this."

She rolled her eyes. "Yes, Pollyanna."

"We'll start the search at the back of Second Chances," I explained as we entered the garage. "The elder was there less than twenty-four hours ago. That'll give my magic the best chance of latching onto its presence."

Raquel climbed into Bugsy's passenger seat and Ariel zipped into the back. "Whatever. You're the one in charge of the magic finding spell."

Bugsy started on the first try. No more troubles from that battery terminal. What a surprise.

Thinking of the battery and Liam's sabotage reminded me of another quandary. "Why do you think Liam hasn't given Conal whatever evidence he has to prove I'm a witch?"

Raquel stared straight ahead out the windscreen, her skin very pale in the darkness of the car. "Who knows? Maybe they get a pay rise or a medal or something for every kill. He might want to keep all the glory of finding and killing you to himself. But it sounded like he's got a vendetta against Conal in particular. He's probably only too happy to frame him as a witch lover."

"Ugh. Soldier politics."

"Don't knock it. It's working in your favour at the moment." She bared her teeth in a frankly unsettling grin. "We can probably find a way to exploit that."

"You have a devious mind."

"I'm a vampire." She glanced slyly over her shoulder at Ariel. "They teach us that at vampire school."

Ariel snorted. "I like her. She's funny."

Like seemed a strong word, but I was definitely warming to the aloof vampire.

When we pulled up in the car park behind Second Chances, the police tape was still there. That was okay; I didn't need to be in the exact spot for the spell to work. We got out, slamming the car doors behind us, and I moved towards the little patch of bush at the back of the empty lot. It would be better not to work magic in full view of anyone coming into the car park.

Ariel was still lingering by the car. Something about the way she was standing struck me as odd—and then it hit me.

I'd heard *three* car doors slam.

"Ariel? Did you just *shut that door*?"

She turned to me, her face alight. "I opened it, too. I felt different. Stronger, somehow. So I tried, and it *worked!*"

Raquel glanced between the two of us, confused. "You two are weird."

"Can you do it again?" I asked, ignoring the vampire.

Ariel seized the door handle, but her shoulders sagged. "It won't move now."

"That's okay. You did it once. It will happen again."

She nodded, but her head drooped in disappointment, and she wouldn't look at me as she walked over to join us among the trees.

"It *will*," I insisted, feeling in my heart that it was true. Everything was changing all at once—but not all the changes were bad ones. "Just be patient. Three days ago, you were invisible, and now Raquel can see *and* hear you. That's progress."

"Actually, progress would be getting on with finding this elder," Raquel said. "All Raquel can see is time slipping away here, and the queen told me to keep you safe. So let's hurry up with the woo-woo stuff so we can leave."

I glared at her but knelt to clear a spot in the dirt and drew my circle with a stick. I laid out the same cards as last time—the Three of Earth next to the Four and Seven of Air, with the Ace of Air over the top—but this time I added the Ace of Earth as well, to ground the magic and make it stick. Then I tapped on the Aces and blew gently on them to activate the spell.

The light that sprang up nearly blinded me. It was the fierce white of a spotlight, and it whipped up into the air like a massive snake uncoiling, towering over the treetops. I jerked back and threw a hand up to protect my sight, but it was too late. All I could see was brilliant whiteness.

"Subtle," Raquel said. "Very subtle. The whole town will know you're out here doing magic."

"What did you do?" Ariel asked. "Are you all right?"

I blinked rapidly, trying to clear the blinding column of white from my vision, and staggered to my feet. "I didn't do anything. It's just a normal finding spell."

"Oh, honey," Ariel breathed. "There is *nothing* normal about this spell."

As my sight finally cleared, I stared up in awe at the massive twisting column of light. I'd added another Ace, but that wouldn't have had this kind of effect on the magic. *Nothing* should have had this much of an effect on my magic. Ling was the strongest cartomancer I knew, and she couldn't produce anything even close to this powerful. I could feel the pull of the spell in my chest, tugging me forward, and it seriously felt as though my heart might get ripped right out of my ribcage.

The towering snake rippled and bent toward the ground, and then it was off, streaking through the darkness, away from the town.

"There's no way we can keep up with that." I ran back to Bugsy. "Let's go!"

The other two piled in—Ariel without opening the door this time—and I sped out of the car park, following the violent pull in my chest as much as the light.

"Can you tone that thing down?" Raquel asked. "We might as well announce to the elder that we're on the way."

I wasn't sure I could, but I tried tugging on my end of the connection, reeling some of the power back into myself, and the distant light faded to something more discreet, though the pull inside me was still so strong that there was no chance of losing the trail.

"There are going to be *so* many reports of UFO sightings," Ariel said gleefully. "I bet Kurranderra becomes famous!"

I groaned inwardly. Just what we needed—even more eyes on our little town.

Though I guess it wouldn't be *my* town for much longer. I didn't want to think about that, so I bit my lip and tried to focus on the pull of the spell inside me instead. This might be the last thing I could do for my friends in Kurranderra, and I didn't want to mess it up.

The trail led us back along Ridge Road, in the direction of my own place. I had a sudden vision of the elder holed up in my apartment. I mean, why not? All the other monsters liked to hang out there lately.

I wondered where Liam was and what he was doing. That wasn't a productive train of thought, so I thought about Conal instead, which wasn't much better.

Despite everything, I still felt an undeniable attraction to him. Maybe if we'd been two different people, our story could have ended more happily. As it was, there was no way things could ever work out between us. Logically, I knew that. Logic said that the best outcome I could hope for was never to see him or his bloodthirsty, bigoted friends again. But Logic wasn't the only voice clamouring for attention in my head. Longing and Desire had very different views on the situation. There was a connection there, and I was pretty sure it wasn't one-sided.

I slowed Bugsy as we neared the turn-off to the old Rogerson place. All the houses along this section of the road stood on huge, tree-filled blocks. It wasn't far from here that Conal and I had first met.

Stop thinking about Conal. You have a job to do.

A thrill of anticipation ran through me—but that was the magic, not anything to do with a stupid werewolf. The elder was somewhere close by. I could *feel* it.

I pulled over and turned off the motor. The ticking of the cooling engine sounded very loud in the sudden silence.

"Why are we stopping?" Ariel asked.

Raquel cocked her head at me. "Here?"

I nodded. "It's very close."

We were parked next to a long driveway that led

through the trees to a dark brick house. The light in the front room was on, illuminating the driveway like a welcoming beacon, and a white car was parked in the carport. Someone was home.

Raquel got out of the car, and after a moment's hesitation, I joined her. She still needed my help. I dialled the light of my spell back down to nothing, focusing on the tugging in my chest.

"This way."

We walked briskly up the driveway, the cold already seeping beneath the layers of my clothes.

"Is it in the house?" Ariel whispered.

"No. I think it's round the back." A faint noise, like a TV or radio, carried to us on the night air. We were close enough now to see that there was a *Baby on Board* sticker in the rear window of the car. I shuddered. Were there children inside? My mind painted vivid pictures of the carnage the elder could wreak.

"You're sure it's here?" Raquel asked, pulling out her phone.

I nodded. "What are you doing?"

"Calling for back-up. I'll admit, I didn't expect you to find anything."

"We can't wait for back-up," I protested. "There are people in there! It could move on them any time. We have to save them."

"Well, Pollyanna, I've got news for you. One vampire, a witch, and a whatever-*she*-is are *not* going to be enough to take down an elder. If you want to walk away from this little adventure, we're waiting for back-up. Hello? Ethan, it's me." She walked a few steps away to continue her conversation in a low voice.

Something slipped in my chest. "It's moving."

"Where?" Ariel asked. "I'll go look."

"In the backyard somewhere." Panicked, I led the way through the carport and eased open a gate to the backyard. It was closer to the house. I *knew* it.

"Where are you *going*?" Raquel hissed. In a flash, she was at my side. "Are you crazy?"

"I just need to see." I had to know what it was doing back there. Maybe Ariel could scare it away if it was about to strike. We couldn't afford to wait for Ethan and the other vampires.

I wished Conal were here. He did this kind of thing all the time.

Wait, no. The last thing I needed right now was a Soldier complicating everything. It was bad enough that Raquel's long nails were digging into my arm, though I knew she wasn't really trying to stop me. If a vampire wanted you stopped, you stopped.

We came around the corner of the house and heard a hiss that put Raquel's to shame. Enough light spilled from the back windows to illuminate a wooden deck attached to the house, its steps leading down onto a small section of lawn. A clothesline loomed in the dark next to a small garden shed. Beyond that, most of the block was taken up by trees.

And in the shadows by the shed stood a woman. She wore a long, flowing dress in such a dark fabric that she blended into the night. It was only when she hissed again that I spotted her.

She took a threatening step toward us, teeth bared. Long, jagged teeth, in a mouth that was far too big. Her eyes were also oversized for her gaunt face, and they glowed red and wild, with no whites at all, above a slit where her nose should have been.

Raquel stepped in front of me protectively at the same time as Ariel raised a sudden gale that whipped sticks and dead branches from the trees and hurled them at the woman. Her matted hair streamed back from her face, showing grey, leathery skin and a disturbingly long neck, and she took a wary step back.

Then her body somehow dissolved. Where a woman had once stood, there was suddenly a pile of rats that heaved and squeaked and scrambled over each other, scattering into the night.

"Ewww," said Ariel, letting her wind drop as the last rats disappeared into the trees.

Raquel frowned at her. "Did you do that with the wind?" Then she turned to me. "Is she an elemental? I thought you said they couldn't live in our world without a host?"

"They can't, which means she's not."

"But she seems to be connected to you," Raquel persisted. "Maybe *you're* her host."

"I'm right here, Vampirella," Ariel said, pointing at herself in a big, exaggerated gesture. "Don't talk about me as if I can't hear you."

"If I were her host, I'd be walking around as a prisoner

in my own body while she occupied the driving seat. She wouldn't exist separately from me."

"Still here," Ariel said, sounding grumpy.

A rat squeaked somewhere in the bushes and I shuddered. "I didn't know vampires could turn into rats like that." I gave Raquel the side-eye. "That was *gross*."

"They can't." Her expression was grim. "That was no vampire. That was a bruxsa."

     I'd heard of bruxsas, of course, but I'd never expected to meet one in the flesh. Not and live to tell the tale, anyway. They were a rare kind of vampire, more superpowered even than an elder, and almost impossible to kill because they had some handy magic tricks that protected them. They had such powerful healing magic that you couldn't even stake them.

"That ... complicates things," I said after a pause.

"You could say that." Raquel looked more irritated than alarmed, which gave me hope that the vampires knew something I didn't about killing bruxsas. "As well as the rat trick, they can also turn into a cloud of bats and fly off. It's like trying to catch water in a sieve."

Just as well Conal had agreed to team up with the vampires. He and Liam alone wouldn't have stood a chance against a bruxsa. As far as I was aware, the Soldiers had no magic beyond the ability to change shape. Teeth and brute strength were feeble weapons against the kind of magic a bruxsa could wield. It was like bringing a knife to a gun fight.

"Why did she run?" Ariel asked. "I thought bruxsas were like the tanks of the vampire world."

"Probably conserving her strength," Raquel said. "The number of kills she's made lately suggests she's gearing up for something big. She won't waste magical energy on fighting unless she has to."

Inside the house, a dog was barking. Raquel and I looked at each other, then turned as one to hurry back through the carport before someone came outside to investigate.

"I can still feel her," I said when we'd gained the safety of Bugsy.

"Where?"

I started the engine and drove slowly along the road. "She hasn't gone far."

Raquel pulled out her phone. "If we can find her lair, that will help. But I'll have to call the hive off. We can't take her at night—that's when she's strongest. We'll have to wait for daylight. Preferably midday, to give ourselves the best chance."

I was only half listening. Spidey senses that I'd never felt before were tingling. "I think ..." I slowed Bugsy to a crawl as I reached the old Rogerson place on the hill, its dilapidated splendours half-hidden among the trees. "I think she's there."

"Want me to go check?" Ariel asked.

"Don't let her see you," I said. "We'll meet you back at home. Be—" But she was already gone. "Careful."

Raquel was busy texting someone, probably Ethan. "We shouldn't go back to your place."

"I need sleep. I'm dead on my feet."

"Then we'll go to Ethan's. The rest of the hive is gathering there to wait."

"Umm, no offence, but I'm not sleeping in the middle of a hive full of vampires."

She sighed. "Usually when people say *no offence*, it means they're about to say something truly offensive. And you just proved my point. Do you really think we'd attack you?"

"Well, not you and Ethan, obviously. I trust you guys."

Surprise flickered across her face. "You trust me?"

"Is there some reason I shouldn't?"

"No, of course not. I mean ... it's just ..." I'd never seen her flustered before. It was kind of adorable. "Humans don't usually trust vampires. And you don't know me very well."

"You just jumped in front of me to protect me from a *bruxsa*. A bruxsa you'd already told me you wouldn't be able to take down on your own. I think it's pretty safe to assume you're not about to snack on me while I'm asleep. But I can't say the same for the rest of your hive. I wouldn't have trusted that guy Miguel as far as I could throw him."

"Miguel was a douche. No one trusted him. But the others aren't so bad." Raquel studied me as if I were a puzzle she had to solve. "But I can see how you might be nervous, since you don't know them. I'll get Ethan to meet us at your place with a couple of the others. They can stay outside and keep watch, in case that Liam guy comes sniffing around again. That will give us enough warning to get you out."

And so it was that I fell asleep to the sound of two vampires at my dining table plotting the death of a bruxsa. Weirdest guardian angels ever.

When I woke, morning light streamed through my window, and Ariel lay with her nose almost touching mine. I squeaked and flinched back.

"Shhh," she said. "We've got company."

"I know. Ethan and Raquel." I stretched luxuriously, feeling wonderfully refreshed. Ready to take on a bruxsa or two. I sniffed the air. I'd been dreaming of bacon, and it seemed I could still smell it ... no. Not bacon, but definitely something meaty and delicious. "Are they cooking? Surely not."

"No, that's the company. Your favourite carnivore's here."

I sat up. "Conal? Did he see you?"

"I'm not stupid. As far as he knows, you're the humanest human around. Nothing funky going on here, no sirree."

I should have been worried. Why did he keep coming back? Surely he was suspicious? But I was distracted by whatever Conal was cooking out there. Had I actually eaten anything last night? My stomach was rumbling, and that delicious scent was calling my name. I got up and threw some clothes on.

"Morning, sleepyhead," Ethan said when I opened my door. He was lounging with one elbow against the kitchen bench, appearing very relaxed—except that he was watching Conal, who was busy at the stove, with great intensity. Almost as if he expected the Soldier to turn wolf any minute. Raquel was on the couch flicking through a magazine, but she looked up, also suddenly alert, when I appeared.

"Morning," I replied, then turned to Conal. "What are you doing in my kitchen?"

"She doesn't wake up firing on all cylinders, does she?" he said to Ethan before turning to me. "I'm cooking, obviously."

Both vampires subtly relaxed at Conal's cheery response, as if they'd been ready to leap to my defence if he'd turned nasty on me. Which made me wonder why they'd let him in at all. So much for keeping watch and spiriting me away if the wolves approached.

"I can see that. But *why* are you cooking? And in my kitchen? Shouldn't you be out Soldiering with your buddy?"

"The vampires found our rogue last night," he said, flipping meat over so that it sizzled. "And it's a bruxsa, so there's no Soldiering to be done until we get a full Hunt up here. In the meantime, we still need to eat." He glanced at Ethan. "Well, some of us do."

A full Hunt? That was thirteen wolves. This was *not* good.

"He turned up an hour ago with a bag full of food," Raquel said. "Just walked right in as if he owned the place."

"He seemed friendly," Ethan added with peculiar emphasis, staring at me as if he were trying to convey meaning by wiggling his eyebrows. "And you did want us to work together."

I frowned.

"What?" Conal asked with an air of innocence.

"No, that's fine," I said. "Make yourself at home. Just break in any time you feel like it. I mean, your buddy does, so why not?"

He grinned. "I figured you wouldn't mind."

Impossible man. Clearly, Liam hadn't changed his mind about offering Conal that *proof* he said he had. Or he had and Conal was biding his time, waiting until my vampire protectors weren't around to take me out.

No. No Soldier was that good at acting. If he'd found out I was a cartomancer, I'd know it from the way he looked at me.

"What *are* you cooking?" That smell was driving me wild. "Is that steak?"

Steak hadn't been on the menu for a long time. Had it always smelled so divine? How had I lived without it for so long?

"I'm making steak sandwiches. Want one?"

"Try and stop me."

He laughed and got busy assembling sandwiches. The open, friendly expression on his face reassured me. He truly didn't know.

Guess I got to enjoy my steak sandwich without fear for my life, at least for now.

There were thick slices of toasted bread, as well as beetroot, lettuce, and tomato to go with the steak—and was that camembert? It all smelled so good my mouth started watering. He was surprisingly handy with a knife, too. Or maybe that should have been unsurprisingly. I snuck the odd glance at his capable hands as he flew through the task of slicing tomatoes. He exuded a sense of authority and competence in everything he did, despite his often mocking manner.

When someone shows you the kind of person they are, believe them, Ling used to tell me when I was a kid. *It doesn't matter what people say, it only matters what they do.* She'd been talking about the kind of kids who said nice things to my face but spread gossip about the odd new girl behind my back. But now I felt confused.

He was a Soldier, a man who protected the human world from preternatural threats—but also went around indiscriminately killing completely unthreatening women like me.

To hear him talk, he was a joker, a man who took nothing seriously—but he'd applied himself pretty seriously to the task of keeping me alive since he'd taken his vow. Feeding me seemed to be part of the deal, as if he were afraid I would waste away without liberal applications of bacon.

He'd said he wouldn't trust the vampires and didn't need them—but here he was working with them anyway. It was as if he didn't want anyone to know that he actually cared about doing a good job. If he hadn't been a Soldier, he would have been damn near perfect.

Shame about the Soldier thing. It was kind of a deal-breaker.

I hardly knew him, but he'd already saved my life

twice. This odd fluttering in my belly every time I saw him again was just some messed-up kind of hero-worship thing, that was all.

It didn't hurt that he always looked good enough to eat. This morning he wore faded blue jeans and a black T-shirt that skimmed lightly over the muscles of his chest. His hair was tousled, and a pronounced five o'clock shadow darkened that Superman jaw. He'd probably spent the night on watch. Ethan had said something before I'd crashed about setting up a perimeter around the old Rogerson place, far enough out so as not to alarm the bruxsa but close enough to make sure she didn't slip away.

I entertained a brief fantasy of living like this every day. Having breakfast served to me by a gorgeous man with laughing green eyes. Pity about the murderous wolf part.

And speaking of murderous wolves ... "Where's Liam today?"

"Don't worry about him," Conal said. "He's run back to the Grand Master with his tail between his legs to whine about my supposed heresy."

Ariel popped into view, perched in her favourite spot on the kitchen bench. No one reacted, so clearly I was the only one who could see her. "It sounds like chess. Ask him if there's a Grand Mistress too."

I ignored her, troubled by a twinge of guilt. "Are you in trouble with ... the Grand Master?"

He certainly would be when the truth came out.

"Usually," he said with a shrug. "I'll clear it up once we've contained the threat here."

Considering that half the people in the room weren't

going to eat, he'd made a mountain of food. Ling would approve.

Well, no. She wouldn't. That murderous wolf thing again. It was surprising how disappointed I felt every time I came up against that inescapable fact.

The doorbell rang, and Raquel leapt up to answer it.

It was Bethany. She peeked around Raquel, and her face relaxed into a relieved smile when she caught sight of me.

"Oh, hi! You're okay?"

I frowned as she came into the room. "Sure. Why wouldn't I be?"

She glanced uncertainly around at the other three. "It's just ... you had work this morning. Cheryl tried to call you, but you didn't pick up, so she rang me to see if I could cover for you."

I hurried back into my bedroom to check my phone. Dead. I'd been so tired and distracted last night I'd forgotten to charge it.

And I'd *completely* forgotten about work.

I came back out, feeling stupid. "Is Cheryl mad at me?"

"More worried," Bethany said. "Considering everything that's going on. I said I'd come over and check on you before I came in." She eyed the two vampires and the hulking werewolf in the kitchen. "So ... *is* everything all right?"

A full Hunt of Soldiers was on the way. Everything was *marvellous*.

"Never better," I lied. "We just ... ah ... got a little side-tracked."

Conal stepped out of the kitchen, carrying the two tastiest-looking steak sandwiches I'd ever seen in my life. Bethany's eyes widened as she looked up at him. I'd gotten used to how tall he was and didn't notice it so much, but Bethany was shorter than me.

"You must be Conal," she said.

"Must I?" he asked with a straight face.

She shot me an uncertain look.

"Ignore him," I said. "I do. Would you like a sandwich? Conal's made enough to feed a small army. I'm going to go out on a limb and say you slept through your alarms and haven't eaten yet."

She flashed me a grateful smile. "That sounds awesome, thanks."

"Save some for me," Ariel told me. "Maybe if I solidify enough I'll be able to eat one of those. They smell *divine*."

She was still perched on the bench, not far from where Ethan leaned against it, arms folded. I'd been getting definite disapproval vibes from him, but Bethany's arrival seemed to have distracted him from his dislike of Conal's presence.

"Sit down, Ethan, you're going to ruin my digestion." That was a bald-faced lie. One bite of the steak sandwich and I was in love. I was going to marry this sandwich and have its babies.

"Good?" Conal asked, eyeing me with approval as I bit into it again, barely restraining a moan of pleasure.

"The *best*," I said around a mouthful of heaven.

"So, Bethany," Ethan said, dropping into the seat next to her. "What happened to your pink hair?"

I looked up quickly. I hadn't even noticed she'd changed her hair again. It was all black now, sleek and sophisticated in its bob.

"We can't *all* have pink hair," she said, smiling shyly at him. He was perfectly positioned to stare down her cleavage, but either she hadn't realised that or she didn't care. "Once Sunday changed hers, I decided to do something different."

He reached out and curled an ebony lock around his finger. "I like it."

Her cheeks coloured a little, but her smile widened.

I waved my sandwich in Ethan's direction. "You'd better not be putting any vampire moves on her."

"Are you suggesting that all this magnificence isn't enough on its own to dazzle a woman?" He gestured at himself with an outraged expression, but his hand dropped away from Bethany's hair all the same.

"This sandwich is really good," Bethany said, still blushing.

"I do my humble best," Conal replied.

She tilted her head, considering him. "You remind me of someone, but I can't think who."

"Jason Momoa?" he asked drily.

"Oh! No, not really. Although if you had a beard, maybe ..." She eyed him assessingly. "Where *did* you get that scar? It looks just like his."

"Long story," he said, touching a finger to his eyebrow, "but it involves a buck's night gone terribly wrong and a hedge trimmer."

So much for the Swedish grandmother story. I

wondered why he always avoided answering this question. The real answer was probably either humiliating or horribly mundane. Maybe both.

He looked up, suddenly alert. "Someone's here."

I paused, steak sandwich frozen in mid-air. "How can you tell?"

"Big vehicle just pulled up outside." He shot a speculative look at Ethan. "Did you call for a truck to carry your ego?"

I choked back a laugh at the unexpectedness of the attack and got up to peek out the window.

And then my blood ran cold. Son of a beech tree—Ivy and Ling had just arrived. Ling had said they wouldn't be here until *tonight*. And here I was with a Soldier in the house.

"Everyone stay put," I said as I rushed out the door. "Someone I know—nothing to worry about! I'll be back in just a minute."

I'd tell them to drive into town. I could meet up with them as soon as I got rid of Conal.

Big Bertha, the motorhome that had been my home for years, rumbled and coughed as Ling switched off the engine. Ivy waved through the passenger window, her face lit by a big smile, as I hurried down the front steps. Her hair was longer than last time I'd seen her, but still a vibrant shade of purple.

"Hi, cherub!" she called as she opened her door. "I hope we're not too late."

"Told you I'd get us here early," Ling said as she got out and slammed the door, pushing straight dark hair back from her face. "I don't know what you were fussing for."

Ivy got out and stretched, making all the silver bracelets she wore jangle. She was a big, solid woman, and her usual method of dressing seemed to involve standing in front of her wardrobe with her eyes shut and throwing things on at random. Today that meant she was in an eye-searing combination of a green flowery shirt and bright red leggings. "I must be getting old. My back doesn't like the long distances as much as it used to."

"Rubbish," I said, bracing myself for her usual bone-crushing hug. "Fifty-nine isn't old. But you can't stay. I'll meet you in town at that coffee shop you liked last time."

"Why?" Ivy peered down at me suspiciously. "What's the problem?"

"Is it the Soldiers?" Ling asked, immediately on the alert. She was tiny and dressed like an undertaker in her usual sober black. She and Ivy were a classic example of the saying *opposites attract*. "Have you seen them?"

"No! Well ... yes, but it's fine." I wilted under Ling's ferocious stare. "Truly. I just need you guys to leave. I'll explain everything later."

I tried to shoo Ivy back towards Big Bertha, but she wasn't budging.

Ling's brows drew together over sharp brown eyes that had never missed anything I was trying to hide. "What's the matter? Are you being *coerced*? Is that Soldier here?"

A flame sprang to life in the palm of her hand. What on *earth*? She wasn't even holding her cards. How had she *done* that?

"Put it away," I begged her, but it was too late.

She looked past me, and her face drained of colour. "Get behind me."

A growl behind me raised the hairs on the back of my neck, and I spun around. A black wolf stalked down the path towards us, its hackles raised, its eyes glowing golden.

"Conal!" I shouted, backing toward the dubious safety of Big Bertha. "Back off!"

This was the first time I'd seen him in daylight, and in other circumstances I might have said he was magnificent, with his long silky black coat, powerful shoulders, and those luminous golden eyes.

Oh, who was I kidding? As if there were any circumstance where a cartomancer seeing a Soldier in wolf form could be a good thing. What a fustercluck this was. Out of the corner of my eye, I saw Ling's flame double, then triple, in size.

Ethan, Raquel, and Bethany tumbled out of the apartment block behind the wolf. Bethany's face was as white as a sheet.

"Stop!" Ethan shouted, darkness billowing about him. He and Raquel rushed down the path, fangs lengthening, trying to herd the Soldier away.

I stepped into Conal's path, determined to halt that menacing advance, though my knees shook.

Conal owed me his life; he wouldn't hurt me. Would he? It was difficult to persuade my body of that, faced with a snarling wolf. He was so *big*. And those teeth were so *huge*.

All the better to eat you with, my mind helpfully supplied.

"Get away from him!" Ethan called. His eyes glowed red from the centre of the black cloud that swirled around him. His body seemed to be disintegrating into the cloud. *Cool*, some distant part of my mind noted. *Vampires really can become smoke.*

"Conal, what are you doing?" I tried for a confident tone, though my knees had turned to water. "These are my aunties. This is Ivy, and this is Ling."

Why couldn't Ling have held her fire for just a few minutes more? No way to convince the Soldier that she was a harmless human now. I looked away hurriedly, blinking spots of fire from my vision.

A wind whipped up from nowhere, flicking pebbles from the road into the wolf's face, but Ariel didn't have much to work with.

The wolf growled, low and menacing, and gathered himself to spring. Did he mean to leap right over me to get to Ivy and Ling?

"Oh no you *don't*," I said, planting my feet and holding my ground.

"Get out of the way, Sunday," Ling snapped.

Behind me, fire flared, and its heat warmed my back. Dancing flames reflected in the wolf's yellow eyes, and something fizzed in my veins, sending a violent shiver through my body.

"Conal Clarke!" I shouted at him. "You owe me your life! You said it was a debt that could never be repaid. You swore to honour it. Is *this* how you're gonna repay me? By attacking the only family I have left? Stop this right now!"

Fire blasted past my ear, so close I felt its sizzle. Little fires ignited in the dry winter grass of the lawn, and the wolf yelped and rolled. Some of that silky black fur had been singed a bit shorter. Bethany screamed and hid her face in her hands while the cloud of smoke formerly known as Ethan surged across the ground.

"Everybody *stop it!*" I shouted.

Suddenly Conal was a man again, but the laidback, mocking guy was gone. In his place stood a stranger, his eyes burning with hatred. "Witches!" he snarled. "Your aunts are *witches.*"

17

That strange feeling zipped through my veins in the silence, like the bubbles in champagne. Was it only a moment ago that we were eating steak sandwiches together like civilised people? What had gone so wrong?

"We are *cartomancers*, dog," Ling said. "Your kind turned the word *witch* into a weapon to wield against us."

"What is a Soldier doing here?" Ivy muttered in an urgent undertone.

"He was *supposed* to be helping coordinate an attack on a bruxsa," I said, giving him a filthy look. "But clearly he's no longer welcome."

I rubbed at my arms. It felt as though tiny insects tramped up and down just under my skin, tickling me with insistent feet. What was wrong with me? I'd felt like this just before the Fool had turned her painted head and looked at me.

Suddenly, everything was too bright, too big. The

world pressed in on me, and I made a little noise of protest.

"And *you*," Conal said in a tone of utter loathing. "Liam was right. You're one of them, and I was too blind to see it. You tricked me. You've been laughing at me this whole time, haven't you?"

My temper flared. "Oh, sure. Because this whole situation is absolutely *hilarious*."

"To think I swore a life vow to *you*. I should kill you."

"Thereby proving exactly what your word is worth."

"Just try it, dog," Ling said, fire flaring menacingly from her hands again. I *really* had to find out how she was managing that without her cards—but maybe later, when Conal wasn't losing his wolfy mind.

Ethan and Raquel circled around him and joined my aunts, forming a wall of steel at my back. Ethan had resumed his normal bodily form, which was a relief. Watching bits of him dissolve into nothingness had given me the heebie-jeebies.

"Just go," I said, sagging as a great wave of weariness rolled over me, threatening to drag me under with it. "I don't want to see you again."

Conal stared at me. His eyes still glowed yellow instead of their usual green. For once, I found absolutely nothing appealing about that scarred eyebrow, which was drawn into the fiercest scowl I'd ever seen on his handsome face. All I felt was sadness.

Why did the world have to be like this? Why were the Soldiers such *jerks*?

Then he strode down the street to where he'd parked

his rental car. We all stood there watching as he got in and drove away, the engine loud in the sudden silence. Ling waved her hand, and all the little tongues of flame licking at the grass went out at once as if someone had turned off a light.

"Is everything all right down there, Sunday?" a querulous voice called.

Mr Garcia was standing on his balcony, his blue beanie pulled down to the bridge of his nose, surveying our odd little tableau beneath him.

"We're all good, Mr Garcia," I called, giving him a little wave. "Sorry if we disturbed you."

"If you need me to come down there and give someone an ass-whooping, I will."

That brought a reluctant smile to my lips. I could just see Mr Garcia and his walking stick squaring off against a werewolf. "I think we're fine for ass-whoopings at the moment. Thanks for the offer, though."

"Any time," he said, giving each of the others a stare that he no doubt meant to be menacing, though he looked more constipated than anything else. "You just let me know if you need me, Sunday."

Then he hobbled back into his unit and slid the balcony door shut behind him. Had he even seen the werewolf? Or the vampire dissipating into smoke? Quite possibly not, given the thickness of the lenses on his glasses. But it was nice of him to be concerned.

After a few beats, Bethany broke the silence. "Umm ... could someone please tell me what just happened?"

Poor Bethany. Every time she came to my house lately there were some preternatural shenanigans going on.

"Come inside," I said. "We've given the neighbourhood enough of a show already."

"Sunday, you need to leave," Ling said in that *this is not up for negotiation* tone I remembered so well from my childhood.

"I need to pack first," I said, walking toward the apartment block. Anger and unhappiness swirled within me. Running away. Again. Was this all my life could ever be?

"We have a lemon meringue pie," Ivy said. That was Ivy for you, always trying to offer comfort.

"Bring it in."

If ever a situation had called for lemon meringue pie, this was it.

Everyone joined me inside a moment later, and Ling locked the front door behind them. I got plates and forks out and brought them to the table, where Ivy set the lemon meringue pie in the centre.

My saliva glands sprang to attention at the sight of it, and I felt sorry for the vampires that they would miss out. As always with Ling's cooking, it was perfection. Meringue was mounded high on top, its folds crisped to a warm brown. When I cut into it, the bright yellow of the lemon filling beneath was exposed. I served a slice to each plate, then stuck my fork into my own.

The delicious tartness of the lemon exploded onto my tongue first, followed by the sweet fluffiness of meringue. To finish off the taste sensation was the buttery goodness of the pastry, not too soft and not too crunchy. Just right. I closed my eyes and savoured it for a moment.

"This is really good," Bethany said, though she looked shell-shocked, her face almost as pale as Raquel's.

Raquel and Ethan had propped themselves side by side against the kitchen counter, watching the four of us eat. Raquel's expression held a certain wistfulness, which I could totally understand. Lemon meringue pie had that kind of effect on people.

"Ling's a good cook," I said.

"And she's also ... a witch?"

"A cartomancer," Ling said firmly. She indicated Ivy. "We both are."

Then she cocked an eyebrow at me in silent question, leaving it up to me how much to reveal.

I sighed. "And I am, too."

Bethany put her fork down, her eyes widening. "What's a cartomancer?"

"We use special cards to help us focus our magic."

"And you can ... throw fire?"

"It depends which element is your forte," Ivy said. "We use elemental magic, but not everyone is as good with Fire as Ling. I can barely light a cigarette, but I'm good with Earth."

"Are you preternaturals?"

"No," Ling said.

"Yes," Ivy said at the same time.

"Well, we're mostly human," Ling insisted.

"*Mostly* human?" Ariel popped into being, sprawled across the couch. From the lack of reaction in the room I gathered I was the only one favoured with her presence. "Isn't that like saying you're a little bit pregnant? You're either human or you aren't. There's no *mostly*."

Shush, I told her. *This is not the time.*

"We're definitely human," I said firmly. This was an old argument among cartomancers. "We just have this unusual ability. It's like how some people can see colour and some can't. Just a trick of genetics. Doesn't make us any less human."

"An ability that allows you to throw fireballs," Bethany said slowly.

Man, she was really stuck on those fireballs. "Sometimes. I've never seen it done without cards like that, though." I raised an eyebrow at Ling, but she folded her arms and stared right back, not to be diverted from her mission of getting me out of here. Fine. I could winkle the secret out of her later. "We can manipulate the elements, though it's not usually as spectacular as that. Most of us have very limited powers, really."

Raquel gave me a sceptical look over Bethany's head, and I recalled the explosion of light that had led us to the bruxsa earlier. Not exactly *limited*.

Okay, so my powers were a little crazy lately. Must be the stress.

"So why does Conal hate you?" Bethany asked.

I flinched, then was annoyed with myself. *Yes, Conal hates you now. Get used to it.* "Because he's a Soldier, and Soldiers are a bunch of jerks."

"Everything you say just leads to more questions."

Ling gave her a look as tart as the pie. "If you keep

asking questions, we'll be here all night, and we need to get Sunday out of here."

"I'm not going anywhere until I've had at least one more slice of this pie," I said.

"I'd like to know, too," Ethan said. "I've heard rumours that the Soldiers used to work with the wi—cartomancers. Must have been a long time ago."

"It was," Ling said.

"What happened?"

"A man felt threatened and destroyed everything to prop up his own sense of self-worth," Ling said. "As they do."

Ivy put her hand over Ling's on the table and spoke to Ethan. "You won't get an unbiased version from us, but the gist of it is that cartomancers and Soldiers did work together once, even it was only briefly. We were the force that held back the darkness and kept the more dangerous preternaturals in check. It was our sacred duty to protect humanity, and we did that work together. Our magics were stronger, together."

"I sense a major *but* coming," Ethan said.

Ivy sighed. "Yes. Male and female formed two halves of a greater whole. The women were the cartomancers, and we wielded the magic of the elements to defend our world from incursions from the magic plane. The Soldiers, who were all male, were our bodyguards, protecting us while we kept the elementals in check. It was just about a perfect system, but in the seventeenth century, it all fell apart."

Bethany raised her hand. "What are elementals?"

"Creatures made of pure elemental magic," I said. "They inhabit the magic plane."

And our world looked like a place full of tempting snacks to some of them, who'd managed to sneak through the portal and cause trouble. Their incursions had created the first preternaturals when their elemental magic had warped humans into things like werewolves and vampires. But Bethany didn't need to hear all that. She had quite enough to take in already.

"What happened in the seventeenth century?" Raquel asked.

"The Church happened," Ivy said with a glance at Ling.

"Not the Church," Ling cut in. "We had worked with the Church's blessing until then, though only a handful in the highest echelons of the Church even knew of our existence. But, as always, people find ways to ruin everything."

Ling wasn't exactly the biggest fan of people at the best of times.

Ivy shrugged. "All right, it wasn't the whole Church. But it didn't need to be. Up until then, we'd been led by the leader of the Soldiers, who was a Cardinal. We cartomancers had our covens, which each had a leader, but no coven leader was above any other. Our strength lay in cooperation, whereas the Soldiers were organised along more military lines, reporting to their Cardinal. As a result, he had a lot of power, even if his position was a secret to most people."

Ling took up the story. "So, sometime in the seventeenth century, Bertram, the Cardinal of the day, took a cartomancer as his mistress, and they had two children, a boy and a girl. The boy grew to become the most powerful Soldier who had ever lived, twice as strong as his formidable father. But the girl, Elizabetta—she inherited both her mother's magic and her father's werewolf strength. Bertram looked at his beautiful daughter and instead of rejoicing in her power, he saw only a threat."

"And something he craved but couldn't have for himself," Ivy added.

Ling nodded, tapping her fork gently on her plate, which still held a pristine slice of pie. I admired her restraint. I'd finished my second slice and was trying to calculate how much longer I'd have to exercise tomorrow if I had a third.

"Yes. He'd always been jealous of the cartomancers' ability to control the elements, and here was Elizabetta, who not only could do that but also outclassed him physically." She shrugged. "He felt threatened. Seeing that this new hybrid of Soldier and cartomancer was more powerful than one or the other, he grew bitter, foreseeing a future when a simple werewolf like himself would be relegated to the position of a second-class citizen. Hybrids and their double power would rule."

"What about the boy? You said he was extra strong. Did he also have both powers?"

"No, see, that was the real kicker. It turned out that male hybrids were only Soldiers, though they were much stronger than their Soldier fathers. But if girls were born of a mixed union, they got all that Soldier strength *as well as* inheriting their mother's elemental magics."

"You said the cartomancers and Soldiers only worked together briefly," Ethan said. "How long did it take for them to start getting it on with each other?"

"The stories are unclear," Ivy said, "but it might have been as long as fifty years."

"I'm surprised it took so long."

"Well, in those days, the Soldiers were an order of warrior monks," Ivy said. "Strictly celibate."

"So there was no bonking of their co-workers," I said helpfully.

"Except for the Cardinal," Bethany pointed out.

I snorted. "There's always a different rule for the plebs than the man at the top."

"And that was the start of the witch hunts that killed so many thousands of innocent women," Ling said. "All because one man envied a woman's power."

Bethany frowned at her. "But how did he persuade all the other Soldiers? And what about the covens? Didn't they object?"

"He was aided by a magical plague that hit the Soldiers about the same time," Ivy said. "It almost wiped them out."

"Shame it didn't do a better job," Ling added darkly.

Ivy gave her a reproving look. "Now, now, darling. The plague didn't affect cartomancers at all, and Bertram started a rumour that they had actually caused it with their magic, which turned the Soldiers against them."

"Once he had the Soldiers onside, he used his position in the Church to turn the general population against 'witches'." Ling sighed. "You have to remember, these were superstitious times. Most people had no education. They got their news and their guidance from the man in the pulpit of their local church. All he had to do was whisper a few alarming rumours in the right ears. See that the right people made the appropriate sermons. Suddenly women were public enemy number one—especially unmarried women, which cartomancers almost always are, because of the nature of our work."

"Couldn't they protect themselves with their magic?" Bethany asked.

"Some of them did. Some of them were overwhelmed by sheer weight of numbers. Others refused to use their magic against the people they were meant to be protecting. And once enough of us had died, the powers of the surviving cartomancers waned. Magic fell out of balance, and more of the elementals began breaking free of the tethers we'd placed on them."

"It became a vicious circle," Ivy said. "The more of us who died, the weaker the powers of everyone who was left grew—and the greater the danger posed by the elementals became."

Seeing that Bethany was looking overwhelmed, I said, "Okay, let's leave the history lesson for now. Basically, we used to work together, it all fell apart centuries ago over political power plays, and now we hate each other."

"Wow," said Bethany, her eyes huge and round. "So where do you three fit in? Are you some kind of magical crime fighters?"

"We've been continuing the work as best we can," Ivy said. "We have a coven, but there aren't many of us, and the area we have to defend and protect is immense. That's why we're always on the road."

Ling nodded. "That and the fact that we always have to hide from the Solders. If they discover us, they'll kill us. We believe that's what happened to Sunday's mother."

Ethan stirred. "I thought she died in a car crash?"

Ivy shook her head. "Dana left Sunday with us while she tracked a particularly vicious elemental. She sounded excited the last time she called—she said she'd located it, but there was a hunting pair of Soldiers in the area, too. We warned her to be careful, but we never heard from her again."

My heart clenched with familiar pain, and I put my fork down, deciding that actually, two slices of lemon meringue pie were quite enough to fill anyone up. Then I sat back in my chair and frowned at them both.

Ivy looked anxious. She was the one I'd always run to for comfort as a child. She was the snuggly, caring aunt. Not that Ling didn't care—she just hid it well. She was firmer than her partner, and thought Ivy had spoiled me. *She* frowned right back, as if I had done something she disapproved of.

I cleared my throat. "Well, anyway. That's in the past. We need to talk about what happens now."

Ling nodded. "You start packing. That's what happens now."

Ariel glanced at me. "Are we sure about this?"

Bethany screamed and leapt up from the table. My aunties gasped, and Ethan was at Ariel's side so fast I didn't even see him move. I was caught completely unprepared.

After all, Ariel had been popping into my conversations forever. I actually jumped and looked around for the wolf attack before realising the truth.

Everyone could see her.

She got up, practically vibrating with excitement, and looked from one astonished face to another.

"It's okay, Ethan," I said. "Everyone, this is Ariel."

The Dynamic Duo exchanged shocked glances. "Your invisible friend?"

"Not so invisible now," Ariel crowed, strutting over to the table.

Ivy's face was white. "This changes everything."

Ling stood up decisively. "This changes nothing. Sunday, go and pack."

Everyone else was on their feet, so I got up, too, and poked Ariel. She felt astonishingly, *miraculously* solid.

"Ow." She gave me the side-eye as she rubbed her arm. "Don't damage the merchandise."

And then her eyes widened as the significance of the moment hit her. I'd never touched her before. She swallowed hard and collapsed into the chair I'd just vacated.

"Well, this is a day of surprises," Ling said, eyeing Ariel. "You also mentioned a problem with Dana's Tarot deck. Where is it? You said the image on the card moved?"

I got *The Lord of the Rings* from its place on the bookshelf. "Don't sound so sceptical. It did move. It looked right at me."

"The cards aren't alive."

"Perhaps you imagined it." Ivy was always the peacemaker. "You've been under a lot of stress lately."

"They think you're crazy again," Ariel said, drawing a quelling look from Ling.

"Typical Dana," Ivy said when I opened the book to reveal the cards in their hiding place. "She always loved that book."

"Why didn't you tell us you had these?" Ling asked, lifting them out almost with reverence. "Oh!"

"What?"

"They feel ... charged. I can feel power in the deck still." She held the cards out to Ivy, who touched them briefly before drawing her hand back.

"That's not normal. Perhaps we should consult the coven."

Ling nodded, then her face softened into a rare expression of tenderness as she turned each card over, as if she were greeting old friends. A lump formed in my throat as I watched her arrange the deck into suits and separate out the major arcana from the minor.

"You said on the phone that some were missing," Ivy said. "Which ones?"

"The Three of Air and the Queen of Air."

They exchanged glances, as if that were significant somehow. I had often found my aunts' silent communications annoying as a child, but this was next level.

"What? Does that mean something?"

"Dana probably had them with her when she died," Ivy said, but she wasn't talking to me.

"The queen?" Ling replied. "She wasn't crazy."

"What?" I asked impatiently, looking from one to the other. "What's the problem?"

But Ling was leafing through the deck, faster and faster. "Where's the Fool?"

"Oh, she's—"

On the floor under the bookcase, because I'd been too scared to pick her up and put her back with the rest of the deck. Only when I got down on my knees to look, there was nothing under there except dust bunnies.

The Fool was gone.

18

"That wolf took it," Ling said instantly, a look of horror on her face.

"Conal? No, that doesn't make sense. If he'd seen it, he'd already have known I was a cartomancer." And he definitely hadn't known, because he'd been treating me with the same mocking good humour as always. "It wasn't until you guys arrived that he ..." Looked at me as if I were the lowest pond scum imaginable, as if I were filth to scrape off the bottom of his shoe. "That he lost it."

"Who else has been here?" Ling asked in an urgent tone. "Who might have taken it?"

Her gaze raked the room, and Ethan held up his hands. "Don't look at me."

No one in the room would have touched it—and no one else had been here.

"The other Soldier," I said as realisation hit me. "Liam. He was lying in wait for us when we got back from the hive last night. He must have found it."

Quickly, I filled them in on my dealings with Liam, from the time he'd appeared in the shop, through his attack on the road the night I'd walked home—though I toned that down for the aunties, since they were looking traumatised enough—up until that last fight in my lounge room. Ivy's eyes widened with horror as the tale progressed, while Ling's expression grew more and more grim.

"Conal said he'd gone back to their headquarters, wherever that is," I finished.

"The part I don't understand," Ivy said, "is why he was already convinced you were a cartomancer before he found the card. Why was he after you that night in the woods? And why did Conal stop him? If one thought you were a cartomancer, why didn't the other?"

"Raquel thought it might be Soldier politics," I said. "Conal and Liam don't seem to like each other very much. But as to how he knew I was a cartomancer, I think he sensed my magic the night Ethan and Raquel and I were looking for the elder, and he came sniffing around town until he found me."

"Well, never mind," Ling said. "It has no bearing on the present situation. Every minute we spend in this house brings us closer to disaster. Sunday." She jerked her head towards the bedroom, the command implicit. *Go and pack.*

"First I need to help the vampires with—"

"Don't be ridiculous," Ling snapped.

"Thou shalt not suffer a witch to live," Ivy said softly, just as Liam had the other night. It sent chills down my spine to hear the words from my gentle aunt's lips. "Those are the words they live by. You can't help anyone if you're dead."

"You should probably change your name, too," Ling said with ruthless efficiency. "We have some contacts who can get you false ID."

Change my *name*? My mother had given me this name. It and her cards were all I had left of her. I stared at Ling in horror.

No. There had to be another way.

"It won't take long," I said, almost pleading. "I just need to find a place to lie low until this is settled."

"You could all come out to the farm," Bethany said. "We've got plenty of room. And the barn is big enough to park the motorhome in. No one would even know you were there."

I flashed her a grateful smile, then glanced at Ethan and Raquel. "And the hive will protect me."

But who would protect *them*? What if one of them died in the battle against the bruxsa? The bruxsa had magic and they didn't. I'd never forgive myself if someone died when my magic could have saved them.

"Queen Nessa has already offered her protection," Ethan said.

"She won't stand up against the wolves if they demand she hand Sunny over," Ling said dismissively.

"Are you calling our queen an oath-breaker?" Raquel demanded, a glint of steel in her expression.

"Guys, guys." I held up my hands before Raquel and

Ling got into a fight. "We're on the same side, remember? We should be supporting each other. The real enemy here is the bruxsa."

"And the wolves," Ling muttered.

Ivy looked at me. "What bruxsa?"

Poor Bethany looked totally confused. She probably didn't even know what a bruxsa was.

"Well, we thought the rogue was an elder, but it's actually a bruxsa," I said. For Bethany's sake, I added, "It's a kind of vampire on steroids."

"Worse than an elder?" She sounded like she might be sick.

"Much worse," Raquel said. "They have special protective magic that makes them very hard to kill, and that magic is powered by blood."

"Raquel and I found her last night," I said, "but she escaped. She's hiding out at the old Rogerson place."

Ethan sighed, rubbing the bridge of his nose. "She's killed five people ... so she's strong."

"And getting stronger," Raquel added. "That many kills so close together suggest she's building up power for some big move—maybe she's pregnant, or maybe she's trying to muscle in on something else's territory."

"Or perhaps she feels the decline of magic the way we do," Ivy said thoughtfully. "There's been a lot more activity among the monsters in the past decades. I think they're all trying to shore up their powers."

"It's a monster eat monster world," I said.

"If only they *would* eat each other and not the

humans." Ivy looked worried. "Bruxsas like cartomancer blood, too. It boosts their power more than non-magical blood. I wonder if she's been drawn to the area because of you?"

Great. Something else to feel guilty about. I gave Ivy a pleading look. She had always been the first to cave when I wanted something as a child. "That makes it even more imperative that I help stop it. The vampires have no defence against her magic. They need our help."

"Absolutely not," Ling said. "Do you think the wolves are going to stand around watching you work magic and say *thanks very much, goodbye* when you're done?"

"Conal might be grateful for the help, at least. He was willing to work with the vampires, and he must know how dangerous a well-fed bruxsa would be. The Soldiers *need* our magic."

Ling shrugged. "That's their problem. They're the ones who hunted us almost to extinction."

"*I* can protect Sunday," Ariel said. "I've been doing it for years."

Ling shot a glare in her direction. "*You* are a problem."

Ariel bristled visibly, and I felt my own hackles go up, too. "What do you mean?"

"She's obviously an elemental. She makes you more of a target."

"*Obviously* an elemental?" I repeated. "Don't you think I've considered that possibility?"

"How could she stay in our world this long without a huge, constant influx of power?" Ivy asked doubtfully.

Elementals couldn't survive for long outside their own magic-rich world, unless they found a human host. That was how vampires and werewolves had begun in the first place. They were humans changed forever by elemental magic.

"I don't know, but it's the only answer," Ling insisted. "There must be something we're not seeing here. How else do you explain her abilities?"

"Don't talk about her as if she's not here," I said fiercely. "Are you still trying to pretend she's not real?"

Ivy laid a placating hand on my arm. "I'm sorry we didn't believe you about Ariel when you were little. We thought you were just a lonely little girl inventing a friend. But Ling's right. I don't understand how, but if she's using mini tornadoes to protect you, she must be an Air elemental."

"Must I?" Ariel folded her arms across her chest, looking mutinous. "And what's wrong with that?"

"What if the wolves see her?" Ling asked. "More to the point, what if her magic draws them to you?" She glared at Ariel. "You should leave Sunday alone."

"Ling!" I snapped.

How could she say that? Ariel had been my only friend for so long, but she was more than a friend. She was like a sister to me, a sassy and comforting presence that was always there. And nobody got away with causing that stricken look on her face, not even my aunt.

"Ariel won't be going anywhere. Her magic has never been a problem before."

"There haven't been wolves in town before!"

I took a deep breath. Shouting at Ling wouldn't help, much as I might want to. "This is non-negotiable. Ariel stays."

And then I stalked into my room to throw a few clothes in a backpack, slamming the door behind me.

19

en minutes later, I was backing Bugsy out of her parking spot, still fuming. I had put my foot down on leaving town immediately, so in the end Ling had reluctantly agreed to regroup at Bethany's place. Bethany said she'd show them the way. Ethan had headed off on vampire business, but Raquel had insisted on coming with me. She took her orders to look after me surprisingly seriously.

Ariel had disappeared, and I wasn't very good company. I barely saw the road, relying on habit to get me to Bethany's place. "I can't believe Ling flat-out refused to consider helping."

"Don't sweat it," Raquel said. "Vampires know how to look after themselves. So a few wolves might die bringing the bruxsa down. Is that such a bad thing?"

I'd been thinking of my vampire friends, but now Conal's handsome face popped into my mind with that scarred eyebrow quirked in its usual mocking way—*not* the way I'd last seen him, with that look of loathing on his face. My heart twinged at the thought of *him* dying at the bruxsa's hands. Because he'd be right there in the thick of the fight.

"Look, Conal is a bigoted jerk. But that doesn't mean I want him to die."

She studied me thoughtfully. "How much do you care about his safety? Enough to risk your own? Because your aunt's not wrong. The wolves aren't going to thank you for helping. In fact, they'll most probably kill you before you even get a chance to offer. It's not worth the risk."

I glanced at the clock on the dash. "It's only nine-thirty. When did you tell Conal about the bruxsa?"

"When he turned up this morning. A bit after eight."

"So the rest of the wolves aren't here yet. We could deal with the bruxsa now, before they arrive."

She looked doubtful. "It would be safer to wait until midday."

"Safer for who? Come on, the sun's shining. The bruxsa's probably fast asleep." I fished my phone out of my handbag one-handed and tossed it to her. I could feel my mood improving as I settled on a course of action. "Do me a favour and call Conal. His number's in there. We can set something up and it'll all be over by the time the rest of the Soldiers arrive."

She still didn't look convinced.

"Please? You said yourself the vampires will be okay."

She rolled her eyes and started searching my contacts. "You must be seeing something in this wolf that I'm not. He's not worth all this trouble."

But she dialled the number anyway.

Was he worth the trouble? He'd saved my life twice now. Before this morning's debacle, the answer would have been a definite yes, in spite of his questionable career choice. He was funny and thoughtful, and I'd actually almost trusted him, even knowing what he was. He made me laugh, and sometimes when he looked at me with a certain light in those luminous green eyes, he left me breathless, too. I'd never met anyone like him before. He seemed like someone I could rely on, and that had been rare enough in my chaotic life that giving it up caused a physical ache in my chest.

Plus, he seemed more open to change—or at least compromise—than I'd expected from a Soldier. He'd agreed to meet the vampires when I'd pushed. He'd even agreed to work with them, despite believing that he really didn't need them. If I could convince him that he needed *me*, perhaps he'd be open to changing a little more. I felt he'd trusted me, deep down. Could that trust really have been destroyed so quickly?

Along with his good opinion. I was still reeling from the one-eighty he'd pulled there. To be perfectly honest, I was pretty sure his opinion of me had been more than merely good. Unless I'd completely misread him, he fancied me, and his interest hadn't been as unwelcome as it should have been.

Was I putting myself in danger for a fantasy? What future could a witch and a wolf have together?

I'd known for years that Soldiers hated cartomancers, but it had never been so *personal* before. Conal wasn't just a

Soldier. He was someone I cared about, whether that was stupid or not. My feelings didn't care about logic. They only cared that his rejection hurt.

"He's not answering," Raquel said.

I pulled over, then made a U-turn. I had to at least *try* to change his mind. If only he could see that magic was a force for good in the right hands. Centuries of hatred would only continue unless something changed. *Someone* had to make the first move.

"What are you doing?" Raquel asked. "I thought we were going to Bethany's?"

"I've got a better idea." The Rogerson place was only a couple of minutes away. Actually, most things were only a couple of minutes away in Kurranderra.

Conal's rental car was parked a few hundred metres down the road from the old house. Another car was parked opposite. That must belong to the vampires on watch.

Good. My hunch that I'd find him here had panned out. I switched off Bugsy's engine.

Raquel gave me a scathing look. "*This* is your better idea? Do you have a death wish?"

I ignored her and got out, closing the door quietly behind me. We were far enough away that the bruxsa should have no idea we were here, but there was no sense taking chances.

The properties on this road were big, two or more acres each, so the houses were few and far between. Mostly it was just your standard Australian bushland—scrubby undergrowth and gum trees.

I had a nasty flashback to the night Liam had stepped out of the trees onto the road, and a shiver ran down my spine. That was *not* going to happen again. He was still down in Sydney—and even if he wasn't, I had Raquel for backup now, and the sun was shining. Let him try something. I was ready to take him on.

I rubbed absently at my arm where he'd bitten me. It was itchy, so I pulled off the Band-Aid. The skin was smooth, not even scarred, as if the whole thing had never happened. Weird. I bet it had something to do with my strange new boost in magical power. Most cartomancers came into their full strength at puberty, but apparently, I was a late bloomer. I felt so good, brimming with health. If I were a dog, my nose would be wet and my coat super shiny.

As we approached the driveway up to the big white house on the hill, a vampire appeared, emerging so quietly from the trees it was as if he'd popped out of the air. He was one of the guys I'd seen on my visit to the hive, a tall, thin man with a long face who looked as though he never smiled. Raquel stopped to talk to him, and I ventured a little further up the driveway, keeping close to the trees.

You could tell that the house had once been magnificent. Single storey with a red tiled roof and a long colonnade of arches in the front, it looked as though it could have been some millionaire's home on the Costa del Sol. Instead, it sprawled on a hill here in the Blue Mountains with cockatoos screeching overhead, its once-white walls grey with dirt. The fountain in the middle of the circular driveway leaned drunkenly to one side, the water in its tiled pond long since dried up. Weeds grew from cracks in the concrete, and a couple had even found a foothold in the gutters of the roof.

"This is a dumb idea," Ariel said, appearing at my side. "If the wolf doesn't eat you, the bruxsa will."

I didn't ask her where she'd been, since she never told me anyway. And one look at her closed-off expression suggested that it wouldn't be a good idea to ask her how she was feeling, either. She'd taken Ling's rejection hard.

So all I said was, "The bruxsa will be sacked out at this time of day, probably dreaming of her next meal. Don't worry so much. That's what the aunties are for."

"And the wolf?"

"I'll deal with him."

"Who are you talking to?" Conal demanded, sounding crankier than a toddler faced with a plateful of broccoli.

We both spun around. He'd approached as quietly as the vampire—I hadn't heard a thing. But now he stood on the cracked concrete behind us, scowling at me. He paid no attention to Ariel, so I assumed she was only visible to me.

"What are you doing here?" he asked.

Clearly Ariel's fears were unfounded. He wasn't going to eat me. Suddenly, I felt flush with confidence and power. I could do this. I swear I could feel my new magic fizzing in my veins. I didn't know why it had suddenly decided to come to the party, but it had picked a good time if it helped me keep this infuriating wolf's ungrateful skin in one piece.

"Looking for you," I replied.

"I want nothing to do with you."

"Well, that's too bad, buddy, because *I* want to help. This is my town, and people I care about are in danger. Including you, you stupid wolf."

"You think I can't handle myself against a bruxsa?" There was nothing welcoming in his shadowed green eyes. In fact, he looked offended.

Okay, impugning his manhood—or wolfhood—might not have been the best way to start. I tried again.

"I'm sure you're the most ferocious wolf that ever lived, but what about the other Soldiers? Are they all as good as you?"

"That's it," Ariel said, "stroke his ego."

I ignored her and pushed on, determined to convince him. "How many of them will die trying to take this thing down? She has magic, and none of you do. Are your stupid prejudices worth more than people's lives?"

"It's not a stupid prejudice." He folded his arms, his face taking on a stubborn look. "Magic is what caused these problems in the first place. It's a black art."

I eyed him impatiently, resisting the urge to reach out and shake him. "Right. Do I *look* like a demon? Are you afraid I'm going to buddy up with the bruxsa and kill you all?"

"No, of cour— No." His gaze slid sideways.

Of course not? He still trusted me. He knew I would never join forces with a bruxsa. "Then you're afraid of magic?" I asked.

He threw his arms up in a gesture of frustration. "There wouldn't *be* any bruxsas in this world if you witches hadn't used your magic to open the gates to demons."

"That happened centuries ago. How long are you going to punish us for that? I, personally, have never let *anything* through the portal, demon or otherwise. But you still think I deserve to die, just because I *could*?"

"Keep your voice down," he snapped. "The bruxsa isn't deaf."

"No, but you are—and blind and stupid as well. Where do you think the magic came from that lets you turn into a wolf?"

"From God, of course." He half turned away, clearly impatient to be done with this conversation.

I put my hands on my hips. "You do know that wolves and cartomancers used to work together, don't you? Did our magic come from God back then, but someone flicked a switch and now it comes from some other place?"

He whipped back around to face me. "That's a lie."

"What? That we used to work together?" I shook my head and borrowed Ariel's line: "What are they teaching you at Soldier school these days?"

Raquel joined us, giving Conal a wary look. "Everything all right?"

"Just peachy," I muttered. "I'm giving Wolfman here a history lesson. He didn't know that Soldiers and cartomancers used to work together."

Raquel folded her arms and stared at him. "Even vampires have heard that."

"Rumours," he said, but he'd lost some of his certainty.

"You should ask your boss sometime," she said. "I

know you've only been a wolf for a few years. Maybe they don't tell the newbies. Don't want to confuse them."

Interesting. He was a new wolf? Maybe that was why he was still standing here talking instead of trying to kill me. He hadn't had time to develop the rigid way of thinking that other wolves like Liam displayed.

Or maybe it was just his precious life debt that stopped him.

"I called Ethan," Raquel said to me, "and he checked in with the queen. She said if we want to go ahead without waiting for the Soldiers, we can. She said she sensed great power in you."

"Really?" Had Raquel told her about my display last night?

"I suspect she wants to see what you've got." She gave Conal a challenging look. "So, are we doing this or what?"

"The Hunt will be here by midday, as we arranged. We will wait."

I shrugged. "Suit yourself. If the queen thinks I can do it, I'm doing it. You can wait out here if you're scared."

I turned and started walking away.

"Ooh, way to pull on his tail," Ariel said. "You should see the look on his face."

I wasn't going to spoil my bad-ass strut by looking back, but I could imagine. Knowing that I'd gotten under his skin gave me a warm glow inside.

A moment later, he caught up with me. "I assume you have a plan?"

20

*E*than arrived with three other vampires about ten minutes later. Together with the two who'd been on watch, plus Raquel, that made seven vamps, one wolf, one witch, and one whatever-Ariel-was. An elemental, according to Ling. Whatever. She came in handy in a fight, so I was glad to have her at my back. We could work out the whys and wherefores later.

Ethan strode over with his usual confidence, tailed by the other vampire arrivals. He grinned at me. "Who said nothing ever happened in Kurranderra?"

"I *liked* it when nothing ever happened in Kurranderra," I said.

He glanced between me and Conal, and his smile faded. "Are we all good here?"

I flashed a fake smile. My teeth were only *slightly* gritted. "We're good. Soldier Boy has agreed not to eat me, and I've agreed not to slap him upside the head for wilful stupidity. For the good of the mission, you understand."

Ethan rubbed his hands together. "Excellent. And do we have a plan?"

"Sunday hides us," Raquel said. "We make sure the bruxsa doesn't escape, and Conal beheads her."

"Ah." His gaze landed on the naked blade in Conal's hand. It was long and straight with a plain hilt. No ornamentation. Just business. It looked like a soldier's sword, and Conal held it with an ease that suggested he knew how to handle it. "I wondered what the sword was for."

"You're not going to just ... you know ..." I bared my teeth at Conal and made a growling sound.

"Rip her throat out? No." He eyed me as if he couldn't figure out if I was making fun of him or not.

Guess I'd better make it more obvious next time.

"Why not?" Raquel asked with a gleam in her eye that made me think she'd been looking forward to the throat-ripping. That seemed a little bloodthirsty, but I guess that made sense. She *was* a vampire, after all. *Bloodthirsty* was kind of their thing.

"No one wants to get into an extended fight with a bruxsa. Teeth and claws aren't much use against its magic, and they're slower. Better to get it over with as fast as possible. A nice, clean beheading is safest."

A *nice, clean beheading*. Right. There was something wrong with a person who could talk about a beheading as if it were a good thing. And there was definitely something wrong with *me*, that I still found him attractive in spite of it. Why couldn't I have fallen for a nice, normal guy who didn't rate the best ways to kill something?

"Right." Ethan turned to me. "And how are you going to hide us?"

I'd considered my cards while I'd been waiting. Our best chance was to sneak up on the bruxsa and strike before she even knew anyone was there. That way she would have no chance to fight back. Vampires could turn to smoke, but smoke was still visible. If she woke at the wrong time, we'd have a fight on our hands, sword or no sword. And heaven forbid our nice, clean beheading got *messy*.

"I'm going to craft an invisibility spell so that you can get close without it knowing." My fingers stroked the smooth surface of the Seven of Air as I spoke. The sneaky card. It had a lot of applications.

Ethan blinked at me. "You can do that?"

I never had before, but something about the magical energy surging inside me promised that now I had the power for it. I could almost hear it crackling, eager to get to work. I'd chosen the success of the Six of Fire to help us, the blindfolded figure of the Eight of Air so the bruxsa wouldn't see us, and the Nine of Air to dull her mind, just in case she woke up.

"Yep," I said.

"You won't be touching *me* with your filthy magic," Conal growled.

This again. I rolled my eyes. "You *want* the bruxsa to be able to see you?"

"I know what I'm doing." That stubborn look was back. "She won't see me."

"If she gets any magical blood, she'll only get stronger."

"If she gets my blood, I'll have bigger problems than that. But she won't."

We glared at each other for a long moment. Stupid, bigoted wolf. He'd rather risk his life than let me use my magic to help him.

"Fine. It's your funeral." I turned to the others. "Where do you want me to set up?"

"How close do you have to be?" Raquel asked.

"You should stay out of sight," Conal said, indicating the surrounding trees with the point of his sword.

"Why?" I gave him a sidelong glance, baiting him. "Are you afraid the bruxsa will kill me before you get the chance?"

He took a deep breath. "I don't want to kill you." Each word came out slowly and deliberately, as if he were forcing himself to stay calm. "But you're not a fighter. You should stay back so we don't have to worry about protecting you as well."

"He has a point," Ariel said.

I shrugged. "Ariel will protect me."

"Who's Ariel?"

Oops. I'd forgotten he hadn't met her.

"If you want to get this done before the Soldiers arrive, we'd better get started," Raquel said, jumping in before I could answer. "Unless you people want to stand out here arguing until the bruxsa wakes up."

I *definitely* wasn't interested in *that* option. I nodded and walked up the driveway, stopping just before it bent around in the final approach to the house. "This should be close enough."

There was even a clump of gum trees to hide behind to appease the stupid wolf. Most of me was still majorly ticked off with him, but there was a small part that noted his concern for my welfare and got all warm and gooey about it. Some part of him still cared enough to make sure I was safe.

Or else he's still honouring his stupid vow, another part of me pointed out. I told that part to shut up. We had enough negativity happening here already without adding Negative Nellie's point of view. Believing that he still cared about me made me happy, so I was going with that.

"I mean, you *are* eminently loveable," Ariel said, watching my preparations with interest.

I've told you before not to eavesdrop on my thoughts, I said mind-to-mind. Conal had already caught me "talking to myself" once. He'd think I'd completely lost it if I did it again, and I certainly didn't want to draw his attention to Ariel. An actual elemental hanging around—if Ling was right and that's what she was—was bound to spook him.

"Well, no one else is doing anything interesting."

I looked up. I had an audience gathered around me. Conal's face was carefully blank as I laid my chosen cards out on the ground. This evidence of magic was probably horrifying him, but at least he was keeping it to himself. I drew a focusing circle in the dirt around them with the point of a stick, then sat back on my heels.

I could feel the magic gathering, frothing and bubbling inside me. I held my hands over the cards, keeping my intentions in mind. Invisibility. Silence. Protection. I'd hesitated over adding an Ace to the mix. Aces were the raw potential of each element, so they were the workhorses of any cartomancer's deck. But my intuition told me I had a winning combination already.

I blew gently on the cards and tapped them. A pale white light formed around my hands as I called to the magic inside me. In the past, coaxing it out had felt like pulling teeth, but now it surged up like a tidal wave. Wisps of white light wafted up from the cards, adding to the glowing ball that enclosed my hands. The magic pushed at me, trying to burst forth in an uncontrolled rush the way it had when I'd searched for the bruxsa, but I was ready for it this time. I clamped down on the fire hose of power, only letting out as much as I needed. No need to send another bat signal into the sky to alert our prey. My arms shook with the effort of holding it all in.

When the white sphere of light was the size of a basketball, I released it, letting the magic fly out to find its targets. From the corner of my eye, I saw Conal flinch as one of the lines of light flew past, almost grazing his nose.

"You're glowing," Ariel said.

So I was. Well, that was new. Hopefully the effect wouldn't last, otherwise hiding from the Soldiers would be kind of challenging.

Then I looked up and found that everyone but Conal had vanished.

"Guys?" Even vampires couldn't have moved away that quickly.

"Here." Ethan's voice was muffled, as if it were coming from a long way away. "This is pretty cool, Sunny. I never knew you could do stuff like this."

I never *had* been able to. As soon as we finished here, I needed to have a long talk with the Dynamic Duo about *why* my powers had suddenly decided to come to the party. Everything I had heard or read until now said that a cartomancer's powers were pretty settled by the time she made it through puberty, and puberty was so far back it wasn't even dust in my rear-view mirror anymore. Maybe Mum had been a late bloomer, too. She'd certainly had power to burn.

"All part of the service," I said. My own voice sounded as weirdly muffled as Ethan's had, and I stifled an urge to giggle. My body was still limned in flickering white magic. "Can you see me?"

"No," Ethan said.

Interesting. I could see myself, but not the others. Presumably they were having the same experience. It was quite thoughtful of the magic, really. I imagined it would be horribly disconcerting to move around when you couldn't see what your own body was doing.

"Stay right there," Conal said, glaring in my general direction even though he could no longer see me. "We'll be back."

He stalked off, moving silently, and slipped through the front door of the house. Presumably, the vampires followed him, though I didn't hear them moving, of course.

"Hello?" I said after a moment, to be sure.

No one replied, not even Ariel. Knowing her, she'd gone along for the entertainment value. Personally, I was just as happy to skip the whole beheading thing, clean or not. I had no sympathy for the bruxsa, but that was something I simply didn't need to see. I'd be having nightmares for weeks.

Seconds stretched into minutes as I stood there, straining to hear anything that would tell me how they were doing. That was probably a waste of time, considering how well my spell had blanketed the world in silence. I couldn't hear a single bird, or even the rustle of a leaf, though they were shifting in a light wind that had sprung up. It was as if someone had shoved magical cotton wool in my ears.

I drew the Aces out of my pocket as I waited, finding comfort in their familiar smoothness under my fingers. It wasn't that I didn't trust the vampires—or Conal—to get the job done. I just worried that something might come unstuck.

If I'd learned anything about making plans, it was that none of them survived contact with reality unchanged.

The vampires would be scouting through the enormous house, searching out the bruxsa's hiding place. Once they found her, they would stand guard while one of them alerted Conal. The hope was that she would sleep through the whole thing, but if she woke before Conal took off her head, they would try to hold her, which would be no easy task. But they couldn't afford to let her speak or move. Her magic would be just as deadly to them as it was to anyone else. I'd be much happier when they all emerged unscathed and this whole nightmare was over.

The minutes became hours, or so it seemed. My impatience had me shifting from foot to foot. What was taking them so long? It was a big house, but surely not that big?

And why had I agreed to basically hide in the bushes, anyway? My magic might be needed. What if my invisibility spell had a distance limit? I should get closer, just in case.

I checked my watch. They'd only been gone five minutes. Huh. It felt more like five hours. I realised I was stroking the card in my hand repetitively with my thumb and flipped it over. The Ace of Fire.

It held all the potential of the suit of Fire. Fire was all about passion and soul. It had many uses in creating illusions—and also, of course, in calling and controlling the element of fire itself. She'd clammed up when I'd asked her how she'd done it, but the fireball that Ling had thrown this morning probably involved the raw power of the Ace.

I'd never been able to do much with Fire before, but now ... the memory of that fireball called to me. Though my magic still fuelled the invisibility spell, the tank felt full. I had power to burn—and maybe a little burning would be just the thing for a bit of insurance.

Noiselessly, I ghosted up the driveway, following the path the others had taken. It felt weird to hear no sounds at all, as if I existed in a bubble outside time. Pale white magic rippled down my arms and swirled around me as I moved, adding to the unreality of the experience.

My life had become very peculiar lately. I blamed Conal.

I slid through the open doorway and stopped to let my eyes adjust to the dimmer light inside. Terracotta tiles, many with cracks or pieces missing, covered the floor.

Above me, the ceiling soared two storeys high. The upper storey was reached by a spiralling iron staircase. Hallways ran off to the left and right, and straight ahead across the expanse of tiles was an archway that opened into an inner courtyard. It offered a glimpse of bedraggled garden and weeds poking up between the flagstones.

Locked in my silent bubble, I couldn't tell which way the others had gone. Knowing that the bruxsa was somewhere close by made the skin between my shoulder blades itch. I glanced at the Ace in my hand. Now would be a good time to work on that insurance.

Lighting candles had been the limits of my power with Fire until now, and even that had been so difficult that it was easier to use a match like a regular person. But things were different now.

I crouched down and pulled out my chalk. As I drew the circle and laid the Ace inside it, I pictured fire blossoming in my hand, like a rare and dangerous flower. The crackle of flame. The heat. Then I blew gently on the Ace and tapped it.

I was used to a long pause before my spells activated. Half the time, nothing happened at all.

So I nearly jumped out of my skin when the magic playing over my arms rushed straight to my hands and burst into a towering column of flame.

"Holy *crap*." Heat warmed my face, though my hands were undamaged. Guiltily, I pulled the magic in, reducing the flame to the more modest fireball I'd imagined. The paint on the ceiling was blistered where the flames had licked at it.

Awesome. I was Teflon Woman. I could hold real fire without it harming me. Bethany would be *so* impressed.

I couldn't help the grin that spread over my face as I scooped up the Ace. Now, *this* was magic. This was like the stories that Ivy used to tell me when I was little, of famous cartomancers and their exploits. She said that there used to be more magic in the world than there was now, and people had been capable of things back then that we could only dream of, but I had thought the stories exaggerated. Even my mum, whose power had been strong enough that people still talked about it, hadn't been able to do the things those women in the old stories could.

Things like the fire that still glowed brightly in my hand.

I tamped it down even further, afraid its light would attract unwelcome attention. Probably a little late to think of that. Oops. If the bruxsa jumped me now she was getting a faceful of fire for her trouble. Despite its small size, the magic of the fireball still pulsed with power in my hand. When I released it, it would launch at warp speed.

Hopefully, if it came to that, the vampires would have the sense to get out of the way, since I wouldn't be able to see them. That was a drawback of my invisibility spell that I hadn't considered. Still, if fireballs became necessary, we would probably be past needing to stay unseen and way into *trying to stay alive* territory. I could probably drop the invisibility spell.

I eyed the two corridors leading off from the foyer. Was I close enough now to guarantee the invisibility spell would continue to function or should I get closer? But which way?

Something brushed against my magic. It was the oddest sensation, like unseen fingers trailing down my spine—only not quite like that, since I didn't really experience it in my body. I'd felt it before, too, the night Raquel and Ethan and I had gone hunting the "elder" in the bush.

Somewhere, not too far away, something had just touched my invisibility spell.

I pushed more magic into it but, just as she had that night, the bruxsa tore at the spell.

No wonder we hadn't found her that night and she'd gone off to kill somewhere else. With two vampires and a cartomancer running around—plus Liam lurking in the bushes—she had clearly decided that hunting elsewhere was the easier option.

My ears popped, and the spell did, too. Someone shouted, a wordless cry of pain.

I was running down the left-hand corridor towards the sound before my brain had quite caught up. The bruxsa was awake and attacking my spell—what did that mean for the others? The fireball in my hand doubled, then tripled, in size, the magic surging in response to my fear.

I skidded past the top of a staircase leading down into the dark and hesitated. Light from my fireball danced on the wall.

"Look out!" someone shouted. It sounded like Ethan's voice, and it was coming from beneath me.

I hurtled down the stairs and pushed through a heavy wooden door into what must have been a wine cellar. And what a cellar! It stretched off into the darkness, looking as though it ran the full length of the house above, though it was hard to tell in the dim light. Wine racks, empty now, lined the walls, and barrels marched down the centre of the vast room. There was dust and bits of debris all over the packed-earth floor.

At the moment, it was lit by the eerie green ripple of an unfamiliar magic that clung to the ceiling like slime and oozed across it in waves. The bruxsa had made a little nest for herself from what looked like old, rotting curtains, probably scavenged from upstairs. But there was no sign of the creature now.

Where was she? And where were the vampires?

And Conal?

Mustn't forget my furry saviour. I thought about him way too much as it was, but I strained to see any sign of him through the gloom. He'd already shown a clear lack of regard for his personal safety, and an annoyingly macho urge to prove himself. Stupid Soldier. If he managed to get himself killed down here, I was going to be super unimpressed.

I moved away from the stairs, placing my feet as quietly as I could. No need to alert the bruxsa to my presence—or step on an old rusty nail and give myself tetanus. Conal would say I'd try any excuse to get taken to hospital. Even though I most definitely *didn't* have shares in it. A small smile tugged at my lips at the memory of that conversation.

Fluoro green magic clung to the top of a stack of old barrels, as if it had dripped down from the ceiling. Something told me it would be a very bad idea to let it touch me, so I gave the barrels a wide berth, creeping behind an old wooden wine rack that listed drunkenly to one side.

I realised I was holding my breath and let it out noiselessly. Something slammed against the other side of the wine rack, and I swallowed a scream as someone grabbed my arm and jerked me to one side.

"Your breathing is so loud even the dead mice down here can hear you," Conal muttered as he dragged me away.

Something hissed on the other side of the wine rack, and two shadows dropped like stones from the gloom above, landing on top of it. Vampires.

"What are you doing down here?" Conal demanded. "I told you to stay outside."

He was trying to bundle me back towards the dubious safety of the stairs, but Ethan came flying out from behind the wine rack as if he'd been launched from a cannon. He slammed headfirst into the slime-topped pile of old barrels and lay still.

"Ethan!"

I was only halfway to him, heart in my mouth, when he sat up, shaking his head groggily.

"Behind you!" he warned, then as I turned, "No! Don't look into her eyes."

Two vampires grappled with a shadowy pile of old rags. One of them was Raquel, but I barely registered her presence before she was getting the fired-out-of-a-cannon treatment, too. The other guy clung on grimly.

The pile of rags resolved into the bruxsa. I caught a

glimpse of the monster's face, bathed in the sickly green light, then the flash of her hand. Suddenly, a splintered piece of wood that had been ripped off one of the old barrels was standing out from the thin vampire's chest.

The bruxsa shrieked in delight. The poor vampire barely had time to glance down at it in surprise before he simply crumbled away into dust.

Then she turned toward me.

Conal shoved me out of the way so hard I landed on my butt in the musty dirt. Two more vampires emerged from the gloom, but they hung back, spooked by the death of their hive mate.

"Get out of the *way*," I snapped, scrambling up. The fireball in my hand doubled in size, but I didn't want to toast Conal.

The bruxsa crooned at him. He didn't move.

"He looked into her eyes, didn't he?" Ethan said in a disgusted tone.

I snatched at Conal's arm to drag him away, right as the bruxsa sprang at him with another ear-splitting shriek. My fireball flew over Conal's head, expanding as it went until I had to squint against the glare. It engulfed the bruxsa in white-hot light.

For a moment, triumph filled me. But the bruxsa stepped out of the fire, her head wreathed in flame but otherwise apparently unharmed.

Dammit. I coaxed another fireball from the spark still fizzing in my palm.

"Conal! Snap out of it!" I shouted, tugging on his arm. The bruxsa was practically on top of us.

"Look out!" Ethan shouted.

The rattle of wood on wood was my only warning as shards of broken barrels suddenly became airborne. They drove towards us as if we were magnets and they were pins —lethal pins.

Then, a howling gale swept in out of nowhere, sending the bits of splintered wood—and the bruxsa—flying.

A vampire cried out, and I flinched, hoping Ariel hadn't just staked someone. But no, all the vampires were dissolving into smoke. Things were getting too hot in here for them. I pushed more energy into my fireball and stepped between Conal and the bruxsa, who was dragging herself to her feet.

Ariel's gale buffeted us, fanning the flames in the bruxsa's hair. I braced myself and hurled the next fireball, lighting the cellar up like daylight. The bruxsa screamed and darted to one side, red eyes glowing with hatred.

One of the few intact barrels remaining exploded, and fire licked across the ceiling.

"Get out of here!" Ariel shouted.

Whether or not Conal heard her, he suddenly came to life, released from the bruxsa's spell. He charged at the monster, sword raised.

The bruxsa flicked a skeletal hand, and a piece of iron piping behind him lifted off the floor and speared straight for his back. Without thinking, I tackled him in a flying leap and landed heavily on top of him.

The pipe whooshed over our heads and clanged against the wine racks on the far wall. I heard it even over the crackle of flame. While we were untangling ourselves from each other, the bruxsa took the opportunity to skitter up the stairs to freedom.

"What did you do that for?" he demanded, once he'd wriggled out from under me.

I was slow to get to my feet, winded from taking one of his elbows to the gut. I bent over, hands on knees, trying to get my breath, and waved in the direction of the iron pipe. "She nearly ... skewered ... you."

Just as well I hadn't been expecting thanks, because I got none. "But she got away."

I straightened, wincing. "Well, excuse me for thinking you might prefer your liver in one piece."

I coughed. The smoke was starting to thicken, and my lungs were struggling. Conal grabbed my arm almost impatiently and towed me towards the stairs—the only part of the room that wasn't on fire.

"But you had a clear shot," he said over his shoulder. "You almost had her. Why would you save your enemy's life when you could have got what you wanted?

I glared at him and tried to break free of his grasp, but he wouldn't let go. "You think I'd choose getting what I wanted over anyone's life? Well, maybe Liam's. He could be on fire and I wouldn't spit on him."

He urged me up the stairs. "So your tender-heartedness applies to everyone, whoever they are."

"He looks disappointed," Ariel said. She was standing at the top of the stairs above us, hands on hips. But she was clearly back in stealth mode, since Conal didn't react to her presence. "I think he wanted to believe he was special to you."

I staggered up the steps, coughing. "You're the one insisting we're enemies," I told him between coughs. "I knew you were a wolf all along and I still liked you. Maybe wake up and join the rest of us in the real world instead of living in your stupid Soldier bubble."

He paused at the top of the stairs in the clearer air. "You liked me?" A spark of his old easy, mocking attitude resurfaced.

I bent over, hands on my knees, and coughed. "Don't get all excited. I like lots of people."

Not the way I liked him, but he didn't need to know that.

Ethan appeared, his vampire buddies in tow. "Guys, not to interrupt you if you're having a moment, but this old place is as dry as tinder. We should make a move."

"That's twice now you've saved my life," Conal said to me, ignoring Ethan completely.

"You're not going to start banging on about a life debt again, are you?" I demanded. There wasn't much smoke here, but it was getting hot. I wiped a trickle of sweat off my forehead. "Cause we all know how *that* turned out."

Anger flashed in his eyes, then was gone again, like a summer storm. "I guess I deserved that. I haven't been fair with you." He scrubbed wearily at his face, leaving a long smear of soot across his cheek. "I haven't slept in two days, and you can't expect me to be *happy* that you're a witch. I'm a Soldier. Hating witches is what we *do*. This is hard for me."

"Oh, boohoo." The poor suffering Soldier. I straightened up. "Try harder. If you really mean to honour that vow of yours, protecting me from your buddies is going to be a full-time gig. I need you on board with my magic. Which shouldn't be that hard, considering it saved your life." I waved the Ace of Fire in front of his face. "This is what *I* do. Take it or leave it."

He nodded. "I'm working on it. Give me time."

Not gonna lie, I'd been hoping for an enthusiastic *I'll take it*. I sighed. His Soldier buddies would be here soon, and if they were all like Liam ... "You'd better work faster. I don't think we have much time left."

21

"I think you've got a bit of Vaughn on you," Ethan said as he wiped Raquel's cheek, leaving a smear of pale skin amidst the dust that coated that side of her face.

"Eww. Gross." She scrubbed vigorously at her cheek, her eyes wide and horrified.

Looking around at the others, I found the same shell-shocked look on all their faces. The death of one of their number had rattled the vampires. They weren't used to being reminded so forcefully of their own mortality.

To be fair, it hadn't done wonders for my own peace of mind, either. It wasn't every day you watched someone explode into a cloud of dust—and this was my second time this week. I'd be just as happy if I never experienced it again.

"Where did that fire come from?" one of the vamps I didn't know asked, giving me a suspicious look. He had a widow's peak that would have made Dracula proud, but none of his charm. His flat stare sent a cold shiver down my spine. "Was that you?"

I didn't have to explain myself to him. "And speaking of fire," I said brightly, "Ethan's right. We should get out of here before the whole house goes up like a torch."

I kind of spoilt the effect by coughing again, though. The crackle of flame from the cellar was getting louder. Time to leave.

"Just put the fire out," Ariel said. "It's still yours. Command it."

I gave her a startled look. *Command it?* I could *do* that?

I mean, it made sense. I'd created it, so I should be able to kill it, too. Ling's flames on my front lawn had disappeared with a wave of her hand. But I wasn't used to my spells lasting long enough to do anything other than watch in disappointment as they petered out. I could get used to having magic that actually *worked*.

Sure enough, the fire snuffed out with only a thought. The smoke lingered for a moment, then drifted away into nothing, disappearing as if it had never been. Grumpy Dracula eyed me with deep suspicion. I ignored him, drawing in a great lungful of charcoal-scented air. Amazing.

"We can regroup," Ethan said as he led the way down the corridor. "It could have been worse."

"Worse than losing Vaughn?" Grumpy Dracula asked in tones of disbelief and scorn. "He was over three hundred years old."

"I knew we should have waited for the Soldiers," one of them muttered.

"Funny, you seemed happy enough to take all the glory a couple of hours ago," Raquel snapped, and the grumbling stopped. The tapping of her heels on the tiled floors was the only sound until we got outside.

There was no sign of the bruxsa, of course. I hadn't expected there to be, but a girl could always hope, right? How nice it would have been to find her lying in the driveway, perhaps with her head conveniently already removed by some passing lumberjack. Did we even have lumberjacks in Australia?

Probably not, but it was *my* fantasy, so I was going with it.

"Who's going to tell the queen?" Grumpy Dracula asked when everyone was gathered around the dried-up fountain in the centre of the circular driveway. He scowled at me as he spoke, as if the whole debacle could be laid at my door.

"What?" I asked him, scowling right back. "I thought you big, brave vampires were going to restrain the bruxsa until Conal could, er ... dispatch it?"

"Your spell failed."

"I don't think that's quite true," Ethan cut in. "We were doing fine until you walked right into a patch of that green magic, and then Sunday's spell popped like a bubble."

"I didn't walk into it," Grumpy Dracula objected. "It *dripped* on me."

"You knew the bruxsa could do magic," Raquel hissed. "Are you really so stupid that you'd walk blindly through an area she's blanketed with the stuff?"

There was no answer to that—no polite one, anyway.

The vampires continued bickering, trying to figure out what to do next. Conal said nothing. He was casting around, bent low to the ground, apparently trying to pick up the bruxsa's trail.

That seemed like an exercise in futility to me. The bruxsa could turn into bats and fly, after all. She wasn't likely to go hiking through the bush just to do us a solid and leave a nice trail we could follow. I folded my arms and watched him, wondering how long it would take before he caved and asked me to use my despicable magic again to help him.

Eventually, the vampire argument tapered off, and they all stood watching Conal doing his sniffer dog impression. Finally, he straightened and looked back at us.

"We'll pick up her trail and find her again. She can't have gone far; she's wounded."

"Really?" I said. "That's good news. Who wounded it?"

He gave me a dry look. "You did. I couldn't get close enough with my sword and none of the vampires even managed to touch it." He swept a hard gaze across the assembled vampires, his expression saying quite clearly what he thought of their abilities in a fight.

"We should wait for the other Soldiers," Grumpy Dracula insisted.

"Man, this guy is really getting on my nerves," Ariel said. She was standing beside me, arms crossed just like mine. I probably had the same infuriated expression on my face, too.

"At least talk to the queen before we follow this wolf into an ambush," another vamp said darkly.

"Oh, come on," I said, fed up. "Who do you think's going to ambush you? The bruxsa? Because she looked in such good shape a minute ago. I'm sure setting up an ambush is the only thing on her mind right now. What are you so afraid of? It's broad daylight and you're *vampires*. You're all supernaturally speedy and strong and all that good stuff. The scary bruxsa isn't going to be able to sneak up on you. You'll see her coming."

"Probably smell her, too," Ethan added. "You hit her so hard with that flame she'll smell like a pork barbecue."

"He's making me hungry," Ariel complained.

You don't eat, I thought impatiently.

"It's the thought that counts."

"Ethan, ring the queen," Raquel said. "It's the only thing that will shut him up."

"I'm not waiting," Conal said. "The trail will go cold."

"Seriously?" They were like a bunch of kids in desperate need of an adult to organise them. "You don't think you'll be able to follow the overwhelming scent of pork barbecue? What kind of a wolf are you? Just slow your roll for half a minute and let Ethan make a call."

He folded his arms, mirroring my posture. "Fine. Since you asked so nicely."

Ethan pulled out his phone, shaking his head. The other vampires stood around in a loose circle, unashamedly preparing to eavesdrop on the call. Maybe they didn't trust Ethan to report what the queen said truthfully.

He rolled his eyes at them all standing there staring at him and hit the speaker button so we could all hear.

Nessa seemed more interested in the account of my magic fire than in the loss of Vaughn. Perhaps he was another pain in her butt like Miguel had been. She was particularly intrigued to hear that I'd managed to wound the bruxsa, since the monsters were usually so hard to hit. Hence all the vampires standing around looking unenthusiastic about the prospect of facing the bruxsa again. But the queen, it turned out, was keen to proceed. I couldn't help a sneaking suspicion that she was as concerned with finding out the extent of my power as she was with catching the bruxsa.

Ethan hung up. "Looks like you're up, Soldier."

Conal nodded and turned towards the trees. The rest of us followed.

He stopped and glared at me. "Not you."

"Why not? You might need my help. I could track the bruxsa with magic if your nose fails you, and I'm the only one who managed to hit her before."

"And now she's wounded, so we can handle it from here." He nodded at the assembled vampires. "Let's go."

He plunged into the bush, followed by the vampires, and was soon lost to sight. Only Raquel stayed with me.

"So rude," I said, still staring after him, but when I made to follow, Raquel stopped me with a hand on my arm.

"Leave it. He's doing you a favour."

"But my magic's useful!" And there was a sentence I never thought I'd say. "It's stupid for him to ignore it because he hates cartomancers."

She raised an eyebrow, an amused look on her face.

"You really think that's what he's doing? I forget how young you are."

"What's that supposed to mean?"

"It's obvious to anyone with two functioning brain cells to rub together that Soldier Boy likes you, whatever the company line on cartomancers is."

I opened my mouth to object that he most certainly did *not*, then paused. "Wait. Are you calling me stupid?"

"Just naïve. It's cute, really."

"I thought I liked her," Ariel said, "but now I'm not so sure. *I'm* the only one who's allowed to call you stupid."

Hush.

Aloud, I said, "So you're saying he's trying to protect me from the bruxsa? Funny, *he* was the one who needed protecting down in that cellar. I saved his life."

Raquel snorted. "Are all humans this slow to catch on, or is it just you? He's not protecting you from the bruxsa, he's trying to protect you from his buddies. The other Soldiers. They'll be here soon, you know. He's giving you the chance to disappear before they get into witch-hunting mode."

I paused. "Oh."

"You know, I always liked him," Ariel said.

Liar.

"But the bruxsa ..." I trailed off. "I need to make sure Kurranderra is safe."

Raquel raised that haughty eyebrow at me again. "Bruce Wayne died and made you Batman? I never heard that it was your responsibility to keep this town safe. How about we focus on keeping *you* safe first?"

"She's got a point," Ariel said. "You can't save anyone if you're wolf snacks."

All valid points. I was itching to finish off the bruxsa, but maybe that was my excitement over my suddenly new and improved magic talking rather than the good sense my aunties had always drummed into me. And speaking of aunties ...

"I guess we should meet up with Ling and Ivy at Bethany's place. They need to be out of sight, too, before the Soldiers arrive."

"Good plan," Raquel said. "Let's—"

I held up one finger as my phone started to vibrate in my back pocket. I dug it out and saw the caller was Bethany.

"Beth? What's up?"

"Sunday ..." Her voice quivered.

"Are you crying?" My heartbeat kicked up a notch. "What's wrong?"

"They took them!" she wailed.

I stiffened, dread seizing me. "Who took who?"

"The Soldiers. They took your aunts!"

22

*B*ethany opened her front door and practically fell into my arms. Raquel shoved us both unceremoniously inside and locked the door behind us. My heart was still pounding from the wild rush to get here, and a sick feeling was lodged in the pit of my stomach.

Bethany shook like a leaf in my arms, and I guided her to a chair in her living room. She lived in an old farmhouse five minutes out of town, and I'd pushed Bugsy to the limit to do it in four. Raquel had insisted I park around the back of the house, out of sight from the road.

"Tell me what happened," I said.

Bethany nodded, calmer now than she'd been on the phone, though she hugged her arms around herself and her face was even paler than usual.

"We were just about to leave your place, but Ivy decided she needed to use the bathroom. So Ling and I were standing outside waiting for her when three cars pulled up. Big black SUVs with those tinted windows so you can't see who's inside. And then all these guys piled out. Ling set fire to one of them, but there were too many."

I really needed to find out how Ling was prepping her fire spell so fast. She'd never been so quick on the draw before.

Assuming I ever saw Ling or Ivy again.

I took a deep breath, trying to calm myself. Panicking wouldn't do my aunts any good.

"How many were there?" Raquel asked, cool as ever.

"Four in each car. So, twelve. They made us go inside again, and they grabbed Ivy too. One of them—he was shorter and muscly, and his hair was shaved really short—said 'that's not her' when he saw Ivy." She gazed at me with wide, frightened eyes. "Like he was expecting you to be there."

I glanced at Raquel. "Probably Liam."

She nodded.

"He seemed to be in charge," Bethany continued. "His eyes were glowing yellow. It was freaky."

"He's a Soldier, same as Conal. I think that happens when they're angry. What did Ling and Ivy do?"

"Nothing. They had two big guys holding each of them, and another guy came and tied their hands behind their backs."

"They found cards in Ivy's pocket, and the Liam guy said that Ling and Ivy must be part of the same coven." She gulped. "And then they searched me. Ling spoke up then. She said, 'She's human. I don't know who she is, I was just asking directions.'"

That was pure Ling. Of course she would try to shelter

Bethany. My heart swelled with pride, even in the middle of my fear.

"So they let you go?" Raquel asked.

Bethany nodded. "They told me not to go to the police or they'd come back for me, and they wouldn't be so gentle next time. Then they tied me to a chair and took your aunties away."

"You managed to untie yourself?"

"I waited a while until I was sure they were gone, and then I started yelling. Your neighbour came in and untied me."

"Mr Garcia?" She was lucky he'd heard her; he was very hard of hearing.

She nodded. "He's very strong. He just tore the ropes in half."

That didn't sound like Mr Garcia at all, but that was a mystery for another time.

"Do you know what happened to Ling and Ivy?" I asked, all the urgency I felt in my voice. What if they were already dead? What if the Soldiers had taken them back to their headquarters?

She looked utterly miserable. "No. I'm sorry. By the time I got outside they were all gone. I got in my car and called you and drove straight home."

"That's okay." I sat down beside her and put an arm around her. "That was the best thing to do. There's nothing you could have done against twelve Soldiers."

Raquel nodded. "Together with Conal, that's thirteen wolves. That's a full Hunt. They mean business."

"Yeah." Every Soldier belonged to the same pack—just

one big happy murderous family—but they usually worked in pairs. A full Hunt was reserved for the biggest threats. "I'm just not sure if Liam's more focused on me than the bruxsa." I looked at Bethany again. "Did they say anything else while they were there? Anything that might give you a clue to where they've taken my aunts?"

"No. They didn't really talk among themselves."

"Probably the motel or wherever they're staying," Raquel said. "They won't want to leave the area until they've dealt with the bruxsa."

I got out my phone again and rang Conal, but it went straight through to voicemail. He'd probably switched it off while he was tracking the bruxsa.

"It's me," I said after the beep. "Call me when you get this. Your buddies have kidnapped my aunts."

Raquel sat in a floral armchair opposite me, crossing her leather-clad legs gracefully. "I'm sure your aunts are safe for the moment. If they'd meant to kill them, they wouldn't have taken them prisoner. They would have done it straight away."

"Do you think so?" That made me feel a little better. Maybe there was still time to find them. Then my shoulders sagged as another thought occurred to me. "Maybe they want to burn them at the stake. That used to be their favourite means of execution."

Bethany was looking green, but Raquel shook her head. "They've moved on from that. I hear they have more modern methods these days."

"If that's supposed to be reassuring, it isn't." I leapt up, unable to sit still any longer. "We need to find them."

"The queen sent me to keep you safe," Raquel said. "I don't think going looking for twelve Soldiers is the ideal way of doing that."

I lifted my chin in challenge. "Are you going to try to stop me?"

"I'm just saying we need to be smart about this."

"I can help," Bethany said.

Raquel rolled her eyes, but I appreciated the offer. Bethany might not be able to do much against the supernatural forces ranged against us, but I wasn't about to discount her help. I couldn't afford to refuse any offer of assistance.

I dropped my head into my hands, thinking. Where was Ariel? She'd been at the old Rogerson place with us, but she'd disappeared after Bethany's phone call and I hadn't seen her since. Was it too much to hope that she was off doing something useful instead of just randomly disappearing?

Regardless, I couldn't count on her. Her appearances were too sporadic. But I still had my magic, and that seemed like the way to go. It wasn't as though the Soldiers didn't already know I had it—I might as well use it. Otherwise we could be driving all over the mountains looking for them.

And I had the terrible feeling that Ling and Ivy didn't have long.

I lifted my head. "I'll track them with magic, the way I did with the bruxsa."

Bethany gazed at me anxiously. "Won't those men be able to smell the magic and find *you*?"

She seemed thoroughly spooked by the Soldiers, and I could hardly blame her. I glanced at Raquel, but she only shrugged. Likewise, I didn't know how sensitive Soldiers' noses were. How much was too much?

Liam had managed to find me the night I'd first hunted the bruxsa with Ethan and Raquel. He would have caught me, too, if Ethan hadn't come back when he did and scared him off. He hadn't wanted to take on a vampire just to get to me—he'd preferred to wait until he could get me alone. Maybe having Raquel along would help discourage him this time, too.

Except this time, he had a full Hunt of his buddies with him.

"I'll be careful," I said. "I'll keep it small. They'll never even know I'm there."

Raquel gave me a look that questioned my ability to do any such thing. "Just don't set off any fireworks this time."

23

I was getting lots of practice at tracking spells lately.

For this one, I laid the Seven of Air in my circle to represent secrets and skullduggery, next to the Four of the same suit, which represented the Soldiers' safe place. Crossing them both, I laid the Two of Water, to represent Ling and Ivy and our deep connection. The Ace of Earth grounded the spell.

As I blew on the cards to activate the magic, I focused on keeping a tight rein on my power. Raquel was right— we didn't want any repeats of the giant searchlight of magic that had accompanied my last attempt.

"Small and subtle," I muttered to myself as I let a trickle of magic seep into the cards in their circle. "Small and subtle."

Raquel flinched as though she expected the opposite, but I'd managed to keep a lid on it this time. I could feel the pressure of the magic yearning to be released, as if I were a dam with a tiny hole in it. Only a thin stream was making it through, but the rest of the water was still there.

It blew my mind that there was this much power just waiting to be used. Where had it all come from? Why now? Something had taken the lid off my magic, exposing a well deeper than I'd ever dreamed. I'd have to talk to Ling and Ivy as soon as I got them back. Maybe they could help me figure it out.

To my eyes, the magic was a bright thread of gold that looped into the sky then bent towards the east, but judging by how both Raquel and Bethany were still watching the cards expectantly, I was the only person who could see it.

Well, that was an improvement over last time.

I stood up from my circle in the dirt of Bethany's driveway. "Let's go."

Raquel straightened. "You've got something?"

"Yep." I squinted into the distance, following the golden thread as far as I could see. "We'll take Bugsy."

"What do you want me to do?" Bethany asked. She'd had a cup of tea while I was preparing the spell and now seemed more like her usual self.

"Stay here and be safe," I said.

She frowned. "But I want to help. I can't sit here doing nothing while you're out risking your necks."

"No offence, but you're human," Raquel said, with more politeness than I'd come to expect from her. "There's not a lot you *can* do."

But Bethany wouldn't give up so easily. "But being human means that I'm safe from the Soldiers, right?

They're all about protecting humans. I can at least drive around and see if I can spot their cars."

"Fine," I said after a moment. "But lock your doors. Don't stop the car and don't get out. Just text me if you see them."

"Okay. I can do that."

Ariel popped into view as I was packing up my cards. Bethany screamed, and even Raquel jumped.

I scrambled to my feet. "Relax! It's just Ariel."

Bethany leaned forward, her eyes narrowed. "You're the one I saw in the bathroom mirror that time."

"Guilty as charged," Ariel said.

"I thought you were a ghost."

Ariel tossed her floating silver hair. "I'm way too good-looking to be a ghost."

"Not to mention alive," I said, giving her a warning look. *No showing off for Bethany*, I added. *She's already fragile.*

Ariel gave me a curt nod. "So, what's the plan?"

"You don't happen to know where the wolves took them, do you?"

"That way," she said, waving vaguely in the direction my golden thread was headed.

Just as I'd thought, she was no help at all.

I sighed. "Right. Well, Bethany's going cruising looking for wolves, and the three of us are following my tracking spell."

"And then we get to bust in and break some wolves' heads?" Ariel asked.

"Not quite," Raquel said drily.

"No busting or breaking until Ivy and Ling are safe," I warned. "Let's go."

Back behind the wheel of Bugsy, I felt a little calmer. At least I was doing something to help now, and I had a plan. Well, a proto-plan, anyway. It mainly consisted of *find aunties and rescue them*, which was admittedly short on details, but I figured I could work out the rest once we found them.

The spell led me all the way into Katoomba. Driving and keeping my eye on the golden thread at the same time was challenging, and Bugsy wandered out of her lane a couple of times. But Ariel couldn't drive, and I didn't trust Raquel to take the wheel either. In my experience, people who are virtually immortal don't take road rules as seriously as those of us who are a little more breakable, Conal Clarke being a prime example.

I didn't want to think about Conal Clarke, yet my mind kept serving up images of him willy-nilly: Conal smiling at me, the light of laughter in those beautiful green eyes. Conal looking fierce and feral as the black wolf, snarling and snapping on the floor of my apartment as he defended me from Liam. Conal wounded and exhausted, sacked out on my bed.

And, worst of all, the look of disgust on his face as he accused me of being a witch.

I mean, I'd known all my life that Soldiers hated us, but I'd never actually met a Soldier before. It was different knowing something in your head and actually experiencing it in real life. Now it was personal, a hatred I'd felt all the way to my bones. No one had ever hated me that much before—not even Louise Hammond that time I'd accidentally tripped her onstage in third grade. And for what? Just because I'd been born with an ability that I'd never asked for and had no choice in? Might as well hate me because my eyes were blue.

The fact that I'd spent a few daydreams on wondering how it would feel to kiss him—and even thought he might have been wondering the same once or twice—made the hurt cut deeper.

My own stupid fault. I should have known better. I *did* know better. Leopards didn't change their spots, and wolves didn't lose their teeth just because they had a nice line in flirtatious banter. History had shown that the Soldiers of the Light would never forgive us for being women with power, and a few smiles from a smoking hot werewolf didn't change that.

The pull of the magic in my chest was getting stronger. I could cry into my pillow all I wanted after I'd rescued Ling and Ivy. Right now, I had a job to do.

"I think we're getting close," I said, slowing Bugsy for a corner.

There was a motel halfway down the next block, one of the more modern ones in Katoomba. It had a restaurant that was supposed to be five-star, though I'd never been there, and even a swimming pool. Though why anyone would want a swimming pool in Katoomba, I wasn't sure. Even in summer, it didn't get that hot up here in the mountains.

I drove slowly past the sign with its improbable palm trees—also something you didn't see much of up here—

and watched the magic arch up over the entryway and disappear somewhere behind the main building.

"They're there." I parked further down the block and switched off the engine.

"What now?" Ariel asked. "Is it time for the head-breaking yet?"

"Not quite." I cast her a stern look, which she completely ignored. She was practically bouncing in her seat with excitement. "First we need someone to sneak in there and scout out the situation."

Ariel's hand shot up. "Ooh, pick me, pick me!"

"Won't they smell her?" Raquel asked. "She's made of magic, isn't she? I'll do it."

"Oh, sure," Ariel said. "Because no one will notice vampire smoke appearing out of nowhere."

"Ariel can do it," I told Raquel. It was true, Raquel couldn't make herself completely invisible the way Ariel could, and I didn't want to risk putting the wolves on high alert. "She'll be perfectly safe. The wolves smell the opening of the portal when a spell is performed, not the magic itself. Otherwise, Conal would have realised straight away I was a cartomancer, with Ariel all over the apartment. I don't think she has any scent at all."

"Yeah, baby, I'm the invisible woman," Ariel crowed.

Raquel rolled her eyes. "Pity you're not the inaudible woman."

"Don't let anyone see you," I said, to forestall an argument between them as Ariel drew breath.

"What do you think this is? Amateur hour?"

She disappeared, leaving a tense silence behind her.

My gaze roved between the rear vision mirror and the two outside mirrors. I was wound tight as a spring, expecting wolves to jump out of nowhere any minute. Would they have guards this far out from the motel? Surely not. But still, my shoulders stayed hunched up around my ears.

Seconds ticked by, the only sound the faint tapping of Raquel's long, red fingernails against her leather-clad leg. Maybe I wasn't the only one who was tense.

"Why do you think the queen was so sure we could take the bruxsa without waiting for the Soldiers to arrive?" she asked at length. "She seemed to think we were strong enough with just you."

"I don't know." My eyes followed a man walking towards the car from behind. He was muscled enough that he could have been a wolf, but he never once looked at Bugsy or altered his stride, apparently wrapped up in his phone. I let out a slow breath once he disappeared around the corner. "It's not as though I've ever shown any evidence of power before. Did you tell her about me helping you with the hunt for the elder?"

Her full red lips turned up in a brief smile. "The elder who turned out to be a bruxsa instead? No. I promised Ethan I wouldn't mention you, and I keep my promises."

"Well, the joke was on her, I guess. Trusting me cost her Vaughn."

Raquel laughed. "You know, maybe that's it. She never liked Vaughn much. Or maybe she just wanted to see if a witch and a wolf really could work together."

"If you keep calling me a witch, I'll start calling you a bloodsucking fiend."

Raquel smirked. "If the shoe fits ..."

"What shoe?" Ariel asked, suddenly appearing. "Are we going shopping? We could do a whole girls' thing with a shopping spree and a slumber party."

"No one over the age of eleven has slumber parties," I said. "What did you find? Are they there?" I swallowed a lump in my throat. "Are they safe?"

"Yep, they're there. And they're safe, but Ling looks *mad*, so I don't know if everyone *else* is safe. They're tied up in a room that's got, like, fifty wolves in it."

"*Fifty?*"

"Well, maybe ten. But it felt like fifty with them all pacing around looking like they were just jonesing to kill something. The place is crawling with Soldiers."

"Could you untie them?" Raquel asked.

"Not without turning solid, and somehow I don't think the wolves would stand around watching while I untied Ling and Ivy and waltzed out with them."

"Were they armed?" Raquel seemed to know all the right questions to ask. I was still stuck on my aunties being trapped in a room with a bunch of murderous Soldiers.

"I saw a couple of guns. But the Soldiers weren't all in human form. There were a couple there all furred up, watching Ivy and Ling. Like watchdogs. Watchwolves."

"That's bad," I said. "We don't want to start a gun fight."

Raquel nodded. "We need a distraction. If we can get some of them out of there, we'll have better odds."

I chewed my lip. I didn't like our odds if there was even *one* Soldier left in the room, but we had to do something. At least Ling and Ivy were still alive.

"I did get these, though," Ariel said.

She opened her hands. A Tarot deck lay in each one, both as familiar to me as my own.

"You're kidding me." I stared at her open-mouthed. "You picked them up?"

Her grin was bursting with pride. "Yep. Carried them all the way."

She'd never picked up anything before—not with her hands, at least. She could use the wind to hurl things around, but that wasn't the same thing.

"How did you manage to lift Ivy and Ling's Tarot decks from under the Soldiers' noses?" Raquel asked.

She grinned, enjoying our astonishment. "They were in the next room. The wolves have four rooms booked. They're all in the one where Ivy and Ling are now, but the decks were left in one of the empty ones, so I grabbed them when I was scoping the place out. I'm feeling so much stronger now it's easy to control who can see me and when I take physical shape."

"You're a legend," I breathed, taking the decks from her and hefting their familiar weight.

"I know. I'll be signing autographs later if you want one."

"So. A distraction," Raquel said, clearly impatient to move on. "Any ideas?"

"I could whip up a little somethin'-somethin'," Ariel said.

I glanced at the afternoon sun. "We should wait till it gets dark."

"Maybe we could get Ethan to tell them he's found the

bruxsa," Raquel suggested. "Most of them should clear out then."

That wasn't a bad idea. While I was considering it, my phone rang.

Conal was on the other end of the line. "I've got some bad news."

24

"Colour me not surprised," I said as I put my phone on speaker. "What is it now?"

The fact that he was still talking to me was good news, at least.

"Liam's just let me in on his genius plan to catch the bruxsa. You're not going to like it."

"Quit stalling and just tell me already. What's the plan? Human sacrifice?"

I'd meant it as a joke, but the awkward silence that followed clued me in.

"Wait, seriously? How is killing my aunts going to help him catch the bruxsa?"

"*He's* not killing them. He's leaving that to the bruxsa. He's going to use your aunts as bait to lure the bruxsa out of hiding."

My heart was pounding, but I forced myself to stay calm. "How's that going to work? Bruxsas don't have a weird cartomancer fetish like you wolves do."

He ignored the question. "The plan hinges on the full moon."

"What happened to midday?" Raquel asked, leaning closer to the phone.

"It's out of my hands," he said, and I could picture him shrugging, a frown on his handsome face. "Liam's been put in charge of the operation, and he says we're doing it his way."

"But the bruxsa's powers peak with the moon," Raquel said. "That's ridiculous."

"Liam says she'll be desperate to feed, to boost her power to the max. She knows we're after her, and she's injured, so she won't come out until the moon does."

"So you've found her again?" I asked.

"No, but the smell of blood will draw her."

I did *not* like the way this plan was shaping up, but I had to ask. "What blood?"

"He's going to cut your aunts." I must have made a small noise of protest, because he quickly added, "Not badly. Just a small cut. Enough so that the bruxsa will be drawn to the magic in your aunts' blood."

I shook my head. "Ivy said something about magic in our blood being attractive to bruxsas, but that doesn't make sense to me. Blood is blood. How can ours smell any different?"

"Call it DNA, then, if it makes you feel better," he said. "But I can tell you it will be irresistible to a bruxsa. She'll know it will make her even stronger."

"Even though she's hurt?"

"It could be enough to cure her."

"Then it's an even stupider plan than I thought!" I said hotly. "If the bruxsa manages to get to Ivy or Ling, it will be unstoppable."

"Hey, I didn't make the plan, I'm just telling you what Liam said."

"Can't you talk him out of it? Why can't you just track the bruxsa the normal way? There's got to be some benefit to being able to turn into a wolf. Use your stupid noses!"

"Liam's not listening to me, and he's got more than half the Hunt convinced I've gone over to the dark side. He tried to order me back to headquarters, but he's not my boss. He can't make me leave, but he's the Huntmaster on this now, and what he says goes."

I took a couple of deep breaths. Liam was a skid mark on the underwear of the universe. Someone should slice *him* open and leave him for bruxsa bait. But my dreams of vengeance would have to wait. Right now, Ling and Ivy were my only concern.

"Okay, tell me the rest of the plan."

"He's taking them up to the old Rogerson place. He thinks the bruxsa is most likely still in the area. Then at moonrise, he cuts them up a little and leaves them staked out in a nice open area, making a blood scent to lure the bruxsa in. The Hunt will mostly be hidden inside the house until the bruxsa arrives."

"And then what?"

"Then we strike when the bruxsa is distracted with your aunts."

Distracted with. That was a convenient little

euphemism for what the bruxsa would likely be doing to my aunts at that point.

"And after you've killed the bruxsa, what happens to Ling and Ivy? Assuming they survive the bruxsa attack?"

His voice was soft and reluctant as he said, "You know what happens, Sunday."

Yep. Liam would kill them with even more glee than killing the bruxsa, as if Ling and Ivy were just another kind of monster.

"Well, that's not happening," I said firmly. No way was I letting Liam and his pack of psychopathic wolves kill my precious aunts. "What time is moonrise tonight?"

"About five-thirty."

I glanced at my watch. So, less than three hours. That didn't leave me much time to come up with the genius plan that would pit me against thirteen wolves and somehow come out on top.

Well, maybe twelve wolves. I had to believe that Conal wouldn't actively work against me, even if he couldn't do a lot to help me. At least he was telling me all this. That was something.

"So, there's twelve other wolves besides you? No more?"

"Yep. Just the twelve. Most of them will be close by, inside the house, but Liam will have a few spread out on the property, well hidden, to watch for the bruxsa's approach and give us some warning."

"What are they going to do if they see her?" Ariel asked, loud enough for him to hear. "Howl? Cause that won't be obvious."

"Never mind about that," Conal said. "You have to get your aunts out now, in daylight."

"They're surrounded by wolves," I said.

"Wait until tonight," Raquel suggested. "It will be easier if we do it when the wolves are distracted by capturing the bruxsa."

"Right!" Ariel leaned forward between the seats, face alight with eagerness. "We can create a diversion and then they won't know where to look, with the bruxsa in the mix as well. It will be easier than trying to grab Ivy and Ling now, when the wolves are in a safe place and literally standing guard over them."

"I'll leave you to your planning, then," Conal said.

"Wait!" I wasn't too proud to beg, not if it helped save Ivy and Ling. "Won't you help us? You owe me a life debt twice over!"

Silence stretched at the other end of the phone. "I wish I could. But I can't betray the Hunt. Bad enough that I've told you all this."

He ended the call.

"So he'll just betray *me* instead?" I said bitterly into the silence.

Ariel patted my arm. "It's not like it's a *surprise* that Soldiers are lying, two-faced monsters who only care about themselves."

"You're right. It's just business as usual for them." I covered her hand with my own. She felt warm and solid and completely real. It was bizarre. Why was everything changing all at once? I felt like I couldn't catch my breath. I squeezed her hand. At least some of the changes were good.

I started the car and pulled out. No point sitting around so close to the wolves. Bethany's place would be far safer.

"So what's the plan?" Ariel asked as we left Katoomba. "I could create a tornado to distract the wolves. I reckon a few uprooted trees flying around would draw their attention fast enough. Especially if I could scoop up a wolf or two at the same time," she added darkly.

"You can do that?" Raquel asked, casting a surprised glance over her shoulder.

It was a bold claim. I'd never seen Ariel uproot a tree before, even in her wildest windstorms.

Ariel flexed her arms to show off biceps that, frankly, needed a lot of work before anyone could be impressed by them. She was a skinny wisp of a thing, even now that she seemed more corporeal. "I reckon I could chuck a house. I'm feeling *strong*, baby. Hey, maybe I *should* do that."

"Do what?" I glanced at her in the rear vision mirror. She had that expression she always wore when she was dreaming up mischief. That face had landed me in trouble countless times as a kid.

"Go all *Wizard of Oz* on their furry butts and pick up the whole house. Chuck the whole thing, wolves and all. Now *that* would be a distraction."

"Assuming you could even do that—and feeling stronger doesn't prove anything—that sounds like a bad idea. You could drop the house on Ivy or Ling, and we don't want *that* much similarity to *The Wizard of Oz*." I glared at her in the rear vision mirror. "No ding dong the witch is dead, thanks."

"I'm no engineer," Raquel said, "but I'm pretty sure real houses aren't as aerodynamic as the one in the movie. It wouldn't stay together. There'd be a pile of building material falling out of the sky."

Ariel got a mutinous look on her face. Now that she'd had the idea, she wanted to run with it.

"Let me think about it," I said, and silence fell in the car.

"Just a little tornado?" Ariel asked as we turned into Bethany's road.

I sighed. "The problem is that we don't want to do anything to scare off the bruxsa. We actually want it to be caught, remember?"

"And if the bruxsa is there, the wolves will be distracted by it," Raquel said.

"Not as distracted as if their house were *in the sky*," Ariel muttered.

"Let's focus on things that we're sure we can achieve." I pulled into Bethany's driveway and parked Bugsy around the back.

Bethany came out of the back door as soon as I switched off the engine. "Did you find them?" she asked.

I slammed Bugsy's door. "Yep. They're holding them at the Mountain Rest Motel in Katoomba."

I gave her a brief rundown of what Conal had told us, and her face paled.

"Thirteen Soldiers?" She looked at the three of us, and

I could see her doing the math and coming up short. "That's a lot."

"We have some resources," I said.

"To fight wolves?"

"I'll come up with something." I glanced at Raquel. "Will the vampires help us, do you think?"

"Officially, the queen won't stand against the Soldiers," she said.

"And unofficially?"

"I'm here, aren't I? I'll do what I can."

"Ethan will help, too," Bethany said, with complete and possibly misplaced confidence in her crush.

"Ethan's a great guy," I said, "but he's kind of in charge of the vampires the queen sent. Him getting involved might be considered an official stand."

I raised an eyebrow at Raquel, who shrugged. "Try and stop him."

"Won't you get in trouble with the queen?" I asked. "Both of you?"

"We can deal with that later."

She looked bored, as if she didn't care what we were talking about, but I felt a rush of gratitude knowing she was actually sticking her elegant neck out for me. Quite a long way out.

Bethany stopped at the back door and chewed her lip, fingers resting on the door handle. "There's something else."

"What's up?" My mind immediately went to ambushes and hostages. Were there wolves inside, waiting for

Bethany to deliver us to them on pain of some terrible threat? I took a deep breath, tensing for action.

"We have visitors. Friends of yours," she added quickly, seeing my reaction.

Ariel immediately blinked out of existence. As Bethany opened the door, she reappeared in the doorway, grinning hugely. "You're not going to believe who's here."

Was it Conal? Had he changed his mind about helping? I hurried inside, practically stepping on Ariel's heels in my eagerness to get to the lounge room and see.

"Sunday!" Mr Garcia said, rising unsteadily as I entered the room. Nicole was sitting on the lounge beside him, his walking stick propped between them. "You're the best day of the week!"

I stared at them, mouth open. What on earth?

"Mr Garcia," I finally managed. "And Nicole. This is unexpected."

I glanced at Bethany, as if she could make this make sense somehow. Why were my neighbours here, now of all times? They barely even knew Bethany.

"You'll have to excuse us," I said. "This isn't a good time for a visit."

"We're not here to visit," he assured me, a twinkle in his eyes. For the first time, I noticed they were the same deep blue as the beanie he always wore.

"That's right," Nicole said. "We're here to help."

25

She was serious, wasn't she? I stared into her determined eyes, totally at a loss.

"That's, um, really nice of you." I cast another uncertain look at Bethany. How had Nicole—and Mr Garcia, of all people—come to be here, offering help? Did they have any idea what they were even offering to help *with*?

"Those Soldiers are getting too big for their britches," Mr Garcia said firmly. "It's time someone stood up to them."

I blinked. "You know about the Soldiers?"

They weren't exactly a *secret*. Most humans had heard of them, but the Soldiers kept a very tight control over their image, and humans, if they thought about them at all, thought of Soldiers as *those nice men protecting us from monsters*.

Nicole nodded. "Going around persecuting perfectly decent people like your aunts for no reason. There are more monsters than ever before, but instead of focusing on that, they're pursuing this stupid vendetta. It's time the preternatural community took a stand."

"The preternatural community?" I felt like I was just repeating everything they said, but I didn't know how else to respond. I was getting a growing feeling that I had no idea who my neighbours were at all.

Mr Garcia started to laugh. "Look at her face! It's all right, Sunday, you don't have to pretend anymore. We've known all along that you're a cartomancer."

They had? But I'd never used my magic around them. I'd never shown it to anyone until the night I'd tried to help Ethan find the "elder". Now, all of a sudden, it seemed as though every vampire and his dog knew about it.

Nicole smiled. "Surely you knew we weren't human either?"

"Um ... no?"

"He's a bluecap, and I'm a dwarf."

My gaze went straight to Mr Garcia's beanie. I'd never seen him without it, even in summer, but I'd thought that was an old man's vanity in not wanting to show his balding head.

I sat down on one of Bethany's armchairs. "Wow, I feel stupid. You're a *bluecap*."

Of course he was. That was why he never took the stupid beanie off. Bluecaps always wore their hats—they were more than headgear to them. More even than a uniform. For every soul they saved, their hat turned a deeper blue. It was an intrinsic part of their magic, something they could no more go without than a vampire could go without blood.

And Mr Garcia's beanie was such a deep, *dark* blue. He must have saved a lot of people. Had he saved them from Soldiers?

I recalled him standing on his balcony this morning when my aunts rolled into town and Conal went all furry and feral on them, offering to come down and kick somebody's butt. I'd been touched by the offer, but I hadn't taken him seriously. He was a frail old man! What could he possibly do against a werewolf in his prime?

Probably quite a lot. Bluecaps were ridiculously strong. I looked into Mr Garcia's smiling blue eyes and realised that the whole *frail old man* thing was just an act. He probably did it to fit in better with the local human population.

I gasped as a thought occurred to me.

"You mean I've been taking your garbage bin out all these months for *nothing*?" I stared at him in outrage. "That thing weighs a ton! And you could probably lift it with one hand."

He burst out laughing. "I wondered when you'd wise up to that. But it was sweet of you to offer, and I didn't want to disappoint you."

"*Disappoint* me? What do you put in it? Rocks?"

"Sometimes," he admitted. "It's good for you to get a workout."

I turned my glare on Nicole. Her garbage bin was almost as heavy, and she was a dwarf. Dwarves were renowned for their strength.

She held up her hands, laughing. "Come on, I never asked you to take out my bin. You decided on your own that you were going for the Good Neighbour Award."

"Because *he's* a frail old man—or so I thought. And it seemed rude to put out two bins and leave the others."

"Sounds like a you problem," Ariel said, appearing on the couch next to Nicole.

"Oh, hello," Nicole said without batting an eyelid. "Who's this?"

I waved a hand in Ariel's direction. "My best friend. Nemesis. Pain in my—"

"Her better half," Ariel said firmly. "Hi, I'm Ariel. Nice to be corporeal enough to finally say hello."

"You've been around for a while, then?" Nicole asked. She was taking this very calmly.

"Years," Ariel said. "But no one else could see me until recently."

Mr Garcia studied her thoughtfully. "And what are you?"

Ariel grinned. "A party waiting to happen."

I rolled my eyes. "Ling thinks she might be an Air elemental."

Ling was barking up the wrong tree there, but I had nothing else to offer him.

"I like blowing things up," Ariel added. "Get it? *Blow* things up?"

Bethany gestured towards the kitchen. "I'm going to make some tea. I know *I* could do with a cuppa."

"Got anything stronger?" Mr Garcia asked with a wink.

"Like Type O?" Raquel added.

Bethany shot her a nervous glance and hurried out. "Just tea," she called from the kitchen.

Raquel took a seat and crossed one long, elegant leg

over the other. "So, what can a bluecap and a dwarf do against a full Hunt of Soldiers?"

"I don't know yet, but I know what we *can't* do," Nicole said. "And that's sit idly by while the Soldiers abduct people in broad daylight."

She sounded scandalised. I almost pointed out that it wouldn't have been any better if the werewolves had taken my aunties at night, but decided that wasn't a nice thing to say to someone who was offering help with something as dangerous as this.

"I'm not as fast as I used to be," Mr Garcia said. "By the time I realised there was a problem and got downstairs, they were already gone."

"Mr Garcia told me all about it after Bethany left," Nicole said. "We decided we had to come and offer our help."

"Do you know where they took your aunts?" Mr Garcia asked.

"They've got them in the Mountain Rest Motel in Katoomba at the moment," I said. "But Conal says they're planning to move them to the old Rogerson place tonight at moonrise."

"They're going to use them as bait to catch the bruxsa," Raquel said. "Typical fur-brained Soldier plan."

Mr Garcia frowned, his usually genial face taking on a fierce expression. "Trust Soldiers to come up with a plan that poses the least amount of risk to themselves at someone else's expense."

Nicole considered me thoughtfully. "Are you sure we can trust intelligence from this Conal character? He's the

Soldier who threw the tantrum at your place this morning, isn't he?"

That was one way to put it. I felt an irrational desire to stand up for Conal but reined it in. He was a big boy. He didn't need me to protect his honour.

"I trust him," was all I said. *Mostly.*

Bethany came back in carrying a tray and started handing out mugs. "Sorry, I mostly drink herbal tea. This was the only black tea I had. It's nothing fancy."

"We don't need fancy," Nicole said, accepting a mug.

"As long as there's plenty of sugar," Mr Garcia said. "Three teaspoons, please."

Bethany thrust a mug at Raquel, who accepted it, looking a little bemused to be included in the tea-drinking. Ariel got one, too, and she stared at the mug in a kind of shock.

"I've never drunk tea before." She took a hesitant sip, then pulled a face. "It's bitter."

"Three teaspoons of sugar for her, too," Mr Garcia said, happily ordering Bethany around in her own home.

"Okay," I said when everyone was settled with a mug. "We need a plan."

"Let's hit the motel," Nicole said.

Raquel shook her head. "There are too many wolves there."

"There'll be the same number of wolves at the old Rogerson place," Nicole objected. "Plus we'll have the bruxsa complicating things."

Raquel gave them a quick rundown of the situation at the motel. Mr Garcia looked thoughtful when she finished.

"Sounds like moonrise at the Rogerson house, then. Who do we have on the team?"

Were we a team? I looked around at their determined faces and warmth filled me. It felt good to be part of something. I'd been too long on the road with only Ling and Ivy and Ariel for company. *This* was why I wanted to settle in one place, and why Kurranderra was worth defending. Because of people like this.

"Just the six of us." I glanced at Raquel. "Plus maybe Ethan?"

She nodded. "Definitely Ethan. And a couple of the others won't be sorry to see the wolves get their butts handed to them, either."

"But will they actively work against them?" Mr Garcia asked.

"Not overtly. It would put the queen in an awkward position."

"Doesn't it put the queen in an awkward position if you and Ethan go against them?"

Raquel lifted one shoulder in a graceful shrug. "Not if we play our cards right."

26

$\mathcal{M}$ r Garcia and Nicole left to prepare for their part in the Great Auntie Rescue. I got up and paced around Bethany's living room, turning the plan over in my mind. We'd tried to account for different variables, but we all knew the truth—no plan survives encountering the enemy.

"You're going to wear a hole in Bethany's carpet," Ariel said finally, watching me pace.

"Yes, sit down," Raquel said, draping one pale hand dramatically over her forehead. "You're giving me a headache."

I snorted. "Vampires don't get headaches."

"Well, if we did, you'd be giving me one. Why don't you try to conserve some of that energy for tonight?"

"Yes," Bethany said. "You're welcome to use my bed if you want to take a nap."

I was way too wired for sleep, and the very idea of peacefully napping while my aunts were held captive by the Soldiers seemed obscene. "I'm good, thanks. Just going over the plan."

"Waste of time," Raquel said, yawning. "I hope you're good at thinking on your feet, because something's bound to go wrong, however much you plan."

That was exactly the problem. Cartomancy was a slow magic, requiring preparation and focus—just the things likely to be unavailable once the excrement hit the rotating cooling device. At least, that was the way it had always been. My magic seemed superpowered lately, but my strength was too new for me to be comfortable relying on it.

"I don't like to leave things to chance," I said.

Ariel grinned. "Yeah, she's not a chill person. Going with the flow gives her hives."

"You need to work on that," Raquel said. "Life is just one long series of disasters that screw up your plans."

I flopped into an armchair. "Gee, thanks for the pep talk. Don't give up your day job, because you'll never make it as a motivational speaker."

Bethany picked up the remote control. "Why don't we watch something while we wait?"

And that was how we ended up watching kids' movies to pass the time before taking on the might of the Soldiers of the Light. Probably the weirdest battle prep in the history of warfare.

"You wouldn't happen to have a sketch pad and some pencils I could borrow, would you?" I asked Bethany.

"Sorry. I can probably find a lead pencil and a note-book, though. Why?"

"Just a feeling."

I'd drawn and painted the major arcana many times in my teens, always hoping that *this* time I'd be strong enough to use them. That if only I made them beautiful enough, the magic would respond. I'd done them in pencils, watercolours, pastels and even oil paints. I'd done them in different styles. Different sizes. Nothing worked. The magic stubbornly refused to cooperate.

But now, it felt as though the magic was just in the next room, and all I had to do was open the door and walk through. It was waiting eagerly for me, and it didn't care about beauty or stylistic choices. I had the distinct feeling that any spell I cast would work, even if I drew a bunch of stick figures on a bit of scrap paper.

Not that I would, of course.

I had my professional pride to think of. So while we watched Elsa sing about letting go, I sketched out a battered tower on a piece of paper I'd carefully cut to the same size as the rest of my cards. Lightning blasted the tower out of a stormy sky and monstrous waves lashed it. As I carefully shaded storm clouds I thought with quiet satisfaction about the traditional meanings of the Tower card. Sudden, disastrous change. Violent upheavals. Destruction of the very foundations that were thought to be so secure.

"Why are you smiling like that?" Raquel asked. "You look like you're thinking evil thoughts."

"Just dreaming of the future," I said.

I was putting the finishing touches on my new card when Mr Garcia and Nicole returned. They didn't bat an eyelid at finding us all sprawled in front of the TV, though Mr Garcia did complain that no one had saved him any popcorn.

I thought my anxiety would skyrocket as the clock ticked down to go-time, but I was surprisingly calm as five of us piled into Bethany's car. Bethany was the only human, so she wasn't coming with us, just providing transport. Ariel would meet us once she'd scoped out what the wolves were doing.

Mr Garcia directed Bethany to an unremarkable patch of bushland on Ridge Road. A fire trail cut through it, a little overgrown but still passable. She pulled off the road and stopped on the trail. The only sound when she cut the engine was the screech of cockatoos in the trees and something that sounded like a chainsaw in the distance.

"Does everyone know what they have to do?" I asked. I was squashed between Raquel and Nicole in the back seat.

Everyone nodded, and Mr Garcia reached over to pat my knee. "Don't look so frazzled. It will be all right, you'll see."

I wasn't so sure, but I was grateful for the encouragement. I looked around and saw nothing but determination on their faces, and my heart welled with gratitude. This was no picnic we were walking into, and these people were risking a lot. It was good to have friends.

I couldn't help thinking of Conal. It was too much to hope that he could have been a friend. We were too different, and four hundred years of history stood between us. But it would have been good to have him on board. I hated the idea that I might have to face him as an enemy.

Mr Garcia opened the door and got out. "Meet me here," he said to Bethany.

She nodded, and we watched him walk down the fire trail a little way. He stopped by a towering outcrop of rock and gave us a jaunty little wave, then slipped behind a boulder and disappeared.

"Do you think the tracker will work?" Bethany asked anxiously.

"We'll find out soon enough," I said, resisting the urge to pull out my phone and check the app. The shadows were lengthening, and the need to get moving was making me twitchy. I wanted to see my aunts *now* and make sure they were okay.

"Even if it doesn't, a bluecap never gets lost underground," Nicole said. "He'll find the right place, don't you worry."

"I'm more worried about *me* finding *him*," I said. Not to mention my ability to pull off the level of magic that the plan required. My magic had been like a fire hose lately, so chances were better than they would have been a week ago, but the power was too new to feel reliable.

However, the alternative was letting the wolves have my aunts, and that simply wasn't on, so my magic would just have to do as it was damn well told. I folded my arms over my chest, squashing a weird sensation that fluttered behind my rib cage. I felt as jumpy and wired as if I'd mainlined a dozen cappuccinos, my heart beating an erratic rhythm in my chest. Nerves, I supposed. Only a madwoman *wouldn't* feel nervous about going up against a full Hunt.

Well, half a Hunt, hopefully. Maybe less. Assuming the plan worked.

The cockatoos screeched again, and a flight of them darted through the trees, a flash of white against the green. Bethany checked her watch, trying to be surreptitious about it.

"Ariel will be here soon," I said, and she nodded and looked out the windscreen.

Silence fell as we waited. Tonight was a full moon, which meant the moon would rise at sunset. I chewed my lip and tried to take calming breaths. My brain knew that we still had plenty of time, but my gut was churning, done with waiting.

Everyone but Raquel jumped when Ariel materialised in the front seat Mr Garcia had left vacant. Bethany even let out a little squeak.

"Where are the wolves?" I asked.

"Five of them inside the Rogerson house," she said. "Two outside near the fountain. Another two in the trees— one down at the bottom of the driveway near the entry, and the other out the back of the house. The rest are too far away to be a problem."

Raquel leaned forward. "And the vampires?"

"Also on watch among the trees. They're spread out in a loose circle around the house in a nice little bruxsa early warning system."

"Did you see Ethan?" Bethany asked.

"Not only saw him but spoke to him. He's on watch near the fountain. I filled him in on the plan."

So far so good. I was glad Ethan was all in. The other

vampires would follow his lead. "That wolf stationed at the bottom of the driveway is a nuisance," I muttered. "We'd make a lot less noise coming up the driveway than wandering through the bush."

"Leave him to me," Raquel said.

Ariel's eyes lit up. "Are you going to—" She curled an index finger at each corner of her mouth in imitation of fangs and made biting motions.

Raquel's lip drew up in a sneer. "I don't bite animals. Not even pretend ones like the Soldiers."

"Are they all in wolf form?" I asked Ariel. Men would be slightly easier to deal with.

"The ones in the house are, and the ones in the bush. The two by the fountain are in human form. One of them's that loser Liam. He's got a sword."

My heart lurched until I recalled Conal saying it was easier to kill a bruxsa with a sword than as a wolf. "And where's Conal?"

"He's the other one by the fountain." Her mouth turned down in an unhappy line. "He's got your aunties."

So much for life debts and honour. I might have known a Soldier's word was worthless.

"Are they okay?" Bethany asked.

"Seem to be. Still tied up, though." Ariel opened her door. "We'd better take it on foot from here."

Raquel, Nicole, and I got out, too.

"Stay safe, guys," Bethany said.

I nodded. "You, too. Lock these doors."

I heard the clunk of the locks as we headed for the road. She should be too far away from the action for the wolves to take any notice of her, but there was still a bruxsa running around out here, and Bethany was vulnerable until Mr Garcia rejoined her.

No one spoke as we followed Ariel down the road in single file, keeping to the shoulder. A couple of cars passed, going the other way, but other than that we were the only ones out here.

But try convincing my brain of that. My skin crawled as if invisible ants were marching up and down my arms and crawling across my torso. The sun was low enough in the sky now that pools of shadow were forming under the trees, and I gave them sidelong glances as we passed, half-expecting a wolf to leap out at me. It was a relief when Ariel halted us.

"This is close enough." She looked expectantly at Raquel and made a shooing motion. "Off you go. Time to do your thing."

The Rogerson driveway, where the watchwolf was meant to be stationed, was just around the next bend in the road.

"My *thing*," Raquel said drily.

"Yeah. Whatever it is you're doing instead of the—" Ariel made the same stupid imitation of fangs with her fingers.

Raquel rolled her eyes. "I'm just going to walk right up to him and tell him he's been reassigned to around the back of the house."

I frowned. "What if he won't take orders from a vampire?"

"Then you do the thing?" Ariel asked hopefully.

"Then I take him down. Wolves are under the impression that they're stronger than vampires, but that's only because they haven't tested us."

"If you kill him, the Soldiers will hunt you forever," Nicole warned, looking troubled.

"Please. Do I look like an amateur? One look into my eyes and he'll go nighty-night and sleep for hours. No harm done."

So the rumours about vampire mind control were true. I mean, I knew Ethan had messed with me a little, but this was next level. Probably a good thing that they didn't spread that one around.

Raquel turned to smoke and disappeared into the gloom under the trees. For a moment, we stood there looking at each other.

"Guess I better go with her," Ariel said, and winked out.

I crouched and used a stick to draw a circle in the gravel of the shoulder. Time to work some cartomancy.

I laid out my cards, the same as I'd used before with the vampires, and drew in a series of deep breaths, trying to quiet my mind. My mind wasn't having any of it, convinced that something was watching us, and my skin crawled with tension. I scratched absently at my arms as I focused on the cards, trying to find that Zen state where they were all I could see.

Nicole shifted her weight from foot to foot, watching me. "Are you okay?" she asked when I looked up. "Nervous?"

"Itchy." But it wasn't quite an itch. Certainly, scratching

my arms made no difference. I was jittery, but not with nerves. "My focus is all over the place."

I shook my head and turned back to the cards. Ivy and Ling needed me. That thought helped me settle. Another couple of deep breaths, and I felt my magic bloom like a flower inside me. I tapped the Ace to activate the spell, and Nicole and I blinked out of existence.

"Whoa." Her disembodied voice sounded spooked. "That is so *strange.*"

I gathered up my cards and stood up, shoving them into my jacket pocket. "You get used to it."

"Really?"

"No." I laughed. Our voices sounded weirdly muffled. "This is only the second time I've done this. It's still crazy."

"It's wild. I can't see you *at all.*"

"We'll have to be quiet when we get closer, because the wolves will still be able to hear us."

"And smell us." She sounded nervous.

"Let's hope Raquel can get rid of the one by the entrance."

"Fingers crossed."

I nodded, though she couldn't see me. "Let's go. Wait. Take my hand so we don't lose each other."

After some groping around, we found each other's hands and moved down the road in silence. How long until the moon rose? The trees that leaned over the road hid the sinking sun from view. Impatience bubbled inside me, along with a nagging worry that we'd arrive too late for Ivy and Ling.

No one challenged us as we turned in to the Rogerson

driveway. No wolves sprang snarling from the trees that lined it, so Raquel had done her job—one way or the other. The concrete of the driveway was cracked and pitted. Weeds grew up from the cracks, gradually forcing them wider. Our steps slowed as we tried to move silently, and the driveway felt a million miles long.

I bit my lip as we rounded the curve and the house came into view, as faded and decrepit as last time I'd been here. But last time my aunts hadn't been sitting on the dusty ground next to the fountain, hands tied behind their backs, secured to a stake that had been driven into a crack in the concrete. Liam stood a few paces away, a sheathed sword hanging at his side. I couldn't see Conal.

Ling looked like she had a bruise on her cheek, though from this distance I couldn't be sure. Nevertheless, rage rose inside me, and my hands clenched into fists. How dare the Soldiers touch my aunt?

If they'd hoped to cow her with violence, it hadn't worked. She was glaring at Liam's back with such intensity it was a wonder he wasn't feeling as itchy and uncomfortable as I was.

Ivy was staring into the trees, a look of boredom on her face. Her back was straight. She was as uncowed as Ling. Pride at the fighting spirits of my aunts filled me. They had no way of knowing that help was on the way, but they refused to show fear. I hoped their attitudes bugged the snot out of Liam.

I hoped all sorts of things for Liam, in fact, none of them nice. If the bruxsa chose to make a snack of him, I wouldn't be shedding any tears.

As Nicole and I drew closer, Conal came out of the house. He was still wearing the casual shirt and faded jeans I'd last seen him in, but something in the way he held himself had changed. He stood straighter, moved more warily.

There was the real Soldier. He'd been hiding under the charming guy who'd cooked me breakfast. Hiding so well that I'd almost been taken in, but I knew better now.

"Moon's up in ten," Conal said, and his voice had changed, too. Now he was all business, with no hint in his tone of the laughter that had always seemed to lurk close to the surface.

Liam nodded. "Let's begin."

27

*L*iam closed the distance between him and the fountain and stood glaring down at my aunts.

Ling glared right back. "Cat got your tongue, wolf?"

In answer, he drew a small knife from a sheath hidden inside his shirt. I must have jerked in shock, because Nicole's hand tightened warningly on mine.

I swallowed hard and tried to calm my racing heart. Conal had said the wolves planned to use Ling and Ivy as bait for the bruxsa. Liam was only going to cut them.

Not for the first time, I longed for the kind of instant power that would allow me to smite this sucker on the spot. But that kind of magic belonged in fantasy novels. Cartomancy had never been like that.

"You'll be singing another tune when the bruxsa finds you." Liam bent down and flicked the knife casually across Ling's cheek, opening a shallow cut. Ling didn't react. She just stared at him, a challenge in her dark brown eyes. "The taint in your blood will call to it, and your black magic won't be able to save you then."

He looked like he savoured the prospect of watching them get attacked by a monster.

"You really ought to see a psychologist," Ivy said thoughtfully. "They might be able to help you deal with your mummy issues."

He pulled back his arm as if to slap her, but Conal's voice stopped him. "We should gag them in case their screams attract attention."

Liam glared at Ivy a minute longer, leaning threateningly over her. "Do it."

He stalked away, and Conal produced two lengths of cloth from his pocket that looked like bandages out of a first aid kit. He tied one around Ivy's head with a practised hand. Ling spat at him before he got hers on, but he wiped his face without comment.

I seethed with rage, but Nicole tugged me towards the trees and the remnants of a garden mingled with the natural bushland. We tucked ourselves in behind the low-hanging branches of a massive rhododendron, close enough to have a clear view of the fountain but well hidden from the wolves.

I mean, obviously we were well hidden. We were invisible. But soon enough I'd have to drop the spell—I'd need all my power for what I was about to attempt.

Only ten minutes until the moon rose. We were almost out of time for the Great Auntie Rescue. But I was planning on waiting until the Soldiers were well and truly occupied with other things before losing the protection of invisibility.

Conal ostentatiously tested Ling and Ivy's bonds, checking that they were tied fast to the stake. That jerk. I couldn't believe I'd ever fancied him.

I shut my eyes for a moment, pained. Dammit, I still fancied him.

"Get into position," Liam said impatiently.

Conal headed for an overgrown hedge that had once shielded an ornamental garden, dropped to his stomach, and wriggled his way under it. Liam took up a position roughly opposite, hidden among a dense stand of bamboo.

Silence descended, and I released the invisibility spell. Nicole gave my hand an encouraging squeeze before she let go, and I felt oddly comforted. I gazed through the leaves at my aunts, sitting bound and gagged by the cracked, dry fountain. How long since the wolves had given them any water? From here I could see that it *was* a bruise purpling on Ling's cheek, which looked swollen. The gag must be hurting her. Conal better not have tied it too tightly or I'd kick him halfway from here into next week. Stupid wolf.

They were all stupid. All this because some long-ago wolf had gotten his knickers in a twist over a woman being better than him. We should be working together against the actual monsters like the bruxsa, not fighting amongst ourselves.

Ling looked even tinier than usual, sitting in the dirt next to Ivy. She didn't even have her cards. If the bruxsa really was drawn by the smell of her blood, she'd have no way to defend herself.

I breathed out slowly and checked the position of the sun. Only the barest sliver was still visible. Almost time for the Great Auntie Rescue to kick off. I hoped Ariel was ready.

Nicole had her phone out, checking the app she'd downloaded at Bethany's house. She tilted the screen towards me so I could see, an anxious look on her face. There was no blip on the map on her screen.

I shrugged at her, as if to say, *well, we knew it was a long shot.* Mr Garcia had been living in this area for a very long time, before there'd even been a town called Kurranderra. Before there'd even been white people in this country, in fact. In that time, he'd built a network of tunnels all through the limestone, enlarging natural caves, delving deep in search of the silver he loved. Bluecaps loved mines, and if there were no miners to create them, they would happily do the work themselves.

Bethany had given him her tracker button. It was meant to help you find your keys, but it would show the location of anything you attached it to on the accompanying app. It was currently in Mr Garcia's pocket. He was somewhere beneath our feet in those sprawling mines of his. The hope had been that the app would help us pinpoint his location before I did my big party trick, but the technology had failed us—not surprisingly, considering how much rock and earth was dampening the signal right now. The makers of the tracker probably hadn't intended it to find your keys fifty feet underground.

I scratched my arm—the jittery, itchy feeling was worse than ever—and watched the last sliver of sun sink behind the trees to the west. There was no sign of the moon yet towards the east. It might just have risen, but we wouldn't be able to see it until it climbed above the trees. My legs twitched with the need for action. I didn't know how Nicole could stand so still. Maybe it was a dwarf thing. She was planted like stone, as immovable as the mountain itself.

The wind sighed through the trees, stirring the leaves all around us.

Are you ready? Ariel whispered in my mind.

Bring it on, I replied. *Let's do this!*

Something moved in the trees opposite us, not far from where Conal was lurking underneath the hedge—something dark and fluttery, as if the shadows themselves were creeping through the trees.

You should write horror, Ariel said. *What a creepy thought.*

A strange noise, somewhere between a moan and a whine, had Ling suddenly sitting up straight. Both my aunts turned towards the sound, their faces pale ovals in the gathering gloom.

My heart clenched. I wished there was some way to let them know what was happening. The shadows coalesced into a vaguely humanoid shape that stopped where it was still shielded by the trees from full view.

I knew it was Ariel in disguise, but I still felt a thrill of horror when the thing finally stepped out of the trees. She had the bruxsa down to a T. The elongated limbs, the grey, leathery skin, the rags that hid a body too thin and malformed to be human. And the face! That was *definitely* not human—the eyes red with no whites, huge above a mere slit for a nose and a gaping maw of a mouth set with jagged teeth.

"That's ... that's Ariel, right?" Nicole breathed, barely audible. Now her stillness seemed more like she was frozen in place by terror than any dwarvish oneness with the mountain.

"Yes." Thank goodness Nicole could see her. Ariel had been confident that she could now control who saw her and when, but it was a relief to have that confirmed.

Nicole tore her horrified gaze away to glance once more at her phone, but the app stubbornly refused to show us Mr Garcia's location. It didn't matter. My spell either worked and I found him in the process, or it didn't and his whereabouts made no difference.

But I *really* hoped it worked.

The Ariel bruxsa crept cautiously out of the treeline and inched across the open ground towards the fountain, bent almost double. Her eyes were fixed on my poor, terrified aunts, and I turned my own gaze away, hating to watch them suffer. Besides, it was time for my next spell.

Step Two of the plan called for the biggest spell I'd ever attempted—the biggest one I'd ever heard of, in fact, and that was only in cartomancy legend. Was it a risk to base our whole rescue plan on an untried spell that I had very little basis for believing I could actually pull off?

You bet your sweet bippy it was.

I crouched down and drew a circle in the soft, loamy

earth. In my defence, my power lately had literally been lighting up the sky. If anyone could pull this off, I felt comfortable that it would be me. All I had to do was ignore the little voice inside me that was putting up a trembling hand and saying, *Excuse me, you want me to do WHAT??*

I laid my new Tower card down in the very centre of the circle. It was the first major arcana card in my deck, and I couldn't be prouder of it if I'd spent a month painting it. My power until now had barely been enough to move the needle with the minors; to think of trying the majors had been a joke.

Looked like I got the last laugh after all.

It might only be a pencil sketch on a piece of paper torn from one of Bethany's lined notebooks, but I could feel the power lying dormant in my rough Tower, ready to be unleashed on the unsuspecting Soldiers.

The usual Tower showed a tower struck by lightning, the top of it destroyed and people falling from the wreckage. Instead of people, my version showed two wolves hurtling through the sky. One had a grey coat like Liam. The other was pale. Even in my anger I hadn't wished that kind of destruction on the black wolf.

The Tower stood for plans derailed, for sudden, unexpected disasters, for reversals and upheavals. I had a very specific kind of upheaval in mind today, and I held it firmly in my thoughts as I laid the Ace of Earth across the Tower card.

The Ariel bruxsa had reached my aunts. Liam would be congratulating himself on the success of his plan and getting ready to spring his trap. I closed my eyes and emptied my mind of all thought except the brutal reversal of his fortunes.

Power hovered just out of reach, stubbornly resisting my call. I took a deep breath. There was no use forcing it. Magic was like a skittish horse dancing away from the bridle. I had to lure it in with sugar lumps.

I let my shoulders relax and sank down on my haunches. My right hand tapped the cards, feeling the vibrations of power in the tingle in my fingertips. I focused on the feel of the earth beneath my other hand and imagined sinking down into it, past the loamy soil and the earthworms, through the layers of rock until I found the dark caverns and tunnels of Mr Garcia's mine, laid out like a beautiful spiderweb.

I sensed something, a speck of energy—Mr Garcia himself?—and suddenly, magic bloomed inside me. I thought I might explode from trying to hold in all that power.

I opened my eyes. I was a fire hose bursting with water, waiting to be aimed at the fire. Fists clenched, I reined the power in, curbing its eagerness to be free until the right moment. We weren't quite there yet.

Ariel had circled my aunts so that she stood with her back to the house, bent over them. They had scrambled around to face the threat, though there wasn't much they could do.

The sniffing is a nice touch, I told her.

You like it? Her mental voice sounded self-satisfied. *What is he waiting for? I could lick them, I suppose. Maybe break out into an interpretive dance. Should have worn a T-shirt with "kick here" on the back.*

Liam would be waiting for the bruxsa to actually attack Ling and Ivy, I realised. He wanted to wait until the monster was distracted by feeding before rushing it. We couldn't have that. In fact, the longer Ariel delayed, the more his suspicions might be aroused. She looked every inch a bruxsa, but bruxsas didn't wander around staring at their helpless victims. Time to give him a nudge.

I opened my fist and released just a smidgen of the power I was holding. A rumble filled the air, and the ground shook as if an enormous truck had just driven past. The Ariel bruxsa did a nice job of acting alarmed, head up, eyes darting every which way looking for the threat.

Was that you? she asked. *I nearly peed my pants.*

Nice. Start moving, as if you're going to run away.

I'm getting to that, she said. *You can't rush artistry.*

You remember there's a real bruxsa out there somewhere, don't you? One that will probably be attracted by the scent of Ling's blood? Let's hurry this along.

She grumbled, but backed away from the Dynamic Duo hesitantly, eyes rolling like a skittish horse. She managed to back herself closer to the house, too, offering what I hoped would be irresistible bait.

Come on, I urged Liam. *What are you waiting for?*

The Ariel bruxsa cast a longing glance at the captives, then took another step towards the trees. Clearly, her nerve was failing. I shook the ground again to hurry it along.

That did it. I didn't hear or see a signal, but suddenly

wolves burst from the house, flooding out to cut off the bruxsa's escape. Conal surged up from under the hedge, and Liam leapt out, too, sword in hand.

But before the wolves could close their circle, the bruxsa took a mighty leap over the heads of two snarling wolves and made it to the safety of the trees. The wolves streamed after it.

"Guard the prisoners," Liam shouted, and two wolves peeled off, heading back towards the fountain.

Conal stopped there, too, watching Liam disappear into the shadows of the forest.

Two more shadows drifted inconspicuously across the ground towards my aunts. Conal and the wolves were still watching the trees, so they didn't see them. Ling did, and her eyes narrowed. She knew what they were.

Some of the tension left my body, though I still felt as though I'd drunk a bucketful of caffeine. A sliver of moon was visible above the trees to the east now. We'd timed it just about right, and so far, everything was going according to plan. It would have been nice if all the wolves had left, but I hadn't expected Liam to leave Ling and Ivy completely unguarded while they all hared off into the distance chasing Ariel. Only two wolves to face was probably the best we could have hoped for—assuming Conal wouldn't actively try to stop us.

I started counting in my head, wanting to give the wolves a good, long head start before executing the next step. The shadows lurking around Ling and Ivy bided their time, too, hugging the ground so they wouldn't be seen.

I was up to twenty-three when it all fell apart.

"Is that Ariel again?" Nicole whispered as a new darkness appeared at the edge of the woods, red eyes narrowing with hatred as it saw the wolves that stood between it and its prey.

My stomach sank. "No. That's the bruxsa."

28

riel! I called. *We need you back here. We've got company.*

More wolves?

The bruxsa.

Oops.

Yeah, big oops. For a moment, the tableau held. No one moved. The only sound was the low growling of the two wolves.

Time to bust out my big party trick. I released the magic into the earth and followed it down, feeling for the warm glow of Mr Garcia.

Found him! Power rushed out of me, and the ground shook and bucked like a bull at a rodeo. Nicole and I fell into a tangle of arms and legs, her head bumping hard into mine.

"Ow." I rubbed my skull as I scrambled up. Fortunately, I hadn't lost my grip on the spell.

A grinding noise like a truck dumping a load of rocks

blasted my ear drums. The ground pitched drunkenly as a crack formed, zigzagging from the fountain, past where I stood, and into the trees. My aunts scrambled away from it as it widened, the stake they were tied to having come loose in the upheaval. Conal tried to take Ling's arm to help her away, but she shrugged him off as if his touch were poison.

The wolves kept their feet more easily than the rest of us. They advanced on the bruxsa, though if they were growling, I couldn't hear it over the roar of rocks splitting and grinding together.

"I've got him," Nicole shouted excitedly in my ear, shoving her phone screen in my face. A blinking green dot had appeared, almost directly under our location.

The crack in the ground widened from a splinter into a yawning chasm. The ancient fountain gave up the struggle and clattered down into the depths. I craned to see down there, but I was too far away. That blinking dot said I'd got the right place, anyway, which was good to know.

Somewhere down there, Mr Garcia was waiting. I hoped that fountain hadn't hit him.

Wind roared through the trees like a freight train, announcing Ariel's arrival. Man, this was like an elemental rave party. A massive branch crashed down, just missing the bruxsa, but unlike the Ariel imitation, the real bruxsa wasn't put off by noise and danger. She knew what she wanted. She dissolved into rats and swarmed the nearest wolf.

Both wolves snarled and snapped at them, breaking rat backs and flinging them away like there was a prize for who collected the most rodents. Conal waded into the fray, swinging a sword I hadn't noticed before and stomping on rats with his heavy boots. A few of the rats got through and scampered towards my aunts. Ivy followed Conal's example and started stomping with her Doc Martens.

The Soldiers were so focused on the rats that they didn't notice the two lurking shadows turn into Raquel and Ethan. Each untied one of my aunts and removed their gags, then dissolved into shadow again and swept away, their part of the plan fulfilled.

I shut my eyes on the wolf-rat mayhem, dangerously close to losing my focus and the spell with it. The plan was for Mr Garcia to spirit my aunties away through his mine to where Bethany was waiting with the getaway car. But I hadn't realised how deep his tunnels lay. Jumping down there would be like jumping off a five-storey building. Not likely to end well for the jumper.

I spread my fingers, feeling my connection to the rocks and soil, then swept my arms up as if I were the conductor and the orchestra was about to launch into the big crescendo. But instead of a swell in sound, the rock rose to greet me. I opened my eyes to see Mr Garcia appear like Aphrodite rising from the sea foam.

If Aphrodite had been an old bluecap covered head to toe in dirt, that is.

Now a tunnel led down into the earth, invitingly close to where my aunties stood. Mr Garcia waved cheerfully at me as he emerged, as if this were just another day and he was out for a nice stroll in the fresh air.

Behind him, tree branches crashed down, and the

wolves fought for their lives. For every rat they killed, more took their place. The bruxsa was too strong.

Ariel changed tactics and began scooping up rats with a powerful wind. She dashed a handful against the ground, killing them, and the bruxsa responded by resuming her normal shape. She had one of the wolves pinned to the ground, and she ripped its throat out, burying her face in the blood.

It wasn't looking good for the surviving wolf and Conal.

What could I do? I still had a grip on the earth spell, but opening a chasm under a being that could turn into bats and fly away wouldn't help. And I couldn't release the spell until Mr Garcia had my aunties safely down into the mine, because I still had to close the earth up after them so the wolves couldn't follow.

I wished Ethan and Raquel had stayed, but I couldn't blame them for making themselves scarce. I'd known all along that they were reluctant to move openly against the Soldiers. I itched with the urge to do something. In a moment, the wolf would be overwhelmed, and then Conal would stand alone against the bruxsa.

As I was thinking that, Liam and the rest of the Hunt came pouring out of the woods behind the bruxsa. Here came the furry cavalry.

The wolves threw themselves into the fray against the bruxsa, who now had a real fight on her hands. Any minute now, she would decide the prize of two juicy cartomancers wasn't worth the effort, however delicious Ling's blood smelled, and she would pull her usual fade-into-shadow trick. Liam would have to be quick with that sword if he wanted to behead her in time.

Instead, Liam headed straight for Ling and Ivy, his sword raised and a gleam of triumph in his eyes.

"Uh-oh," Nicole said.

Mr Garcia took one look and lifted an auntie in each arm, throwing them over his shoulders like sacks of grain. Ivy was so tall that her legs almost touched the ground. It looked ridiculous, but also—wow. I'd known he was strong, but I didn't realise he was *that* strong.

Ling and Ivy struggled in his arms.

"Put me *down!*" Ling shouted. She hurled a fireball in Liam's direction, but hanging upside down clearly affected her aim, as it zapped harmlessly into the sky and fizzled out.

"We have to help Sunday," Ivy yelled.

"Just go!" I shouted. "We'll follow."

Nicole and I broke cover, sprinting across the ground towards the tunnel, but Liam would get there before we did. I sent a tremor through the earth under his feet, building up steam for a nice chasm to drop him into. *He* wouldn't be able to fly out.

"Enough!" Mr Garcia shouted at me. "You'll collapse the whole mine."

Ling saw the danger, too, and managed to wriggle out of Mr Garcia's grip. Back on her feet, she sent another fireball straight at Liam's head, but the earth was still heaving and she staggered.

"How are you *doing* that?" I shouted.

She flashed me a wicked grin and held up her hand,

palm facing me. Was that a *tattoo*? Did she have the Ace of Fire tattooed on her hand?

That was genius.

The fireball missed Liam completely and exploded all over the bruxsa instead. She shrieked—

—and Conal took advantage of her momentary distraction to bring his sword down in a well-placed arc.

The bruxsa's head flew off her shoulders and bounced across the ground.

In a perfect world, everyone would have cheered and congratulated each other on a job well done, and we all would have gone down to the pub to celebrate.

But of course, that wasn't what happened. These were Soldiers after all. Though it was supposedly their sacred duty, the eradication of the bruxsa and the danger she represented hardly seemed to matter to them.

The one thing that Soldiers loved more than killing monsters, more than anything else in the world, was killing cartomancers. With the bruxsa out of the way, every wolf there turned his attention to my aunts.

Well, every wolf but one.

To my complete shock, Conal barely paused for breath after delivering the killing blow. He sprinted to my aunts and put himself between them and Liam.

Liam paused, considering this new dynamic. Panting for breath, I joined Conal and my aunts, followed by Nicole. The wolves, as if in response to a silent command, began to circle us menacingly.

They'd cut us off from the tunnel.

But we weren't out of options yet. Ariel had dropped

her wind and branch-throwing efforts, but she was still here, unseen, my little ace in the hole.

I'm not going in anyone's hole, she said in my head.

I hate it when you do that.

Fine. You can yell at me after *these wolves are toast.*

I doubted I'd be yelling at anyone. I was still twitching like a caffeine addict. It must be the adrenaline. I'd probably have the mother of all crashes once this was over, and sleep for a week.

The roar of a car travelling at high speed pinged my brain, and I realised I'd been hearing it for a while. It was getting closer. So close, in fact, that it must have just turned into the driveway.

Bethany's little white car roared up the driveway.

She didn't slow down until the very last minute. The wolves wouldn't give ground, and they ended up playing "flesh, meet fender" and losing. I watched a wolf sail over her bonnet and go cartwheeling through the air, reminding me of the night I'd met Conal. It must be a thing with Soldiers.

The back fishtailed like crazy as she slid to a stop.

She leaned across the seats and shouted out the passenger window, "I saw the tracker appear! Do you guys need a ride?"

"Look at Baby Goth, all grown up," Ariel said proudly. She had appeared next to me, but judging from the lack of reaction, I was the only one who could see her.

"Plan B," I said to Nicole.

She nodded and pulled a small drawstring bag from her pocket. In a flash, she had the bag open and the contents shaken loose. Ariel caught the fine dust with her wind and sprayed it over the wolves.

"Not Conal," I said hastily.

She rolled her eyes, but the stream of dust parted around Conal as if he were a rock in a river. Nicole didn't wait to see the result, jumping into the front seat and slamming the door.

"Come on," she urged.

Beyond our little circle, the wolves had all fallen to the ground and were writhing around in apparent agony.

Mr Garcia had set Ivy down, and now he tried to herd both my aunts towards the car. He'd never make it as a sheepdog. It was like herding cats.

"Are you all right?" Ivy asked me, as if I'd been the one held captive by the Soldiers all day instead of her.

"Want me to hit them with another fireball?" Ling asked, a determined look on her face, though she already looked like she'd run a marathon. Still, when did Ling *not* have a determined look on her face? *Determined* was her thing.

"What was that powder?" Conal asked sharply over his shoulder.

"Silver dust," I said, only then registering that Liam was striding towards us, apparently unaffected.

And then I realised that the wolves weren't writhing in pain. They were actually transforming. One by one, they stood up—even the one that Bethany had hit with the car. He was favouring one leg and looking mighty unhappy about it, but he wasn't dead. None of them were. They all wore black combat gear and, almost as one, they pulled knives from sheaths on their legs.

"I thought wolves were allergic to silver?" I said, moving to Conal's side and eyeing all the knives and hard-faced men. So much for Plan B. Now I needed a Plan C.

"We spread that rumour around," Conal said. "But as you can see, it does us no harm, only forces us into human shape."

"Well, this is a nice surprise," Liam said. "All three witches at once."

Conal stepped out, shoving me behind him. "Touch her and you'll lose a hand."

"He's been watching too many movies," Ariel said in a critical tone.

Shut up. It makes me feel all warm and fuzzy inside.

"Oh, that's what we're calling it these days? You've got the hots for him."

Ignoring her, I said to Conal, "Nice to see your vow actually means something."

Liam's eyes narrowed. "I'll be happy to kill you, too, witch-lover."

"I'd like to see you try. If you even *think* about hurting her, I'll rip your intestines out and feed them to you."

Wow. He sure knew how to make a girl feel special. I leaned against his muscled back as the caffeine feeling suddenly spiked. Was I going crazy? I scratched furiously at my arm as magic fizzed in my veins. My skin was crawling with ants. Invisible ones.

Now they were inside me, too. I gasped in shock and fell to my knees. From far away, I heard people saying my name. Ling's face swum in my vision, then Ivy's, and I was shaking like a nudist at the North Pole.

I was on my back on the cracked concrete, bits of rock digging into me. The sky was beautiful, the deep blue of just after sunset, before true dark arrives. The moon had cleared the trees, full and round, blazing with light.

A wave crashed through my body. I felt my heart stop and restart, beating to a new rhythm. The ants squirmed through my flesh, turning into burrowing rats, chewing me up and spitting me out. I closed my eyes, but I could still see the moon on the inside of my eyelids, glowing gold.

When I opened them again everything had changed. The world looked different. Smelled different.

I was different. Four legs. White fur.

I saw the look of horror on my aunts' faces and I ran, a howl of loss trailing behind me.

29

_I_ streaked down the driveway, stumbling a little until I found my stride. Four legs were different than two, and my centre of gravity was lower. My heart hammered a panicked rhythm, and I thought it might burst from shock. Stars swam in my vision.

I was a wolf.

How could I be a wolf? The one thing I had hated and feared all my life. Was this some kind of divine joke? Why was I being punished like this? A whine of distress trembled in my throat, the memory of my aunts' horrified faces burned into my brain. They hated me now. They were disgusted.

Of course they were. _I_ was disgusted. And confused. I was a cartomancer—how could I be a wolf? What was happening to me?

Gradually, I became aware that another wolf raced at my side, this one an improbable pink colour.

Ariel's voice spoke in my head. _Hey, this is fun._

Fun? Are you out of your mind?

It was lucky there was no traffic on the road, because I bolted across it without even looking. I had no thought but to get away, to lose myself in the bush somewhere and hide.

The pink wolf looked over her shoulder. *Conal's coming.*

I looked and saw the black wolf sprinting after us. He moved gracefully, leaping fallen logs and ducking low-hanging branches as if they weren't there.

Sunday! he called. *Wait!*

The strangeness of it made me falter. I was used to hearing Ariel in my head, but this was clearly Conal's voice. I shook my head, confused, and redoubled my efforts, hoping to leave him behind. I had a good start on him.

Another whine rose in my throat. If I'd been in human form, I'd probably be crying tears of anger and confusion. Did wolves even have tear ducts?

What kind of question is that? Ariel asked in a disgusted tone. *You turn into a wolf and that's what you want to know?*

Why not? I fired back, stung. *It's a perfectly legitimate question.*

A perfectly boring question, you mean.

Fine, what questions do you have?

Do you reckon you could lick your privates?

You're disgusting.

What? Dogs can do it. Wolves should be able to as well.

Sunday, slow down! That was Conal again. *There's no need to panic.*

Easy for you to say. He hadn't just had his whole world turned upside down. *And I'm not panicking.*

What are you doing, then?

Interesting. We could chat mind-to-mind, but he didn't seem to have heard my conversation with Ariel.

I'm ... Running away from my problems. Yeah, maybe I was, but I wasn't admitting it to him. *Can Liam hear us?* I asked instead, as the horrible possibility occurred to me.

Not at this distance.

I slowed down, then stopped. *We have to go back! Ling and Ivy are back there with no protection.*

The black wolf stopped next to me and nuzzled my face. If he'd done that as a human, I would have found it odd, but as a wolf I felt comforted.

Relax. The black wolf's golden eyes stared into mine. It was mesmerising. I could feel my body relaxing. *They got away in Bethany's car.*

I sat down hard, my legs weak with relief.

Beside me, Ariel sat down, too—and started licking her privates. Conal didn't react, so she obviously wasn't visible to him. Lucky bastard. I rolled my eyes and looked away, focusing on the black wolf who now sat pressed against me. He was warm and solid and felt like the only real thing in a world gone crazy.

You're a wolf. His mental tone was full of wonder. *How is that possible?*

Seems pretty obvious to me. Liam bit me and passed on the werewolf bug—just like I thought would happen. But Conal had said it wouldn't, and I'd believed him, like an idiot.

But women can't become wolves. The bite doesn't have any effect on them.

Ah ... excuse me? I looked down at the silky white fur of my chest and my white paws. I twitched my tail, which was so fluffy it could have been a feather duster, and curled it around over my paws. *Living proof right here, buddy. They most definitely can.*

The black wolf huffed out a sigh. *Regardless, you're a Soldier. That's a good thing. Soldiers' families are considered auxiliary members of the pack. Even Liam wouldn't move against your aunts now—at least not while the rest of the Hunt is watching.*

I hardly heard the end of his statement. My mind had snagged on *you're a Soldier now* and it was busy running around in circles screaming.

I leapt up. I hadn't been panicking before, but I was now.

I'm not a Soldier. I'm a cartomancer. You could offer me all the money in the world, and I still wouldn't be tempted to join your merry little band of butchers.

But you've already joined. He got to his feet, too, sounding puzzled. *You're one of us now.*

No! I refuse.

We're not some country club that you can resign from, he said. Frustration coloured his mental tone, and something else, too. Maybe a little bit of hurt that I could reject his fabulous offer? *The moon called, and you answered. You're a werewolf now, end of story. What did you think would happen?*

My heart was pounding like a drum in my chest. I

hadn't thought anything. I hadn't known it was going to happen until it was done and dusted.

What, you think I planned this? Sure, why not? I'll just get that rabid dog Liam to bite me so that my entire life can get flushed down the toilet! That'll be a good time! You think that's how it went down?

Of course not. Poor choice of words. My bad.

You sounded pretty sure of yourself. The moon was in my blood, urging me to run, and I danced on my clawed feet. *End of story, you said, as if you think I'm going to fall in line like the rest of your mindless troops. But I won't.*

You tell him, Ariel said admiringly. *Bite him. That'll show him you mean business.*

I won't be part of your little gang of killers. I'm a cartomancer, and I help people. I don't go around murdering innocent people.

Neither do we!

You killed my mother!

I took off, unable to spend a moment more in his company. Smug, irritating furball.

I've never even met your mother.

Not you personally, you idiot, Ariel said, and I felt his shock through our link. She must have shown herself to him. Bet that was the first hot pink wolf he'd ever seen.

A moment later, I heard them both racing after me. Even a wolf has trouble moving completely silently at top speed. My heart thundered in my chest as I ran, leaping fallen trees and swerving around obstacles until suddenly I burst out onto another road.

I simply turned and followed the road, hugging the

shadows at the edge. There were no streetlights here and it was full dark. No cars passed, and I settled into a long, loping stride. Conal drew level with me, but he didn't speak. Thank heavens for small mercies.

All I could think about was getting home, as if the whole tangled mess would disappear if I could only shut my front door on the world. There were plenty of were-wolves in the world who didn't belong to the Soldiers, and I refused to become part of an organisation dedicated to killing people like me. There had to be a way out, but all I could think of now was my bed, like a wounded animal seeking its den.

Streetlights started to pop up as we reached the more densely populated part of town. A man out walking his dog saw us and stopped dead to watch us pass, dragging his little yapping thing close to his legs as if that would be any kind of protection. Shocked faces stared at us from passing cars.

None of that was my problem. We finally reached my street. I'd never been so glad to see our little unit block before. I hurled myself up the front stairs and into the foyer and abruptly discovered what *was* my problem—no more opposable thumbs.

I leapt up against the front door of my unit, raking my claws down it in frustration, but I couldn't open it.

You're going to lose your bond if you keep that up, Ariel said. *Look at those scratches.*

How do I change back? I demanded, eyeing Conal in a fury. A whine rose in my throat.

You can't.

What? I'm stuck like this? The whine turned to a howl.

Only for the rest of the night. You'll change back automatically when the moon goes down.

You can change at will! I objected. This was outrageous.

Ask to speak to the manager, Ariel said.

This isn't funny!

It's only because it's your first time, Conal said, his mental tone soothing. He rubbed his face against mine again, and I felt the same subtle relaxation at the gesture. Probably wolf pheromones or something. *Your body didn't know how to become a wolf until the moon showed you, and it won't learn to return to human form either until the moon leads the way. After the first time, it will come as naturally as any other reflex.*

Ariel changed back to her regular form and opened the door. I surged past her, relief blooming inside me, then stopped in shock.

Everything I owned was scattered over the floor. The dining chairs were overturned. It looked like it had been snowing, because the cushions from the couch had been ripped open and fluffy white stuffing carpeted the room. I stared around in shock. Every kitchen cupboard hung open, the contents scattered willy-nilly across the countertop and spilling onto the floor. Every book in the bookcase had been thrown down, as if a tornado had passed through.

Or as if the place had been tossed.

A strong smell of rosemary hung in the air. All my little herb jars had been smashed on the kitchen floor. Beneath it lay another scent that I recognised as Liam's. I growled, and the hackles rose on my neck.

What had that jerk been doing in my house? I padded over to the books, my eyes searching through them with increasing alarm. Where was *The Lord of the Rings*?

Ariel pushed past me and fished it out from under a pile. She held it out to me with a stricken look on her face, showing me the empty cavity inside it.

My mother's Tarot cards were gone.

30

___

*C*onal found my car keys in the mess and hustled me downstairs to Bugsy. He held the back door open and gestured me in.

"Come on. I assume you don't want to see Liam again in a hurry, and this is the first place he'll come looking for you."

Where are we going? I asked, but there was something off about the mental bond we'd shared. I no longer had the sense of his presence at the other end, though he was standing right in front of me.

"If you're talking to me, I can't hear you," he said. "That only works when we're both in wolf form. Get in."

"She wants to know where you're taking her," Ariel said.

"Somewhere quiet she can sleep it off."

I was still staring dubiously at the open door. It wasn't that I didn't trust him, exactly. He'd just defied Liam and defended us all. It was just ... well, no, scratch that. Actually, I didn't trust him. Not completely. If he thought he was going to drag me off to join the Soldiers, he was in for a surprise.

He hunkered down beside me and rested his forehead against mine, his hand tangling in the soft fur at the back of my neck. Even though he was in human form now, it still gave me that strange sense of comfort. He smelled *right*.

"The first change is traumatic for your body." His voice was soft and gentle. "Pretty soon now, you're going to feel like you've been run over by a truck, and you'll be more exhausted than you've ever been in your life. I'll take you somewhere safe to sleep it off. You need twelve hours of solid sleep and a lot of red meat when you wake up."

I stiffened. No way was I hunting down some poor animal and eating it.

"What kind of red meat?" Ariel asked suspiciously.

He laughed. "The kind you buy from the butcher's shop." His hand moved in soothing strokes down my back, and I leaned into him. "Relax. Maybe trust me a little? I just want to look after you."

Yeah, because he wanted a new recruit for his stupid Soldiers. But I *was* feeling tired—drained, even. It had been a rough couple of days. I yawned and climbed into the back seat, curling up with my nose tucked under my tail. My *tail*.

The last thing I heard was the slam of the car door before I was out like a light.

When I woke again, it was broad daylight. I was lying in an unfamiliar bed, and the delicious aroma of cooking steak filled the room. My tummy rumbled loud enough to shake the building. I practically jack-knifed out of bed.

I stumbled from the bedroom into a lounge room painted a cheery blue. Raquel was seated on a butter-yellow lounge, flicking through a magazine. She tossed it aside as I entered.

"Sleeping Beauty's awake," she called into the kitchen.

"Breakfast is nearly done," Conal called back.

"How are you feeling?" Raquel asked. "You looked like a dead dog when Conal carried you in last night."

"I feel ... I feel great, actually." It was true. Apart from the ravenous pit that used to be my stomach, I couldn't recall the last time I'd woken up feeling so refreshed. "Where are we?"

"My place," she said with just a hint of defensiveness.

I glanced around in astonishment at the cheerful colours and little homey touches. There were even embroidered *pillows*. And there she sat, on that bright yellow lounge, looking like a crow that had got lost in a tropical paradise.

"*Your* place?"

Admittedly, she was a stylish crow, but she wore black from head to toe, as she often did. This was the kind of place I'd expect Cheryl and the twins to live in, not chic Raquel. Especially as I had a sneaking suspicion that she'd embroidered those pillows herself.

"My weekender. No one knows about it. I don't normally have guests here, but Conal said you needed somewhere to lay low."

"It's lovely." I looked around, admiring the framed prints on the walls and the soft rugs underfoot.

Then Conal came in with a plate of steaks that were bigger than my head, and I lost interest in soft furnishings. The table was set for two, and I took one of the chairs, salivating at the smell of cooked meat. There was way too much steak for two, but maybe more people were joining us later.

"Do you mind if we eat in front of you?" I asked Raquel, belatedly remembering my manners.

"Be my guest," she said, and that was all the encouragement I needed to dive in.

I was almost finished my second steak before I slowed down. I hadn't been a big meat-eater in years, but I'd never tasted anything as delicious before. It was as if my tastebuds had suddenly come alive. I forked a third steak onto my plate, drawing an approving smile from Conal.

By the time I'd finished that one, there were no more steaks left, as Conal had matched me steak for steak. So much for being too much for two people. Finally, I sat back, the gnawing ache in my stomach appeased.

I tapped the edge of my plate with a fingernail that had so recently been a claw. "So, about this werewolf thing."

He leaned back in his chair. "Yes?"

"I thought you said I couldn't possibly become a werewolf because I didn't have a penis."

"I did say that."

"I assume you realise I haven't magically sprouted a penis overnight?"

His eyes gleamed with amusement. "Perhaps I should check."

"Men," Raquel said with deep disgust, pulling out one of the spare chairs and joining us at the table. "They're obsessed."

"*She's* the one who started talking about penises," Conal objected. "How is it *my* fault?"

It occurred to me that Ariel was usually in the thick of any talk about penises, but there was no sign of her.

"Where's Ariel?"

Conal shrugged. "She disappeared not long before you woke up. No doubt she's off causing mayhem somewhere."

"Yeah, that sounds about right. So ... werewolves and penises?"

He grinned. "Obviously not as strong a connection as I'd been led to believe." His smile faded as he shook his head. "Although I've never heard of a female wolf before, and there have been plenty of women bitten over the years."

I regarded him with suspicion. "So, you *weren't* lying to me?"

"No, of course not."

"Of course not? There's an *of course* about it?"

"Look, I may not have a perfect relationship with the truth, but that was the truth as far as I was aware. I was just as surprised as you were."

"Then why me? And what are we going to do about it?"

He frowned. "What do you mean?"

"I should have thought that was obvious. There's no way I'm staying a wolf. You guys *suck*."

"I hear it's a one-way ticket," Raquel drawled. "No take-backsies."

I bit back a sharp retort as we all heard a car pull up outside. "Are we expecting anyone?"

Raquel went to the window and twitched the curtain aside. "It's your aunts. And Bethany."

Ariel popped into existence in the middle of the room. "Oh, good, you're less hairy. How are you feeling?"

Outside, doors slammed.

"Did *you* bring them?" I asked, gesturing wildly towards the sound of approaching footsteps.

"Yep. I didn't want them to worry about you."

"That's really sweet, but maybe you should have *checked with me first*." I whirled, looking for a way out. There must be a back door. I'd get out before I had to face that look on their faces again.

"What's wrong?" she asked.

Conal was on his feet, too. "Relax, Sunday."

"Relax?" I rushed past him into the kitchen, but there was no back door in there. He caught me by the arms as I hurtled back into the room. "Easy for you to say. No one looked at *you* like you were dirt on their shoe."

"Sure they did." His grip tightened, pulling me against his broad chest. "You do that every time you see me, and you don't see *me* running away. And no one thinks you're dirt on their shoe."

Raquel went to let them in, and I closed my eyes, stiff as a board in the circle of his arms.

"Sunday." His breath whispered across my cheek. "Look at me. Your aunts love you. Everything will be fine."

"Liar," I mumbled into his shirt.

Then they were there. Even with my face buried in Conal's chest, I felt the change in energy as Ling and Ivy came in, trailed by Bethany.

"Sunny!" Ivy cried, then she was dragging me from Conal's arms so she could wrap her own around me. "Are you all right? We were so worried!"

Her hug was as enthusiastic as ever, and she *sounded* normal. I risked a peek and found her beaming at me. She took my face between her hands and checked me over for signs of damage, the way she used to do when I was little and I'd been in a fight at school. Once she was satisfied, she pulled me into her arms again, half-smothering me against her ample chest.

"Why did you run away like that?" she demanded. "We spent half the night looking for you."

"I was ... in shock, I guess. I didn't know what else to do." I chewed my lip, circling around the heart of the problem. "And you didn't seem very happy with me."

I hadn't meant to sound accusing, but the hurt was clear in my voice.

"Oh, cherub." Her arms tightened. "It was a shock for us, too. That's all it was. You're still our darling girl, whatever shape you're in."

My heart felt lighter, but Ling still hadn't said anything. I raised my head and found her shaking her head at me.

"You're an idiot," she said sternly. "Did you really think that anything would make us love you any less? Come here."

I came, and received a brief and very rare hug from

Ling as my reward. I wiped my eyes hastily on the back of my hand afterwards, and she didn't even comment. Truly a momentous occasion.

"Now that's settled, we need to talk." Ling's gaze was decidedly less friendly as she turned it on Conal.

"That was her *I give the orders around here* voice," Ariel said helpfully as she popped into view beside me.

She got a look that was almost as bad as the one Conal had received. "Already I miss the days when I couldn't see you," Ling said.

"Oops." Ariel covered her mouth with one hand, her eyes dancing with laughter. "Was that my outside voice? My bad."

You're not helping," I told her. Unlike her, I used my inside voice.

Ling needs to lighten up, she replied. *We fought the Soldiers and nobody died. We should be partying.*

Forgive me if I don't find becoming a werewolf a cause for celebration.

"There's not much to talk about," Conal said coolly, his gaze holding Ling's in challenge. "Sunday's a Soldier now. She'll be coming with me."

"Hold it *right* there, buster." I jabbed my pointer finger into his chest. "This is my life. You don't give the orders."

Ling hadn't stopped glaring at him. "She'll be coming with *us*, wolf. She's a cartomancer."

"Did you not hear what I just said?" I asked her. "It's my life. I won't be going anywhere with anyone."

"You can't stay here!" Conal and Ling said in such

perfect unison that they looked at each other in horror. Imagine that—they actually agreed on something.

"Seriously," Conal continued, "there are things you don't know about being a wolf. You'll need help adjusting to the change. The safest place for you now is with us."

"Seems to me the hardest part is over," Ivy said, "and she didn't need your help for that. She turned into a wolf all by herself."

"That's right," Ling said. "We'll take it from here. She doesn't need any interference from the likes of you. This is all your fault, anyway. She wouldn't *be* a wolf if it wasn't for you."

I felt compelled to defend him. "Conal didn't do this. Liam's the one who bit me. Conal saved me from him."

"He didn't do a very good job, then," Ling said.

"It doesn't matter," I said. "I'm not staying a wolf."

"Sunday," Conal said gently, "there's no cure for lycanthropy."

I lifted my chin. "How do *you* know? You're the guy who told me that women couldn't become wolves. There must be some way out of this."

"Why don't we all have a seat?" Raquel suggested.

"I can make some tea," Bethany said. "Do you have any?"

"No."

"In Big Bertha," Ivy said, and Bethany scampered out.

I dropped onto the nearest yellow lounge, and after a moment, Ivy and Ling sat together on the opposite one. I hadn't thought that through, because Conal immediately sat down next to me, and I wasn't very happy with him right now.

"Have you ever heard of a way to reverse lycanthropy?" I asked Raquel as she took a seat in a floral armchair.

"No. I can ask around, but you people would know if anyone would, surely. You're the ones who can work magic."

"You're barking up the wrong tree," Ariel said. "Forget being a wolf—the bigger problem here is being a Soldier."

"Not going to happen," I insisted.

"The alternative is we hunt you down and kill you," Conal said.

"What happened to *we're all one big happy family*?" I asked.

"New wolves need other wolves around to keep them sane. If you went off alone, then next full moon you'd be killing your aunts, or Bethany. Whoever was closest. Anything to satisfy the bloodlust."

"That's rubbish," Ling said. "How many people did she kill last night?"

"I was with her last night," Conal said. He took my hand and, despite everything, I felt a little shiver at the contact. "Sunny, you don't have a choice. You have to come with me, for everyone's sake."

"So that lunatic Liam can finish what he started and kill her?" Ivy asked.

"We don't kill our own," Conal said. "She'll be perfectly safe."

"We only have your word for it about this bloodlust," Ling said.

"My word's good. Isn't it, Sunny?"

I nodded reluctantly. I had no intention of joining the Soldiers, but I didn't want to hurt anyone either. Perhaps I could stay with them until I figured out a way to reverse this curse.

"Think of it as an opportunity," Conal said. "This is a chance for you to change the culture of the Soldiers from within. You could achieve what you wanted. No more hunting wi—cartomancers." He corrected himself, but we all noticed the slip-up. Ling scowled. "You could be a force for good. There's never been a Soldier before who was also a cartomancer. Think what this could mean."

"Soldiers never change," Ling said bitterly.

I studied Conal's face. For once, there was no mocking light in those green eyes. He really thought we had a chance to make a difference. But I'd have to live with the *Soldiers*. Ugh.

"I don't know." I could feel myself weakening. I hated everything about this—but if I could end the vendetta against cartomancers, shouldn't I at least try?

"Remember Elizabetta," Ling warned.

Yes. The girl from the lost history books, whose father had been the leader of the Soldiers. He'd killed her because she had the powers of a cartomancer and the strength of a werewolf.

All of a sudden, I itched to get my hands on one of those history books, to read the story for myself. So many details had been lost over the centuries of persecution. Maybe she'd had more than just a werewolf's strength.

Maybe she'd actually *been* a werewolf, too, and I wasn't the first cartomancer-turned-wolf after all.

Either way, it didn't bode well for me. The Soldiers weren't known for being accepting of change.

Still, she must have only been a child when her father killed her. I was a grown woman, and my magic was super-charged.

Wait.

I stared at Ariel. My magic had suddenly gone crazy ... and my hair had turned completely white ... and Ariel had had her big Pinocchio moment ... all around the same time.

"Right after that stupid wolf bit you," Ariel breathed, her eyes wide.

That was your inside voice, right?

"Yes."

Good. I wanted to keep this to myself until I'd had a chance to think it through. Something about becoming a werewolf had boosted my power beyond anything I'd ever heard of. Beyond anything the Soldiers would expect. Conal might be trying to help me, but he was still a Soldier. No need for them to know I had an ace in the hole.

"I told you," Ariel said firmly. "I'm not going in anybody's hole."

Hush, you. Aloud, I said, "I'll do it."

Ling leapt up. "Over my dead body."

Bethany came inside, carrying a kettle and tea-making supplies from Big Bertha. She took one look at Ling's face and headed straight for the kitchen.

Raquel stood up. "I'm going to help Bethany."

Coward.

"Trust me," Conal said. "If Sunday doesn't come with me, it probably *will* be your dead body."

"We'll figure something out," Ling said. "The risk is too great."

"I'm prepared to take it," I said.

An odd expression crossed Ling's face. "You don't know everything, Sunday."

"What do you mean?"

"It would be playing right into *his* hands." She looked at Ivy for support.

"Whose? Conal's?" She made it sound as if he'd come up with some Machiavellian plot to turn me to the dark side.

"No." She hesitated a moment, which was strange. Ling never hesitated. "Austin."

"Who's Austin?"

But Conal was staring at her incredulously. "Austin Madden? The Grand Master? What's he got to do with this?"

Ling gave a bitter laugh. "Everything."

"Who's Austin?" I repeated.

She sighed. "Your grandfather."

Conal opened his mouth to say something, a look of astonishment on his face, but nothing came.

I blinked. "The Grand Master of the Soldiers is *my grandfather*?" Ling and Ivy were both nodding. "How —how ...?"

"Whoa," Ariel said softly. "Mind. Blown."

"On your father's side," Ivy said. "Obviously."

Ah, yes. The mysterious father my mother would never talk about. *Obviously*.

No wonder Ling wanted to remind me about Elizabetta. I was Elizabetta Mark II, only instead of being the Cardinal's daughter, I was the Grand Master's granddaughter. I was bursting with questions and a hysterical urge to laugh.

"Nothing about this is obvious," I said. "But if Bethany and Raquel ever stop hiding in the kitchen, you can tell me all about it over a cup of tea. Although, honestly, this conversation needs a serious injection of alcohol." I glanced at Conal. "But it doesn't change the fact that I'm now a werewolf and apparently in need of a pack."

"Don't be scared," he said. "I'll protect you."

"Oh, yeah? Maybe I'll protect *you*."

Ariel rolled her eyes. "Can I punch him? *Please?*"

"But who's going to protect the Soldiers?" I asked.

He cocked his head to one side. "What do you mean?"

I folded my arms and stared him down. "Because they won't know what hit them after I finish with them."

EPILOGUE

Conal

Sunday's apartment still looked like a bomb had exploded inside it.

I paced through the wreckage, back and forth, back and forth, eager to be gone. I could smell Liam everywhere. Knowing that he'd been here, poking through Sunday's life, touching all her things with his filthy paws, made my lips skin back from my teeth. I'd never liked him, but this urge to rend and tear was new. I'd rip his throat out if he so much as looked at her sideways. That smug piece of—

"I'm ready."

She'd appeared in the door of her bedroom, a backpack over her shoulder, that ridiculous pink hair tied back like a long tail. And just like that, I saw the white wolf again instead of the woman. I'd chased that silken white tail through the bush, my only thought to catch her and keep her safe.

Which was a big job, given her habit of marching headlong into danger.

I eyed the backpack with distaste. "That's all you're taking?"

She lifted her chin in a defiant gesture. "I'm not planning on staying. I'm getting Mum's cards back from your douchebag friends and figuring out how to break this curse. And then I'm leaving."

Had there ever been a more infuriating woman in the history of the world?

"I told you." I tried for patience, I really did. She'd been through a lot lately. "There *is* no way to break it."

Her lip curled. "Don't talk to me as if I'm seven. We've already established that you don't know as much about it as you think you do, so we'll see about that, won't we?"

"Fine. But don't complain when you run out of clean underwear."

Lord, why did I say that? Now I was thinking about her underwear and imagining what she would look like as I took it off.

"Why? Don't Soldiers have modern conveniences like washing machines? Will I have to take my clothes down to the river and beat them clean on the rocks?" Her hips swayed almost insolently as she strolled towards me, a mocking smile on those soft, full lips.

I jerked my gaze back to her eyes. *Focus, you idiot.* "Have you got your cards?"

The smile vanished instantly. "Of course. They're

coming with me, end of story."

The way she said it made it clear she was bracing for an argument, but that wasn't why I'd asked.

I knew my own people. Liam wasn't even the worst of them. There would be objections—some of them violent —to her joining us. I would kill anyone who touched her, of course, but I had to sleep some time.

Yesterday, those cards had made me shudder. Today, I saw them as just another weapon in the arsenal. I'd vowed to protect her with my life, and I would take anything that helped me keep that vow, even her magic.

I'd never felt such a visceral drive to protect anyone before. Of course, I'd never owed anyone a life debt before, either.

That was all it was.

If you'd like to receive the exclusive free ebook *A Taste of Magic*, sign up at www.marinafinlayson.com for my news-letter. It contains a story about Sunday's first encounter with the Soldiers, as well as a story set in my world of the Thirteen Realms, plus a novella featuring werewolves, dragons, and an impossible heist.

Reviews and word of mouth are vital for any author's success. If you enjoyed *Magic on the Cards*, please take a moment to leave a short review at Amazon.com. Just a few words sharing your thoughts on the book would be extremely helpful in spreading the word to other readers (and this author would be immensely grateful!).

AFTERWORD

Thank you for reading *Magic on the Cards*. Out of all the millions of books in the world, you chose mine, and that's pretty special! I hope you enjoyed meeting Sunday and the gang. They'll be back for more adventures in *Magic in the Flesh*.

If you'd like to read more of my work, sign up for my newsletter at www.marinafinlayson.com to receive the exclusive free ebook *A Taste of Magic*.

It contains:

An Unexpected Guest: a prequel to *Magic on the Cards*

Innocent: a short story from the world of the Thirteen Realms

Dragon Tears: a stand-alone novella featuring a dragon, a wolf pack, and one impossible heist.

SHADOWS OF THE IMMORTALS SERIES

Join Greek gods and monsters for a high-octane urban fantasy adventure!

Lexi may be a thief, but she's not stupid. When a crooked fireshaper offers her a job that's a one-way ticket to sleeping with the fishes, she skips town.

All she has to do is keep her head down and pretend to be a regular human. It's going fine until Jake shows up. He's a hot-as hell fireshaper who seems way too interested in her, and not in a good way.

The fireshapers are hunting Lexi, and things are about to heat up. Even her strange magical gift may not be enough to save her from the flames.

See the Shadows of the Immortals series on Amazon

THE PROVING SERIES

Everyone wants Kate dead. Shame she can't remember why.

There's a big difference between wanting to move on from a tragic past and having someone rip the memories right out of your head. When Kate returns from an unusual courier job with no memory of where she's just been, alarm bells start ringing.

Whatever happened must have been pretty wild, because now there's a werewolf in her kitchen trying to kill her—and he's just the first in line.

Kate's caught up in a war between the daughters of the dragon queen. To survive, she must remember the explosive secret she's forgotten—but first she has to live through the night.

See The Proving series on Amazon

THIRTEEN REALMS SERIES

Can a magicless changeling survive the deadly games of the Fae Courts?

Meet Allegra—changeling, outcast, and trouble magnet extraordinaire. She's desperate to get back into the Fae Realms, so she's bending over backwards to please the Lord of Autumn.

Her latest impossible task comes with a partner. The Hawk is a fae knight, as lethal as he is gorgeous—and an unrelenting jerk when it comes to changelings.

Somehow, she has to impress this guy to get back to the Realms. But it's hard to be impressive when you're running for your life.

See the Thirteen Realms series on Amazon

THIRTEEN REALMS: THIEF OF SOULS SERIES

She set out to destroy the assassins. Now she must join them or die.

Half-fae Sage wants revenge on the fae assassins who murdered her friend. But when she's caught spying in the heart of the assassins' stronghold, she has a choice:

Trust Raven, the arrogantly seductive fae noble who promised to help her. Or trust Ash, the steely-eyed master assassin who spared her life by binding her as an apprentice, and who protects her even though he seems to hate her.

Or confront the mysterious deadly being that lurks at the heart of the assassins' power, the infamous Thief of Souls. They are all puppets dancing to its malevolent tune, but when the music stops, who will be left standing and whose strings will be cut forever?

See the Thirteen Realms: Thief of Souls series on Amazon

ACKNOWLEDGMENTS

Heartfelt thanks to my beta-reading crew, Mal, Connor, and my dear friend Jen Rasmussen. As always, their comments and suggestions have improved the book and, in some cases, saved me from my own errors.

Thanks also to my editor, Isabella Jack Pickering, for her helpful suggestions and for her endless patience in fixing all my commas. And a huge thank-you to Heather of Book Cover Artistry for the stunning cover. It was love at first sight!

And thank you to you, dear reader. None of this would be possible without you!

ABOUT THE AUTHOR

Marina Finlayson is a reformed wedding organist who now writes fantasy. She is married and shares her Sydney home with three kids, a large collection of dragon statues, and more books than she can ever hope to read.

Her idea of heaven is lying in the bath with a cup of tea and a good book until she goes wrinkly.

She also writes cozy mysteries under the pen name Emerald Finn.

Made in the USA
Las Vegas, NV
27 June 2023